"I'm sorry I left without saying good-bye last night . . ."

"Shelly? Damn. Shelly, this is great. Where are you? Where can we meet?"

"I'm calling because my girlfriend . . . Kathleen. You remember. She was with your friend."

"Yes?" Webster said, holding his breath.

"Well, she hasn't returned and I was wondering if she was still with your friend."

"My friend was murdered this morning and Kathleen is gone, Shelly."

"What?"

"He was shot to death. The police want to talk to you and to Kathleen. Where are you?"

She was silent.

"Shelly, you've got to help catch these killers. Who could have done this? Why? Who are you? Where do you work? Live? Are you a married woman? Is Kathleen?"

"I can't talk anymore, Webster. For your own good, don't look for us."

"Shelly!"

He heard the click.

DEAD TIME

New York London Toronto Sydney Singapore

ANDREW NEIDERMAN

A Novel

DEAD TIME

POCKET STAR BOOKS
New York   London   Toronto   Sydney   Singapore

This book is a work of fiction. Names, characters, places and incidents
are products of the author's imagination or are used fictitiously. Any
resemblance to actual events or locales or persons living or dead is
entirely coincidental.

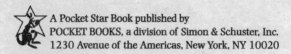 A Pocket Star Book published by
POCKET BOOKS, a division of Simon & Schuster, Inc.
1230 Avenue of the Americas, New York, NY 10020

Copyright © 2002 by Andrew Neiderman

ISBN: 0-7434-1268-0

First Pocket Books printing March 2002

10   9   8   7   6   5   4   3   2   1

POCKET STAR BOOKS and colophon are registered
trademarks of Simon & Schuster, Inc.

For information regarding special discounts for bulk purchases,
please contact Simon & Schuster Special Sales at 1-800-456-6798 or
business@simonandschuster.com

Front cover illustration by John Vairo, Jr.;
photo credits: Stephen Wells/Photonica, Robert Walker
Photography/Photonica

Printed in the U.S.A.

For Emily Grace
Another star to light
up our heaven.

DEAD TIME

Prologue

The phone on the small, light maple nightstand beside the bed shattered the protective walls of sleep that had closed around Kathleen Cornwall. Jolted by the staccato sound, she opened her eyes quickly and looked at the young man beside her. It took her a moment to focus, something that hadn't happened for almost a month. She was afraid of what that might mean, but she refused to pay any attention to it.

Carl hadn't woken. He had been so sweet, so loving, and so vulnerable himself. Now he looked gentle beside her. Kathleen hadn't known many men intimately in her life, but those she had slept with and woken beside all resembled little boys when they slept, especially her husband, Philip. Sometimes she would lie beside him, holding her breath for fear she would wake him, and gaze at his face in repose, taking advantage of the opportunity to look at him without his knowing. A little thing like that used to be titillating.

Like Philip, Carl had been tender and considerate while they made love. She felt confident that Carl Slotkin was a man who would dote on her and make her feel like someone special, just the way her husband had. She had searched and searched for centuries, it seemed, to find someone like Philip. Now that she had, she wondered if she could love him and he could love her once he knew the truth. Would she ever tell him? Could she? She and Dr. Woodruff hadn't talked about this sort of eventuality. She didn't think he would have the answers anyway. He was brilliant, but was he wise?

The phone continued to ring. The persistence of the caller frightened her. When she gazed at the clock, a sword of fear sliced through her heart. She knew they were waiting for her outside. This was the last day of her furlough. Dr. Woodruff had been adamant about the time. She had been here too long; she knew it, but suddenly she felt she couldn't get herself to lift her body off this bed.

Kathleen feared her exhaustion wasn't only a result of the intense lovemaking the night before, even though that had been an erotic marathon. It had gone on into the wee hours until Carl had cried out for mercy. They had laughed about it, but she was disappointed. Her hunger was insatiable. Dr. Woodruff had warned her about this. He had warned her about her excessive appetites.

"You'll drink too much; you'll eat too much. You'll behave like a kid turned loose in a candy store," he had predicted. But that wasn't wisdom; that was just a logical conclusion he had arrived at through careful research.

Finally, Carl opened his soft blue eyes. The phone was still ringing.

Carl smiled the smile of one who had half-expected the woman beside him to be gone, that all he had experienced had been nothing more than a fantasy. Reality filled his heart with joy.

"Hi," he said.

"Hi."

The phone continued to ring.

"Who's calling me this early on Saturday?" he wondered aloud and finally turned to pick up the receiver, but Kathleen put her hand on his arm and stopped him.

"Let it ring, Carl," she said.

He looked at her with a little happy surprise on his face.

"Might be important?"

"Nothing's important but us this morning," she replied. Carl Slotkin liked that. He had suffered a long love drought since Denise Arnold, one of the secretaries at the insurance office, had dropped him and had even taken a job in San Diego. It soothed his ego to believe she had done so because she couldn't work at the same firm and not be his lover. Carl was only twenty-six. Those things were still important.

The phone mercifully stopped ringing and Carl's answering machine kicked on, but that only put a chill of anticipation in her heart. Both she and Carl waited to hear the voice of the caller. All they heard was a click, which they knew meant the caller had hung up. Kathleen also knew they wouldn't give up that easily, but still she neglected the tiny alarms sounding in her heart and mind even though time was running out quickly. She could see the sand falling in the hourglass and she felt as if she were turning into dust and falling along with it.

"I wonder what that was all about," Carl muttered.

"Nothing, or they would have left a message," she said quickly. "Maybe they just don't want to disturb us," she added wishfully. Carl widened his smile.

Kathleen tried to widen hers too, but the skin around her lips felt so taut. Carl saw something troubling in her expression and his smile faded.

"Are you all right?"

"Yes. Just kiss me." Kathleen wanted to drown the sound of her heart thumping wildly in her ears. When Carl continued to stare at her, she pleaded more forcefully. "Kiss me!"

He did so and she wrapped her arms around him. The joints in her elbows seemed to lock, and a small, almost indistinguishable jolt of pain emanated from her lower back. She should have been terrified, pulled herself away from him, risen, dressed and left; but again she forced herself to ignore any warning.

Carl turned into her and moved gracefully between her legs. Then he lifted his lips away to look down at her.

"You look tired this morning."

"Pleasantly so," Kathleen said. It was what should have been; it was what she wished. "You haven't lost interest in me already, have you?" she challenged when he continued to hesitate.

"Hell, no. I'm never going to lose interest in you," Carl pledged.

Again, she attempted a smile. She lifted her lips

toward his instead and they kissed. She knew her lips felt dry to him, so she reached for the glass of water beside the bed and took a sip. He watched, a small smile of amusement on his face.

He kissed her again and then they began to make love. Carl's eyes were closed at the start, but after a few moments, he opened them with curiosity and gazed down at her.

"What's wrong?" he asked.

She began to cry and he stopped immediately.

"Just hold me," Kathleen said. "I'm sorry."

"It's all right." Carl embraced her and she buried her face against his chest.

They lay there like that for a while, neither speaking. He stroked her hair. The Los Angeles morning sunlight leaked in and around the beige cloth blinds, diluting the shadows and turning the dark brown rug into a shade closer to champagne. She felt the rhythm of his strokes begin to slow and she realized Carl had noticed something unusual. It put a deep chill in her. She felt like someone who had been lowered into a grave alive. Was this all a dream? A broken promise?

Indeed, Carl had realized something was very different about her, but before he could speak, he thought he heard the sound of his front door opening. Curious, he sat up to listen.

"You hear something?"

She didn't move. She had half-expected it, but now that it had come, she didn't know what to do.

A moment later there were two men standing in the bedroom doorway, both in dark jackets and ties, both looking more like bank tellers or lawyers than burglars, clean-shaven, hair neatly brushed. The man on the left, stout, bull-necked, wore a thick gold bracelet on his wide left wrist, and the man on the right, taller, but just as wide in the shoulders, was wearing a Rolex. *Is this the new fashion for thieves?* Carl thought. *Yuppie burglars?*

"What the hell . . . how did you two get in here? Who are you?" he demanded.

The man on the left looked toward Kathleen instead of at him, but Kathleen still had her face averted.

"Look at her hair, Satch," he said, jabbing his elbow into his partner's upper arm.

"Jesus!" Satch Norris exclaimed, shaking his head. "You shoulda come down when you were supposed to, Mrs. Cornwall," he said sharply.

"Mrs. Cornwall?" Carl said, grimacing. She had never told him she was married, but that wasn't all that confused him. He looked down at Kathleen and shook his head as if to jar what he saw from his eyes. How could he not have noticed? Could he have been that drunk?

She started to cry. Carl became more flustered and very indignant. He wanted to get out of bed and put on a more courageous stance in front of these intruders, but he was naked beneath the sheets and felt defenseless. Instead, he thought about reaching for the phone and dialing 911, but the look in their eyes told him he would probably not get a word into the receiver.

"What do you want? Who the hell are you two?" he demanded, his voice straining as his heart began to pound. He hated sounding so weak and whiny.

Tommy Murden answered by reaching under his

jacket to produce a nine-millimeter pistol. Carl had no time to react. The first bullet smacked him at the center of his forehead and the second struck his heart.

Kathleen felt the blood splatter over her naked back, but she didn't move. Still facedown, she waited with a weak, sinking feeling in the pit of her stomach.

Satch approached the bed and poked her sharply on the shoulder. She didn't react.

"Is she dead?" Tommy asked, wide-eyed.

"Naw, not quite; but as good as, if you ask me. Why didn't you come down when you were supposed to, Mrs. Cornwall?" he asked with the tired voice of an adult who had been chasing a child all day long. "Look at all the trouble you caused."

Kathleen remained silent, still. Fear had intensified the numbness and fatigue. She wanted to cry, but even that seemed to require too great an effort. Satch looked at his partner and nodded.

"We better get her back. Let's get her moving along, Tommy," he said. Tommy returned his pistol to the shoulder holster and forcefully seized her arm and lifted her from the bed as if she were nothing more than skin and bones. She tried to scream, but the dryness in her throat made her gag. She coughed and swallowed hard, her eyes bulging with the effort.

"I don't want to go back. Just do it to me, too. Just do it!" she pleaded in a hoarse voice.

The two men looked at each other, Tommy's eyes widening and his eyebrows lifting.

"Maybe we should," Tommy said. "Put her out of her misery, huh?"

"Zack said to bring her back," Satch reminded Tommy.

"Yeah, but he doesn't know what we're bringing back. You wanna call him?"

"We'll call from the car," Satch promised, his cold eyes fixed on Kathleen, who gazed down without expression.

She tried to resist, but they dressed her. By the time they were finished, Kathleen could barely stand.

"What the hell is happening to her?" Tommy asked.

"How the hell should I know?"

"She looks ridiculous in those clothes," Tommy said.

"Just keep her jacket closed and hold her close."

"Zack ain't gonna like this," Tommy said, looking at her. "We shoulda been up here faster."

"How the hell were we supposed to know?" Satch said, but he didn't look confident.

Then, actually carrying her between them, they took her from the apartment. Fortunately, there was no one in the corridor or in the elevator. They propped her up between them in the elevator, each supporting her at the elbow. Kathleen was breathing heavily through her mouth and some strands of hair had fallen out and lay on her coat. Satch brushed them off and then blew at the rest. Tommy laughed.

"Zack's going to want to carry her in himself and slap her down on Woodruff's lap, huh?"

Satch nodded, a small smile on his lips.

At the front door of the building, they forced her to walk. Kathleen tried to resist, but they were far too strong. Even so, they attempted to look graceful and concerned as they headed toward the car. They put her in as gently but firmly as possible. It was a bright, warm Los

Angeles morning. Traffic had begun to thicken and they were aware that some people were watching.

Satch got into the backseat with her, and Tommy got behind the wheel of the late-model black Lincoln Continental.

"Move it," Satch ordered.

Tommy started the engine and shot into traffic, intimidating a woman who had the right of way and pulling ahead of her. She leaned heavily on her horn as he accelerated.

"Easy. We don't want to get pulled over with her in the car," Satch said.

"Right."

Tommy slowed.

By the time they reached the end of the block and made the turn toward the 10 Freeway East entrance, Kathleen was having her usual difficulty breathing and the arthritis had her twisting for a more comfortable position.

She would never find one until they laid her out to rest.

1

The beautiful young woman Webster Martin had made love to the night before was gone from his life as quickly as she had entered it. He opened his light blue eyes with every expectation she would be beside him in his king-size, dark oak bed. When he found she wasn't there, he sat up slowly, afraid that if he moved too quickly, he would shake, rattle and roll the brains he had scrambled overdoing everything, especially drinking. Normally, he was very careful about that sort of thing, retreating as soon as he felt a buzz, but last night was far from normal.

He scrubbed the sleep out of his cheeks and stretched. When he looked around, he saw his clothes cast about everywhere, his shirt over the dresser mirror, his pants dangling over the overstuffed chair, his underwear on the floor with one sock near it and the other . . . somewhere. He smiled, recalling how frantic he was, shedding his wardrobe. In the short time it had taken him to go to the kitchen and get her a glass of water with ice, she had stripped and slipped her naked body under his sheet. Just the glazed peaks of her smooth, shiny shoulders were visible, everything else a promise in waiting.

But, he didn't see any of her clothing now.

"Hello," he called. "I'm awake." He waited, but heard nothing.

Confused and curious, he rose to go through his penthouse apartment on Wilshire in Westwood, now expecting to find her in the kitchen, perhaps preparing them breakfast. What better way to greet the day than with her dazzling eyes smiling at him. But she was nowhere in sight.

He searched the bathrooms and then opened the patio door and stepped out onto the balcony hoping she was enjoying the view. There wasn't any marine layer so he could see clearly out to the ocean and even make out some sailboats. When he looked to the east, the Hollywood hills loomed sharp and clear. It was rather cool for April, however, and he was naked. He closed the patio door and returned to the kitchen, wondering if she had at least left him a note. There was nothing, nothing on the table, nothing on the refrigerator, nothing by the phone. In fact, except for the empty water glass by the bed, there wasn't a trace of her anywhere in the apartment. It was as if she had truly been an apparition.

What time could she have gone? he wondered, and thought she might have risen during the night while he was in a dead sleep and slipped out.

Disappointed, he went to take a shower and dress. Although it was Saturday, he still had to visit the job site in

Sherman Oaks where he and his father were construct-
ing sixty-five town houses. Martin and Martin had become one of the biggest residential contractors in Los
Angeles, but at age twenty-eight Webster didn't just in-
herit this good fortune. He had a talent for spotting the
areas that would become desirable and where housing
units would be most in demand. It was how he had put
his expensive East Coast college education, majoring in
the social sciences, to work. He had always been fascinated by what motivated people to make their significant
life choices: where to live and work. He liked to research
areas and scientifically predict why and when people
would be choosing them for residences or for employment. So far, it had paid off and Gordon Martin was very
proud of his son.

A good few minutes before Webster wanted to end his
delightful, multiheaded, life-reviving shower, the phone
rang. Hoping it might be Shelly, the only name she had
given him last night, he stepped out wringing wet and
nearly slipped on the tile to lunge at the receiver on the
bathroom wall.

"Hello."

"How did it go?" Phil Gold asked with a slight twang in
his voice. "Or can't you talk right now?" he asked in a
deep whisper.

Webster, Phil, and Carl Slotkin had gone to Thunderbolt together where he had picked up Shelly, or, as Phil
suggested before Webster had left with her, she had
picked him up. The three had been close friends for
nearly four years now, Webster and Carl the closest. In a
city known for its transient population, a four-year

friendship was like a lifetime. Most young people who came to the City of Angels to fulfill their fantasies were discouraged or defeated in short order and left to pursue simpler goals in a more stable environment.

Webster had left the upscale dance club before learning how Carl was making out with his find. Phil had spent the evening just wandering through the crowd, searching more desperately since his two buddies had, it seemed, struck oil.

"It was great, but she's gone," Webster said, not cloaking the disappointment in his voice.

"Gone? How do you mean?"

"Gone, like in not here. I woke up and she had already left the apartment."

"So? Maybe she had someplace important to go."

"Not a note, nothing," Webster emphasized. "It's almost as if I dreamed the whole thing."

"Wet dream anyway, I hope," Phil said.

"Speaking about wet, I'm dripping all over the bathroom and the shower's still going."

"Carl and I are going to lunch at Dimitri's in Melrose, care to join us?" Phil said quickly.

"Got to go to Sherman Oaks, remember? I don't have as soft a job as you two."

"Nor as soft an income," Phil countered. Webster laughed.

"How did Carl make out?"

"I haven't checked yet, but he left about ten minutes after you did and she was clinging to him like a giant rag doll sewn to his shirt."

"No kidding. She was a knockout, too, wasn't she?"

Shelly had seized his attention so intensely, Webster really didn't look at her girlfriend too closely.

"Yeah," Phil said, his voice full of envy.

"Should I ask about you?"

"No."

Webster laughed.

"What are you doing tonight?" Phil asked.

"I don't know. I was thinking about taking her to dinner, someplace special."

"Two dates with the same woman? You know what that leads to, what that could mean?" Phil kidded.

"Yeah, well, at the moment, there doesn't seem to be any danger of it. Like I said, she's gone without a note, and I don't know much about her."

"What's there to know? You got a name, didn't you?"

"Only her first name. If she told me her full name, I don't remember."

"You're kidding? You got her phone number, right?"

"Thought I would this morning."

"She really didn't tell you anything else about herself?"

Webster thought for a moment.

"Not much," he said. "At least, not much I can remember. We did put away a few Rob Roys."

"A few. Call me later if you don't connect with her. Unlike you and Carl, I went home empty-handed. I've got no grand possibilities tonight either."

"There's always dial-a-date," Webster said, laughing.

"I tried that, remember? They fixed me up with a girl who had a mustache."

"Okay. I'll call you later, but hopefully to tell you I've connected with her."

He hung up and carefully stepped back into the shower. Finally satisfied and awake, he emerged again, dried, shaved and dressed himself. He had some cold cereal with fruit and black coffee. Like most of the people in his generation and especially those in Los Angeles, he was a bit neurotic about his body and his fat content, not that he had much about which to worry.

At five feet eleven, weighing one seventy-five with wide shoulders and a trim waist, he looked as athletic as he was. Twice a week he played racquetball at the Santa Monica Athletic Club with Phil, Carl and Richard Berber, a very successful divorce attorney. They usually played at seven in the morning before everyone went to work. Generally, Webster exercised in the gym two other days a week, depending on his workload.

His hazel-brown hair was always a little too long for his father's taste. The old man continually lectured him about looking like the boss and not one of the construction workers, but Webster was no one to put on airs, even though he lived in a luxurious penthouse apartment and drove a 500SL Mercedes. Despite his father's little criticisms and comments, the two had a warm, close relationship, deepening after Webster's mother's death in a drunk driver car accident when Webster was sixteen. He was an only child, never regretting that as much as he did when his mother died and he had no siblings to comfort him.

His father usually sucked in his emotions. When he cried, his tears fell inside, and when he was in public, he wore a face as stoical as the face on a granite statue. He put all the energy of his mourning into his work, driving himself nearly twenty hours a day during the weeks after Webster's mother's tragic death. When his father raged, he raged at things, cursing building materials, driving the spoons of backhoe shovels deeper into the earth. Those structures constructed during the months that followed their family tragedy were built with a vengeance. They'd stand forever, Webster thought.

Webster decided to try Carl to see if he had been able to get more detailed information from his girl. Since Shelly and she were girlfriends, Webster assumed he could track her down. He punched out Carl's number and waited. The answering machine picked up. He listened impatiently to Carl's outgoing message.

"If you're just lying there in bed, Slotkin, pick up the damn phone." He waited. "All right, I've got to go to Sherman Oaks. Call me on my car phone. I have to talk to you," he said and hung up.

He checked the bedroom once more before leaving the apartment, even kneeling down and searching under the bed for a possible note that might have fallen. He saw some dust and made a mental note to tell Claudia she should stick the vacuum cleaner in not so visible places, too. But there was no written note from Shelly. She hadn't even written her telephone number and address on the mirror in lipstick the way girls in movies often did.

It wasn't as if they hadn't had a wonderful time together, either. He reminisced about the evening as he left the apartment, went to the elevator and pushed the button for the garage. Almost immediately after he, Phil and Carl had walked into the upscale dance club in Hollywood, he saw Shelly gazing at him. She was standing by the horseshoe bar. The string of multicolored bulbs woven in figure eights above her cast a rainbow over her face, but as the lights blinked, her smile flashed. At first he thought she was someone he had met before. She had that friendly of a look.

Indeed, when he drew closer, she apologized for staring at him.

"I'm sorry," she said when he smiled back and tilted his head. "I thought you were someone else."

"I'll be someone else for you," he replied and she laughed. "Were you supposed to meet this someone?"

"No," she said.

"Actually, I thought you looked familiar when I first saw you. Have I seen you here?" Webster asked.

"This is my first time. My girlfriend brought me," she added, nodding toward the young woman beside her.

"Hi," Carl said to her girlfriend before Phil made a move. "I'd be more than happy to be someone else for *you*."

She laughed and Carl squeezed himself in between to start his own conversation.

Most of the girls came in pairs or in small groups of three and four. There was security in numbers and no one was more vulnerable than a girl alone in this city, as well as most. The fact that Thunderbolt was expensive and selective about its clientele didn't matter either. Money and position didn't preclude psychosis.

"I see Sam Gottlieb," Phil said, diplomatically excusing himself. Webster hardly noticed and Carl barely grunted. Webster's eyes were fixed on this woman, who

either really mistook him for someone, or liked him immediately and used it as an introduction. What difference did it make anyway, he thought, as long as the
result was the same?

"Well, should I pretend to be someone else or be myself?" Webster pursued.

"Oh, always just be yourself," she said. He thought she
had the deepest dark eyes he had ever seen. She had
shoulder-length ebony hair, rich and thick, the kind of
hair that gleamed in the light and invited fingers to
stroke it or run through it. Even in the neon brightness,
the healthy youthfulness in her complexion was evident.
She had diminutive facial features and an attractive figure that boldly announced itself in her tight Betsey
Johnson black dress.

Now that he concentrated, he recalled the introduction.

"My name's Webster, Webster Martin," he had said
and she had replied with just, "Shelly."

Then she had given him that warm smile. She hadn't
blown him off. He gazed at Carl, who was laughing and
talking to her girlfriend as if he had known her all his
life. His friend's obvious success encouraged him.

Webster ordered a Rob Roy, which happened to be
what Shelly was drinking, so he ordered her another one
and they made small talk. Reviewing that initial conversation, he realized just how small that talk was. They discussed the dance club and he remarked with authority
how expensive it was to construct it. Naturally, she asked
him how he was so sure about costs and he told her what
he did for a living. Before he could ask her what she did,

she suggested they dance. Carl was already on the dance floor with her girlfriend.

Shelly attacked the dance floor as if it were an aerobics gym, and for a while, he was afraid she was just one of these young women who sought out partners merely to get themselves onto the dance floor to attract someone else. The loudness of the music, the thickness of the growing crowd all made it difficult, if not impossible, to talk while he went through the rhythmic gyrations, hoping, like most other men he saw dancing, that he didn't look like a complete idiot opposite this obviously talented dancer. Most women nowadays had more rhythm than men, he thought, maybe because they became less inhibited when they were out here under the lights. Most of them looked like they were in their own little fantasy, and Shelly wasn't an exception.

He tried holding her attention and occasionally shouted something, but she just shook her head and spun, threading those shapely arms through the air as gracefully as an Olympic swimmer and lifting her feet like someone walking over hot coals. It exhausted him just to watch her, but every time there was a slight pause in the music and he hoped they would retire to the bar for respite, she pulled his arm and urged him to dance just one more.

Finally, he threw up his hands and pretended to hobble off. Reluctantly, she followed. He was breathing hard and he thought he was in good shape. She looked hot, but excited and far from out of breath.

"I get so little opportunity to dance these days, and I love to dance," she said.

"Why so little opportunity?" he asked.

"Just busy."

"Doing what?"

"Things," she said cryptically, "but most of all, I like to dance."

"I had a feeling you were fond of it," he replied between gasps. She laughed. Then she leaned over to whisper.

"Most men I've been with lately don't last that long."

"Why does that make me feel like I'm in a rodeo riding a wild bull?" he said. She laughed again, their eyes met and he saw the warm desire. I'm taking this girl home tonight, he realized, and became very excited, very interested.

As he walked toward his Mercedes in the garage, his mind still replaying the previous night's events, he realized she had countered and eluded almost all his prying. In his car on the way to his apartment, she finally told him she was a personal assistant for a very old but very wealthy man. She couldn't tell him the man's name, he was too famous. She said she hoped he would respect that. It only made him more curious, but he didn't pursue it. He did recall asking her where she lived, but he seemed to remember her saying she lived on the estate, wherever that was. He thought she said she had been born and bred in the Midwest, but she hadn't mentioned a town.

After he had peeled off his clothing, nearly ripping his briefs in the process, she had insisted he put out the lights. He didn't mind. He saw her with his fingers, realized how supple her breasts were and how smooth her skin felt. Her limbs were tight, athletic, and her stomach was flat. All the promises in her sexy appearance were fulfilled. The only imperfection he recalled was a small black and blue mark on her left forearm he had noticed when they were at the dance club. It was the sort of trauma that resulted when one had a blood test. He had made a mental note to ask her about it later, but forgot. At the time he was afraid that questioning her about something like that might turn her off. It was obvious that questions about her personal life bothered her, and he wasn't about to risk losing her. He figured that once they really got to know each other and she saw he was someone she could trust and not a fly-by-night pickup, she would be more forthcoming.

He really did want to know more about her. Despite the lifestyle many men his age followed, he had trouble being intimate with someone of whom he knew little. One-night stands weren't really his style. He wanted a meaningful relationship. Unlike most of his friends, he could marry and have a family without sacrificing the lifestyle to which he had grown accustomed.

Their lovemaking came so quick and heavy, he didn't have time to delve any further into her background. She had as much energy and as much of an appetite for sex as she did for dancing. Once again, he was overwhelmed. He had heard about women who were insatiable, but he had always considered that a myth. The myth quickly became fact. She wasn't displeased with him when he asked for mercy. She laughed and got him to promise he'd be there for her later.

The combination of the lovemaking and the Rob Roys

was enough to put him into a deep, pleasant sleep. He felt her beside him and remembered closing his eyes with the confident belief she would be ready to ring his bell again in the morning. Otherwise, why did she get him to make that promise?

Now, he found he couldn't get his mind off her, even though there was an arm's-length list of things for him to review at the building site. Her face flashed in his eyes, the scent of her perfume and her hair lingered in his nostrils and the memory of her perky breasts lay on his fingers. He recalled she had a unique look in her eyes, a glint that suggested she was wiser and far more intelligent than she pretended. That intrigued him, but everything about her intrigued him.

As he drove, he realized his heart was pounding as if he were about to make love, and he was only thinking about her.

She wasn't just a great night; she was his IT girl, the sort of woman who would cause him to look forward to the morning, make him feel really alive by heightening every one of his senses. There wasn't a sunrise or sunset before he had met her; there wasn't any good music or good food. He had to find her again, see her again, pursue her until he made her part of himself, part of his life.

"My God," he muttered, surprised at his feelings, "I'm head over heels in love with a woman I know nothing about and a woman I might never see again."

Anxious, but excited about this realization, he had to be reminded by the drivers behind him that the light had turned green. He waved an apology and sped up.

She better call, he thought. She gave him every indication she liked him, didn't she? She laughed a lot; she was impressed with his apartment and he recalled her telling him he was a wonderful lover. She has to call. But what if she doesn't?

He'd just go looking for her, go back to Thunderbolt, and then he'd hit every dance club in Los Angeles until he found her, he vowed.

Finally, there was something more than work and play to occupy him, he thought, and that would give his life more meaning. His father was worried that Webster would take so long to find the right woman, he'd never live to see his grandchildren. He tried to explain to his father that men didn't jump into commitment as quickly as they did when his father was his age. It was possible, even common, to have a relationship that didn't result in marriage.

"That's the trouble with this generation," his father insisted. "They dote on themselves so long, they don't know how to care for someone else. That's why you got all these divorces."

"But that's why I don't want to just marry anyone, Dad. I want to feel confident I've found the right woman."

"The right woman," he grunted and then took on that fixed look of determination and said, "Just look for a woman like your mother."

"Easier said than done," Webster retorted. At least his father liked that.

But maybe I found her, Dad, he thought. I don't know if she's as sensible as Mom was or if she has Mom's ability to be somewhat independent and yet make a marriage successful. I don't even know what toothpaste she likes. I only know she made me feel great so I've got to find her again.

I will, he told himself confidently. People just don't come into your life and then disappear like this.

Do they?

2

Dr. Harrison Woodruff gazed lustfully around the ornate sitting room in the plush New Orleans Garden District mansion. His mind clicked off the antiques and collectibles as well as the expensive furnishings like an accountant figuring net worth. The total value of this one room probably could support his program for months. Being in the black was crucial to the continuation of his program, despite the promises it made and the exciting successes he had accomplished in so short a time. The men overseeing his work were not fellow scientists, not poets and dreamers; they were coldhearted businessmen.

Dr. Woodruff crossed his long legs and with his right thumb and forefinger smoothed out the crease in his light brown slacks. He was six feet one and gangly to the point where all of his good clothing had to be custom made. He didn't like getting dressed up; he hated wearing a tie, especially in the sticky late April New Orleans climate, but he was well aware of how important first impressions could be. Besides, he had the feeling Mrs. Forsch only met with men in formal clothing. Her husband had been one of New Orleans's most successful attorneys and had been well-connected politically.

Harrison had read her dossier on the plane from Palm Springs. He was especially happy about her ancestry. On both her mother's and father's side, everyone, with the exception of those killed in accidents and war of course, enjoyed long life. She had a wonderful genealogical tree.

So far, every one of the candidates that Intelligence had recommended proved to be just the type Harrison required. However, because Zack Steiner, the head of Intelligence, personally brought him the names and dossiers, he always anticipated disappointment. It was an understatement to say Harrison wasn't fond of Steiner, but he had to admit the man did his job well.

The white ceiling fan above Harrison clicked annoyingly because it, aside from the occasional gong of the dark oak grandfather's clock in the long marble entryway, was the only sound in the house. He gazed at his watch. It had been almost ten full minutes since the butler had greeted him and had brought him to the sitting room to wait for Mrs. Forsch. He had hoped to recruit this woman in record time and make the early afternoon flight back to Los Angeles and then catch a shuttle to Palm Springs. There were things he wanted to do early tomorrow morning at the site.

Finally, he heard the distinct sound of someone's heels clicking over the tile floor and a moment later, Emma Forsch entered. Her short gray hair had that familiar blue tint he had seen in the hair of so many other older women throughout the country, and even in Europe. However, at seventy-four, Emma Forsch looked like a woman who had aged well. He knew from the dossier that she didn't have any plastic surgery. That was a requirement, of course. However, her face was relatively wrinkle-free. There were the usual crow's feet etched at her eyes and she had some lines in her chin, but her forehead was rather smooth and her cheeks still quite flush.

It was her neck and her chest that showed the age, with spots and ridges of loose skin. There were brown age spots on the backs of her hands as well. She was an elegant-looking woman, statuesque in posture with her shoulders firm and her back showing little of the curvature of the spine evident in so many women of her vintage.

Emma Forsch still had rather youthful-looking, bright blue eyes. Harrison could see that she had once been a very attractive woman, her beauty reminiscent in her small facial features, her high cheekbones and her soft, graceful mouth. She knew how to wear makeup, her lip rouge not too bright, her eyeliner subtle and just a pat of facial makeup here and there to highlight her features.

She was just as subtle about her jewelry. The large diamond ring being the only ring, and one gold bracelet. This morning she wore no earrings, but she did have a cameo on a gold chain around her neck. She wore an ankle length but rather tight-fitting skirt and a light-blue silk blouse. She maintained her figure well for a woman in her seventies, he thought.

All of this cheered Harrison. She fit the profile perfectly: someone with wealth who was concerned about her physical appearance. The dossier said she even had a personal trainer.

"Dr. Woodruff, I'm sorry to have kept you waiting," she said, extending her hand as he rose to greet her.

"No problem," Harrison said. He smiled, his light green eyes as warm as he could make them.

"Please, sit down. Would you like a cold drink or something stronger? Perhaps a mint julep?"

"I'm fine," he said, not meaning to seem impatient or too businesslike. But she appeared to be a woman who understood. She sat across from him on the high-back seventeenth-century Louis Quatorze chair and pressed the tips of her fingers together. He gazed at the doorway. She caught the look and smiled.

"Please, feel free to close the door if you like," she said. He nodded, rose and did so. Then he returned to the settee.

"You look a lot younger than I had anticipated," she said. He laughed, nervously. Youth was ironically not an advantage for him. He had to resemble some wise old scientist. People Mrs. Forsch's age had a built-in distrust of people much younger.

"I've made optimum use of my years, Mrs. Forsch. I'm older than you think."

She nodded, her eyes still a bit narrow, suspicious.

"I make it a point," he continued, "to meet with any prospective participant personally. The project is still small enough that I can have a direct relationship with everyone who is involved."

"That's very good and very reassuring," she said. "Our

mutual friends have told me the same thing. All speak very highly of you. They say that it's inevitable you will win a Nobel prize."

Harrison smiled and shrugged.

"That doesn't excite me as much as the day-to-day work," he said. "If it comes, it comes, but it's only a bonus in my mind."

"My husband used to say beware of people with humility; it's not natural. We all have a need to be in the limelight."

"I'm afraid I'm not going to agree with that, Mrs. Forsch."

"Please, call me Emma."

"Emma. The limelight can be debilitating for some of us and an obstacle to the work and the goals we wish to accomplish."

"Which makes for all this clandestine behavior," she said, smiling and nodding at the closed door.

"Precisely. I'm sure you can imagine what would happen if my work were prematurely exposed. The health of the entire project is at stake as well as the efforts, lives and money of many people."

"I appreciate that. That's also why you call yourselves the Renaissance Corporation, I imagine? Rather innocuous-sounding."

Harrison smiled.

"The one thing security didn't question and trouble me about," he said. He leaned forward to speak sotto voce for dramatic effect. "I don't think they understand the literary allusion."

Emma Forsch laughed and then paused for a long moment before raising her sharp blue eyes and fixing them on him firmly. "If I am to understand what you are proposing, you want me essentially to die."

"Figuratively, of course. But Mrs. Forsch, Emma, life as you now know it will die anyway when I am successful, won't it?"

She thought for a moment, gazed at her possessions in the room and then nodded slowly.

"I suppose that's very true."

"Afterward, you can resurrect yourself anytime, any way you like. Except, of course, as yourself as you now are."

She smiled softly, like one in a dream.

"My husband's been dead for almost ten years. My son was killed in a car accident almost twenty-five years ago. It seems like just yesterday," she said softly. "He wasn't married and he was our only child. I have no grandchildren and a woman my age without grandchildren . . . well . . ."

Harrison nodded. He knew Emma's son had been gay and wouldn't have provided her with any grandchildren anyway. Happily for him, he had heard similar stories. It made them prime candidates.

"Most of my old friends are gone, a few linger in rest homes, and as for cousins and nephews, nieces, that sort of thing, they expect you to just fade away gracefully." She sighed deeply and gazed around the impressive room again. "The house is too big for me, of course, but it seemed like a terrible retreat to sell it and move into something smaller.

"I don't have much reason to buy anything anymore.

I own everything I've ever wanted. What's another diamond ring?"

Harrison smiled, waited. Usually they did this: they talked themselves into it if he were patient and understanding.

"And as far as a man . . ." She laughed and he smiled. "I think about it. I have some acquaintances of course, but they're all one step from the tomb themselves and a younger man . . . why would he be interested except for the money, and how would that make me feel?"

"There's a young woman in you yet," Harrison said, nodding at her. She laughed.

"I'll tell you a secret." She leaned toward him to whisper. "I have fantasies."

"That's good," he said.

She laughed and then she stared at him again.

"This death, how do I do it?"

"You don't do anything. At the appropriate time, after arrangements are made, you will leave and all that will be taken care of by people who are expert in these matters. Frankly, I don't even know the details. It's not my area."

"I see. And my new home?"

"Temporary new home," he corrected. He was forever the optimist. She liked that.

"Temporary new home," she parroted, closing and opening her eyes.

"It's in Palm Springs. Actually, outside of Palm Springs between Palm Springs and Rancho Mirage. On the outside it appears to be just another health spa. Actually, it is. It has exercise facilities, mud baths, beautiful dormitories and grounds, a small lake. There's a very nice dining room and you will be able to socialize with our other candidates."

"Do I know anyone?"

"You might have known someone. Remember?"

"Oh, yes." She laughed. "Imagine going up to someone and saying, I was at your funeral. It was very nice. Too bad you couldn't attend."

Harrison laughed. He liked this woman. She was attractive, intelligent and had a good sense of humor. He thought she might be his best subject.

"What about my servants?" she asked. "My butler and my cook have been with me nearly thirty years."

"Nothing different in the way they are to be treated, I'm afraid. And what would happen to them if you actually did pass away?" he followed quickly. "The same things."

"That's true. Still, this dying is quite a demand," she said, but not with a great deal of conviction. Once again, like a cat licking his lips, he thought: this woman is a perfect candidate for the project. "It's not as easy a decision as one might think, is it?"

She was waiting for some sort of a thoughtful response from him, but this part was always difficult and the part for which he had the least patience. He was a bachelor, the older of two children who had been alienated from his own parents and his younger brother for some time. They didn't even know he lived in California now, and he had no idea what had become of his brother. The last thing he knew, Jason was attending college in Boston. So for Harrison, family, friends, lifelong servants, whatever, weren't ever a consideration. His own short-lived relationships were perfunctory, shallow and without emotion. Even in the throes of sexual intercourse, he felt he was still doing research, and eventually, if not immediately, so did the woman with whom he was making love.

"The end result is worth the sacrifice. At least, in my humble opinion," he replied.

"What did I tell you about humility?" she countered, feigning indignation. He laughed again.

She was pensive. The grandfather clock bonged, its chimes muffled behind the closed door. Nervously, he traced the crease in his pants again and waited like a fisherman, musing about other things, waiting for the float to bob so he could pull in the next fish.

"The results you've had have been exciting, haven't they?"

"Yes, they have been and they will continue to be so," he assured her, his eyes narrow and full of confidence.

"I suppose I have to think it over," she said. He was terribly disappointed.

"You have all the information I can give out," he said, his voice thin, close to a whine. "I have an opening now. You know the arrangements and you know what can be. I don't mean to pressure you, but time is very important."

"Especially when you're my age," she quipped. She paused once more to think. He could almost hear her heart pounding. She was close. "I just say yes and it all starts?"

He nodded.

"The moment I go to the phone and report that yes, it starts."

"How long do I have?"

"I can give you two, maybe three days," he said. "But it's better if you don't linger and wring your hands over the decision, believe me," he added.

"How do you know so much?" she suddenly demanded with more vehemence. For the moment she sounded like a prosecutor, cross-examining him on a witness stand.

"It comes from experience and from confidence. I'm talented, with more than just a touch of brilliance. Whatever it was that gave Einstein, Edison, people like that the edge, gave it to me, too. How's that for lack of modesty?"

"Refreshing," she replied. "All right. If I say yes, what do I do now?"

"Nothing. Someone will call; someone will come to see you and everything will be done. However, financial arrangements are another matter."

"Go on," she said, smiling suspiciously.

"We have someone to take care of that, too, if you need the assistance. He has all the necessary paperwork completed and ready for your signature."

"Won't that attract attention, especially if my family starts raking over the estate with their own attorneys?"

"You have to understand," Harrison said, this time with genuine pride and arrogance, "the people behind me are the best. We have never had a problem and even if we do, they have people who take care of problems."

She nodded.

"Considering the people who have spoken to me, I am impressed. You do reach into high circles."

"Everyone wants me to succeed," Harrison said. "Especially people with power and wealth."

"Um. It's logical, I suppose. They have more to lose and more to live for, don't they?"

"I wish I could offer everyone the benefits of my work, but for now, I'm afraid it has to be this way . . . the chosen few. And you are one of them, Emma," he emphasized.

Emma Forsch thought for a moment and then fixed those piercing eyes on him again.

"You're not the devil, are you?"

Harrison pulled his shoulders back, surprised by her question.

"I hope not."

"So do I," she said. "So do I."

He had that mint julep after all. She took him through the house and showed him her gardens and the grounds. There were beautiful flowers and hedges, a luxurious pool and cabana, banana trees and camellias, a guesthouse with trumpet vines around the windows. It was all well-kept, but deserted, lonely-looking, like a painting.

"Beautiful," he said. He had a scientist's appreciation of perfection. "So well-balanced in color and design."

"Actually, it's painful to look at it. There are no happy children's voices echoing, no wonderful groups of people enjoying a party. I can't remember when anyone swam in the pool last. I feel like a dying breed or something.

"But once," she said, "once this was the place to be."

Harrison didn't share the longing. In his mind all that wasn't really necessary. He vaguely, if ever, recalled his own past. It was almost as if he had never had one.

"I'm sure," he said, smiling, "that you will have a very impressive obituary."

She glanced at him, saw he was serious, and then she laughed.

"I think I'm going to like you, Dr. Woodruff."

He smiled at her sincerity and lifted his light eyebrows.

"Good. It makes it all easier when my people like me," he said. He finished his mint julep. "I take it then that you want to move forward, Emma. I don't want to rush you, but I do have to get back."

She took a deep breath, smiled and nodded.

"Yes."

He went to the phone and made the call.

"The goods are of perfect quality. It's a go here," he said. He felt stupid using the cryptic talk Zack Steiner insisted he use, but he didn't feel like getting another lecture. The less he had to do with the man, the better.

"That's good," Zack Steiner said, "but we've had a problem with one of the products."

"Problem? What sort of problem?"

"The sort I anticipated one day," Steiner said dryly. "You'll have to get right back."

"I'll be on my way as soon as I finish here. Exactly what sort of problem?" he demanded.

"The product has started to spoil, and that created other problems. Mop-up problems. Do you follow, Doctor?"

"No."

"Then why don't you just hurry on back and see for

yourself," Steiner said. Harrison could sense the smug smile on Zack's lips. "It's not the sort of thing we can discuss on a phone that hasn't been properly cleared," he added.

If anyone was paranoid, it was Zack Steiner, Harrison thought. What did the man think, some spy network had tapped into Mrs. Forsch's line just because he had come to see her?

"What about my new candidate?"

"We'll have to put her on hold now, won't we?" Steiner said.

"I can't do that. I won't do that," Harrison insisted. "Whatever the problem is, I'm sure I can solve it," he added.

"I'm not the one you have to convince, Dr. Woodruff."

Harrison knew Steiner was referring to the Renaissance board of trustees and especially the chairman, Ben Stoddard.

"You can be sure I'll be successful," Harrison countered. There was a moment of silence. "You want me just to leave her when I've won her confidence and she is ready? You of all people know how hard it is to find the right candidate. If I give her any indication of a problem, we'll lose her," Harrison whined, regretting the hysteria in his voice.

There was another deliberate moment of silence before Zack spoke.

"Tell her she'll be contacted soon and her code words are: Your phone was out of order," Steiner said reluctantly. "But it's on the record that I am not recommending this action at this time."

"Right. I take full responsibility. I'll be back as soon as possible, if not sooner." He meant it to sound threatening, but Zack Steiner was not easily intimidated by anyone, not even Ben Stoddard.

"That's good, Doctor."

Troubled, Harrison stood by the phone for a few moments. He wasn't sure whether he was bothered more by the possibilities of what could have gone wrong or by Zack Steiner's gloating. After another moment, he regained his demeanor and returned to Emma Forsch. He told her the code words, and when she raised her eyebrows, he shrugged.

"Like I said, I don't have anything to do with this aspect. I do apologize for the histrionics, but they are the experts. You've got to trust them."

She nodded.

"I'll see you soon," he told her and they shook hands.

She paused with him at the door.

"I hope I've made the right decision," she said.

He saw the hesitation.

"You have. You might not realize it yet, but you're a very lucky woman, Mrs. Forsch," he assured her.

"No, very rich," she said.

That's the same thing, he thought.

She had her driver take him to the airport. He was able to catch an earlier flight than he had expected. Anxious because of what Steiner had said, he was happy to be on his way. For a while however, he could sit back and relax. Whatever the problem Steiner referred to was, he was sure he would find a remedy. He was getting closer and closer to perfection.

Mrs. Forsch was right to criticize him for false modesty. If anyone earned his arrogance, he had.

Nothing could or should stop him now.

He closed his eyes, smiled and shook his head.

Wasn't that funny, he thought, when she asked me if I were the devil.

3

Chicky Siegler limped down the corridor toward the crime scene. The corns on his right foot were inflamed. He knew the foot was going to get bad, but he neglected to make an appointment with the podiatrist. He neglected every other part of his body these days, why exempt his foot? he thought. He was usually this sarcastic with everyone else. He couldn't help being sarcastic to himself either.

Chicky had been roused from a deep sleep. A devout insomniac, he usually didn't achieve any shut-eye until nearly morning and on these final days before his retirement, when he expected not to have to report to work until late in the afternoon, he anticipated catching up on the "z's." But how did that poem go . . . "the best laid plans of mice and men . . ."

Looking at himself in the mirror before leaving his two-bedroom house off Pico in West L.A., he thought the sacs under his eyes were big enough to hold two days' laundry, especially his laundry. Surface veins had popped along the crests of his dull freckled cheeks as well as the top and end of his bulbous nose, and his carrottop hairline had receded to the point where he could see the small rise in his skull, also peppered with freckles. To make room for all my extra brains, he thought, and spread his lips to gaze at that molar that cried daily for root canal.

Christ, he was decomposing while yet alive. It was time to make a reservation at the undertaker's. He had a friend in Missing Persons who did just that: Jay Carson, and Jay was only five years older than him. The guy didn't trust his children to take care of his burial needs. He was sure they'd opt for bargain basement prices and maybe even have him cremated to save the graveyard cost. He had gone so far as to pick out and reserve his coffin.

Some people were so obsessed with their own deaths, they neglected themselves and died, Chicky thought. He laughed. However, he didn't really neglect himself. He had been planning for his retirement. He had put the house up for sale and already had an offer that would bring in a handsome profit. He would take the one-time tax exemption afforded people his age, buy the motor home he and Maggie had talked about for years, and just keep an apartment. There would even be a nice bundle left over so he could earn interest to embellish his pension.

Since his son and daughter had practically disowned him, he didn't have to think about leaving them anything, not that either needed it. Bobby was a successful entertainment attorney and Jackie was married to Curt Bablow, the valley's most successful car dealer.

"You can't get a better price at an auction than you can at Bablow's. Sold!"

If he heard it once a day, he heard it ten times on the radio and saw it ten times on local television stations. No, his children weren't waiting for their legacy; they were building their own. God bless them.

Both accused him of neglecting Maggie until her mental condition recently required committing her. Never mind that the psychiatrist was convinced her depression was caused by chemical imbalance. His children believed that the chemical imbalance was initiated by his lifestyle and his lack of understanding. That was their conclusion. He told them if they could live with that belief, fine. He wasn't going to go hat in hand for their love, even though he sure missed it.

He regretted not having been closer with his children. He confessed to himself that to a large extent his lifestyle—more exactly, his devotion to his career—was primarily the reason. Unfortunately, his children viewed him as a policeman more than they viewed him as a daddy. He had put too much of their upbringing on Maggie's shoulders and now he and probably she were paying the price.

Somehow, some way, this too shall pass, he thought, but for the time being he was too proud and too stubborn to look for solutions. His children should be looking for solutions. His age earned him the right to be pampered and humored, whether they liked it or not.

"You look like shit," Raul Torres said after Chicky nodded greetings to the two uniformed patrolmen at the door and entered Carl Slotkin's apartment. The police photographer was just leaving, but one of the forensic detectives was dusting the doorknob for prints.

"You don't look so good yourself," Chicky told his partner. The truth was the thirty-six-year-old was in great physical condition and looked more like an eighteen-year-old. He was a handsome Latino with a dark Cesar Romero mustache and an accent that wooed the ladies. There was something musical to his intonation, and in fact, he had a good singing voice and was always called to join in at the piano whenever there were parties. He was married and had a pair of eight-year-old twin girls.

"The hit on this guy was picture perfect," Raul said and pointed to his forehead. "One here and one here," he said, pressing his finger against his heart.

"And the weapon of choice? Do we know yet?"

Raul held up a bullet in a plastic bag.

"Just dug it out of the wall behind the headboard. Passed right through his heart. Nine millimeter, Teflon-coated, the choice of the more refined assassin these days, since they slip easily through bulletproof vests."

"Your admiration for and infatuation with cold-blooded killers has always amazed me, Torres," Chicky said.

"Just recognizing perfection wherever I find it. I find it so rarely lately, amigo."

"You're not referring to my work, are you?"

"Hey," Raul said, holding up his hands, "when it comes to perfection in police work, I step back behind your shadow. And that is getting to be a bigger and bigger shadow," he added, nodding at Chicky's expanding girth.

"You're going to miss me," Chicky warned him. "Go ahead. What do we have this fine morning?"

"Name's Carl Slotkin. He sold insurance. Worked for Farmers out of Santa Monica. Twenty-six years old, bachelor. Been in this apartment three years. Emanating out of Chicago. No family here."

"Who found him?"

"A friend. Phil Gold. He's in the bathroom throwing up his breakfast."

Chicky started for the bedroom. Raul continued talking as they stood in the doorway watching forensics work.

"Seems the two and another friend were out on the town last night. They hit Thunderbolt on Sepulveda where Carl here picked up an attractive woman. Phil didn't know very much about her, except that her name was Kathleen and she was a friend of the woman . . ." Raul checked his note pad. ". . . their buddy Webster Martin picked up and left with a few minutes earlier."

"Does look like a man surprised during whoopie," Chicky said, observing Carl's prone naked body. "Did his friend know the woman he was with?"

"No. They've got some hair samples from the pillow. Donald says Mr. Slotkin had sexual intercourse and he's found some alien pubics enmeshed in the deceased's."

"Was Donald surprised by that discovery?" Chicky asked loudly.

Donald Hodes, the tall, thin forensics man, gazed at them and smirked. He was a pale man with pocked skin and bony features. Chicky kidded him all the time mainly because Donald Hodes gave him the creeps, especially when he considered the work he was doing. It was surely either this or being an undertaker.

Chicky smiled at him, but Hodes just glared.

"I guess he didn't practice safe sex, huh, Donald?"

"Fuckin' funny, man. Hilarious."

Chicky laughed and turned to Raul, who was smiling. "Any powder traces on his chest?"

"No. Hodes thinks he was shot from about here," Raul said. "Forensics already vacuumed the spot."

"What else do we have so far?"

"Not much. I bagged a glass that was on the nightstand," he said, nodding to his left.

Chicky nodded. Besides fingerprints, there was the possibility the medical examiner would find traces of lipstick, makeup. They would also have to determine if all the blood on the sheet and pillowcases was only Carl Slotkin's.

"What was in the glass?"

"Just water."

"Did you contact this Webster Martin?"

"Not yet. He called this morning and left a message on Carl's answering machine, but I figured we'd start with Phil baby, first."

"Let's go talk to him," Chicky said.

They found Phil sitting in the kitchen, dazed. Although he was five feet eight and twenty-five, Phil had a baby face that gave him that perennial little kid brother look. His dark brown hair was carefully styled and his skin was so soft and clear, it looked like he was yet to take his first shave.

Raul poured him a glass of water. He downed it in a single gulp and looked at the two detectives, his hazel eyes wide with wonder and fear.

"This is Lieutenant Siegler, Phil."

Phil nodded.

"Why would anyone do that?" he asked Chicky, as if Chicky's age and worn look gave him the wisdom to explain the insanity that raged so freely around them.

"We were hoping you could tell us," Chicky said. "Did he have any enemies?"

"Carl? Hell no, at least not like that kind of an enemy. I mean everyone has someone who's not in love with him, but Carl really is well-liked."

"Was," Chicky reminded him.

Phil nodded and swallowed. He looked like he was going to heave again.

"Easy," Raul said. The young man's face was losing color quickly.

"I can't believe he's dead in there. I can't believe it. Even while I was on the phone calling the police, I just didn't absorb it, believe what I was saying, but after seeing him like that . . . Jesus."

"How did you get into the apartment?" Chicky asked.

"I had a key. Carl had a key to mine. We did each other favors from time to time."

"What sort of favors?"

"Take care of each other's things when one of us left town, that sort of stuff."

"So you knew each other long?"

"Almost four years. We work for the same insurance firm."

"You know his family, too?"

"I met his sister when she came to visit. That's about it. His parents don't like flying, so they've never come. Webster met his parents. He went to Chicago for a visit with Carl last year. Jesus," he muttered. "Who's going to give the family the news? I don't think Webster's going to want to do it."

"We'll handle that, Mr. Gold," Raul said.

"This Webster . . ."

"Webster Martin. Close friend," Phil said.

"He didn't come here last night?"

"No. He went back to his own apartment. He wasn't looking for any more company," Phil said with an envious smile on his lips.

"Tell us about last night again," Raul said. "Especially about the girl Carl was with."

"Think she did it?"

"We don't know yet, Mr. Gold. Possibly. Possibly she wasn't here when it happened; possibly she was."

Phil nodded and took a deep breath as if he were about to dive under water.

"She was very pretty, dark hair, brown, wore it nearly down to her shoulders and pinned on the sides, you know. Like a pearl bobby pin or something," he said. "She was in this sexy dress with the front cut out so it ran down between her tits, nearly to her belly button. I remember she had very blue eyes," he added. "Can I have some more water?"

Raul got him another glassful. After Phil took a gulp, he continued.

"She wore pearl earrings, just a big pearl in each lobe,

and I remember she had a slight dimple in her right cheek when she smiled."

"That's a pretty detailed description," Raul remarked.

"She was the kind of woman you looked at, if you know what I mean. I was jealous. She just had eyes for Carl. She hardly glanced at me, and Webster was already involved with someone. Carl . . . he was bowled over immediately. They both were. I felt like a third eye, so I shmoozed with some friends. Carl and Webster danced with their girls for a while, but when I saw Carl go back to the bar, I walked over."

"Did you hear her say anything about herself?"

"Just that her name was Kathleen. Oh, I think she said she worked for some old rich guy. Something like that. They were giggling and being silly, downing Rob Roys like they were Evian water. I felt stupid. They didn't even look at me; so I wandered away again, and when I looked back, they were on their way out. Webster had already left. I had come with Carl, so I started after him, but then I thought, why should I crowd his action, know what I mean?"

"Sure," Raul said.

"I found a ride with someone else. I called Carl late in the morning, but he didn't answer, so I just came over."

"You didn't leave a message on the machine," Raul said quickly.

"I knew how many rings before it came on and I figured Carl was still involved. Know what I mean?" he asked. Whether it was just because he was upset and nervous or whether it was his poor self-image, Phil Gold needed constant reaffirmation, Chicky thought.

"Yeah, I can imagine," Raul said. Chicky raised his eyebrows. "What are you smirking about? At least I can still imagine."

Chicky laughed.

"What did you do then?" Raul asked.

"We were supposed to have lunch down at this place on Melrose with some friends so I figured after a decent amount of time, I would just pop over," Phil continued. "He hadn't called to cancel. I just assumed we were still on."

"Anyone else at the dance club know this woman?" Chicky asked.

"No one in our crowd knew either of the two."

"But you said these two women were definitely together?"

"Yeah, they knew each other, but I can't tell you how close they were as friends, and Webster might not be able to help you right now with any information."

"Why's that?" Chicky asked.

"I called him this morning to ask him about his night and he said his date left before he woke. All he knew about her was her name, no phone number, no address. I don't know if he's learned anything more about her yet."

"Well, a name's something." Raul said.

"Only her first name," Phil added.

Chicky smirked.

"They went to bed together and he knew only her first name?"

"That's what he told me this morning."

"Younger generation is getting harder and harder to understand," Chicky said, scratching his head.

"She didn't leave him a note or anything. She just left," Phil emphasized.

"Maybe she was dissatisfied. It happens," Raul offered dryly.

Phil shrugged.

"Strange pair of women, even for the modern female, don't you think?" Chicky muttered. "One leaves before the guy wakes up; the other's gone after the guy is offed or just before."

Phil nodded and Chicky turned back to Phil.

"How do we reach your friend Webster?"

"He's at a job site in Sherman Oaks right now," Phil said. "He and his father own a contracting company, build apartments, Martin and Martin. I can give you his car phone number."

Raul jotted it down in his note pad.

"We're going to want you and Webster to sit with a police artist and work up a picture we can take around," Chicky said. "Unless Webster can give us something more concrete about the girl Carl was with last night."

"Sure." He thought for a moment. "I do remember overhearing one thing she said about herself while I was standing near them," he suddenly added.

"What's that?"

"They were talking about the music and the way people dress and Carl asked her why she was so surprised. I heard her say it's been a while since she was out on the town. The way she was dressed and the way she looked, I thought that was a strange thing to say."

"Why do you think she said it?"

"I don't know. Carl didn't ask her why when she said it

either. He just looked back at me and winked. I bet he didn't believe her any more than I did. Maybe she wanted him to think she was very naive or something. Weird, isn't it?"

Both detectives stared at him.

"Maybe they were both just sophisticated hookers," Chicky said to Raul. He nodded thoughtfully.

"We haven't noticed anything missing," Raul said. "Still a wad of money in Carl's wallet." He turned to Phil. "But since you know this apartment pretty good, you take a look around the place and let us know if you see anything expensive gone. Just don't touch anything."

"Carl didn't have anything really expensive here. He was doing well, but not that well."

"You remember his jewelry?"

"A few rings, a good watch. The most expensive piece is the diamond in the onyx ring."

"He's still wearing it," Raul told Chicky.

"Got to be some reason why someone wanted him dead," Chicky said. "If robbery's not the motive, and he doesn't have real enemies, it must be a jealous lover. Maybe she was married; maybe that's why she said she didn't get out much. Maybe she ran off and her man followed her here."

"Makes sense," Raul said, nodding. "That's why her friend left Webster, too. They were both married."

"Think so?" Phil asked.

"Maybe. It's just conjecture, but that's what we do for a living," Chicky said. "We're detectives."

Phil shook his head.

"Poor Carl. Just his luck to pick up that woman," he said. "It might have been me in there, but Carl moved on her faster than I did."

"Apparently he didn't move fast enough," Chicky replied.

Phil nodded.

"It's getting real hard to be single in America," he muttered. "If it's not AIDS, or some other sexually transmitted disease, it's jealous lovers."

"Better go back to arranged marriages," Chicky said. "Leave it up to wiser heads."

"I don't disagree," Phil said with a small smile. "At least I would get laid safely. Hell," he added, "at least I would get laid, period."

Chicky nodded, thinking, it's probably true.

4

"What?" Webster shouted into the car phone. A tractor trailer was roaring past him on the 405 toward the Sunset exit.

"We need you to come right to the police station, Mr. Martin," Chicky repeated.

"What happened to Carl? I don't understand. Was he in some sort of accident?"

"Can you come right to the station, Mr. Martin?"

"I would like to know what the hell's going on," Webster screamed into the phone. "Where's Phil?"

"He's here."

Webster thought for a moment, slowing down. Instantly, the driver in the car behind him hit his horn and pulled around him. Webster glanced out the window and saw a young man with a face distorted in rage. There was a strange electricity in the air. It was as if insanity were raining down over the city.

"I want to know what's going on," Webster insisted. "Either tell me or put Phil on the phone."

"Your friend Carl Slotkin was murdered some time this morning in his apartment," Chicky reluctantly told him over the cellular phone.

Webster nearly lost control of the car. He swerved, put on the brakes and then sped up to change lanes.

"Murdered? Did you say Carl was murdered? I'm sorry. There's a lot of noise and . . ."

"I think it's better we just talk at the station, sir. You've got the address."

"But . . . Okay. I'll be right there," he said and cradled the receiver. A woman in an enormous white Lincoln Continental transferred her PMS into the car horn and practically blasted him off the highway before whipping past him and giving him the finger. She looked old enough to be his mother. The shock of it combined with what he just had heard sucked the blood from his face. His head spun and his heart nearly lifted itself out of his chest. He had to pull over for a moment; he signaled, and did so. Traffic whizzed by, the wind from some of the bigger trucks actually rocking the Mercedes.

He thought about calling his father, but he imagined his old man would start screaming about his not going to talk to any policeman without their attorney at his side. "Not in L.A.!" he would shout.

How could Carl be dead? Why would anyone kill Carl Slotkin? He thought about the woman Carl had been with, Shelly's friend, and then he thought about Shelly again, how she had just disappeared as if she had been part of a dream. It was all beginning to frighten him; it was like falling into one of those thrillers peopled with psychotic women à la *Basic Instinct* or *Fatal Attraction*. Jesus.

He checked the lane, waited almost two minutes for an opening, and then gunned it and shot back into the traffic, his heart pounding so hard, it nearly took his breath away. He looked wildly at the drivers who boxed him in on the right and left. This was Saturday. When the hell did the traffic lighten up around here? He battled his way around the line of cars and took the Sunset exit, driving as quickly as he could to the police station. He located the police-business-only parking spaces and pulled in. Now that he was actually here, he just sat for a moment.

Carl, dead? Murdered? He hadn't known anyone who had been murdered. He didn't even know relatives of people who had been murdered. It still seemed like something that happened to other people and reported on news shows that were becoming more and more pure entertainment. It made the news unreal, but this phone call and his being here at a police station . . . this was damn real. Christ, Carl was like the brother he never had. It was impossible to think of him as being dead. He still heard Carl's laughter from last night and recalled the look of glee in his eyes when they gazed at each other at the bar.

Tears came to Webster's eyes. He felt his throat close. The memories of visiting Carl's family with Carl came roaring back. His mother was so sweet and his father so proud, simple people, humble origins, treating Webster as if he were some sort of celebrity because he had lived and worked in Los Angeles all his life. Carl had obviously built him up in his parents' eyes. He bawled him out for it, but his friend was very proud of him and proud to bring him to visit his family. Just the thought of Carl's mother and father hearing this news shattered Webster. He had to reach deeply to find the strength to step out of the car and stand. Then he took deep breaths, closed his eyes, opened them and headed for the front of the station.

Moving slowly in a daze, oblivious to all the commotion around him, Webster found his way to the desk sergeant, who called Chicky and Raul out to meet him.

"Come on back here, Mr. Webster," Chicky said after the introductions and led him to a conference room. Webster contemplated the empty, beige walls and the long table with scratches and chips dug into its surface. He gazed at the mirror to his right, imagining it to be a one-way window. Were there other policemen behind it watching and listening to the things he said? This place nurtured paranoia. He couldn't help it. Maybe he should have called his father and gotten their attorney.

"Please, have a seat, Mr. Martin," Raul said, gesturing. "Can I get you something to drink, a soda, coffee?"

"No. I'm fine," Webster said and sat. "This is all true? Carl is dead?"

"I'm afraid so, sir," Chicky said. "He was shot twice, once in the forehead and once in the heart."

"Jesus." Webster's heart began to pound harder when he envisioned the scene. "Shot?"

Chicky nodded and sat and Raul whipped out his note pad.

"We heard your message on the answering machine. The clock on it says you called at nine-thirteen. Is that correct?"

"Sounds about right. When did this happen to him?"

"Where were you when you called him?" Raul asked instead of answering.

"I was home. When was he shot?"

"We believe about nine this morning, give or take fifteen minutes. It could have been eight-thirty, eight forty-five," Raul said. "Is there someone who can verify you were home at that time?"

"What? No. Why?"

"It's standard procedure to ask our questions completely," Raul said, smiling.

Webster nodded, his eyes directed down.

"Your friend Phil Gold found him around eleven-thirty and called us."

Webster looked up quickly.

"Where is Phil?"

"He's here, in another room with a police artist, giving him the details we need to draw a likeness of the woman Carl was with last night," Raul said.

"Did she shoot him?"

"We don't know who shot him or why just yet, Mr. Martin," Raul said. "Do you have reason to believe she would shoot him?"

"No. Of course not."

"Chances are this woman was the last person to see Carl alive."

"Right, right."

"We'll have you join Phil in a moment and see what

you can contribute," Chicky said. "First, let's talk about last night. The three of you went to this dance club, Thunderbolt? Is that correct, Mr. Martin?"

"Yes."

"About what time?"

"Close to ten, I think."

"You and Carl picked up these two women. Phil said he knew the name of the woman with Carl was Kathleen, but he didn't know her last name. Do you know her last name?"

Webster shook his head.

"I really didn't talk to her. I was occupied with her girlfriend."

"Phil says you told him your date returned with you to your place, but left you without your realizing it and you didn't have her phone number or address, nor did you have her full name," Raul said. "Is that a correct summary?"

Webster nodded.

"And she went to bed with you without telling you her full name?" Chicky asked. He couldn't get this fact through his head. In his day you not only knew the girl's name, you knew her ancestry, her favorite foods and colors. When he considered the length of courting he had done before he and Maggie had made love. "Didn't you ask her for her full name?" Chicky followed.

"I did, but she didn't seem to want to tell me at the time, so I didn't pursue it. I asked her again, later, and she just fooled around, saying things like Shelly Martin, which is my name, of course. We got to giggling and I . . . I suppose I thought I would find out sooner or later. I'm hoping she'll call me today. I gotta check my answering machine."

"All right. We'll let you do that in a moment. Did she tell you anything about her girlfriend?"

Webster shook his head.

"At the time I wasn't very interested in her girlfriend," he said, feeling he had to offer Chicky explanations for every answer.

Chicky gazed at Raul who nodded slightly.

"But you were very interested in the girl you were with, right?"

"I know it sounds stupid, but she avoided talking much about herself."

"Do you think she wanted to keep herself somewhat anonymous?" Raul asked.

"Why?" Webster asked. Clandestine reasons had simply not occurred to him before.

"There are lots of reasons. She might be a married woman out on a fling. Was she a married woman, Mr. Martin?"

Webster considered the possibility for the first time, but shook his head.

"I don't think so."

"Why not?" Raul asked quickly.

"She wasn't wearing a marriage ring. She just seemed . . . uninvolved. She told me she worked for a wealthy old man and lived on his estate."

"That's what Phil said the girl Carl was with told him," Raul remarked.

Webster looked up at him and grimaced.

"She did? Maybe they were deliberately giving us false

information. Maybe they were out on a fling, but who would kill Carl?"

"That's what we have to find out," Chicky said dryly. "You have any suggestions?"

Webster started to shake his head and stopped.

"Maybe a jealous husband who tracked her to him."

"Maybe. Phil has a pretty good memory of the woman Carl was with. What about your memory of that woman?" Raul asked.

"To be honest," Webster said, "I barely gave her a second look. My attention was fixed on Shelly."

"About how old was Shelly?" Chicky asked.

"Mid to late twenties, about my age."

"She and her friend were from L.A.?"

"I can only guess so," Webster replied. "She never gave me any specific addresses or actually confirmed it. I'm sorry. Damn," he said.

"Didn't she say anything that gave you a hint about where she was from?"

"You mean originally?"

"Anything." Chicky was shaking his head, smirking.

"I think she said she was from the Midwest," Webster offered. "She had a slight accent, I guess. Sort of Midwestern, but I don't know." He shook his head. "I'm not good at this sort of thing."

"You don't seem to know much about the woman you slept with," Chicky said. "What do you people do, just meet, dance and fuck?" Chicky asked, astounded.

"It all happened so fast. I usually know more about the women I'm with," Webster said defensively. "Just this time . . . it was different, but I was having a good time. I wasn't concerned." He paused. "I had had a few drinks and I was . . ."

"Feeling no pain?" Raul suggested with a smile.

"Yeah," Webster said. "And I thought, expected, we would spend time with each other today and learn about each other. It happens that way sometimes," he insisted. Chicky looked at him as if one of them were from a different planet. "That's just the way it is nowadays!" he said, his face turning crimson. Right now, Chicky reminded him of his father.

"Easy," Raul said. "Your mating habits aren't in question here."

Webster reached for his handkerchief and wiped his face, gazing irately at Chicky, who still stared and smirked.

"Did she have a car, follow you to your place?" Raul asked.

"No. She just agreed to leave with me when I told her where my place was. She said she wanted to see the view at night, something like that. I felt pretty lucky and I guess I didn't ask a lot of questions because I thought it might spoil the moment, if you know what I mean?" Webster said, searching for an explanation that might satisfy Chicky.

"He hasn't the slightest hint," Raul said, nodding at Chicky.

"If this is what it means to be young nowadays, I'll stick with my arthritis and the corns on my feet," Chicky muttered. Raul laughed. The light moment helped Webster to relax.

"So how did she leave your place?" Chicky asked. "Someone pick her up?"

"I don't know. Maybe. As I told you, when I woke up, she was already gone. I never heard her leave. It was like I was drugged," he muttered.

"Could she have put something in your drink?" Raul quickly followed.

"Why would she do that? No. I made the drinks at the apartment. Besides, we didn't really drink once we got there," he added.

"Did she call anyone while she was at your apartment?" Raul asked.

"Not that I know. She might have after I passed out," Webster remarked.

"She probably called a cab. We'll check it out," Chicky said. Raul nodded and wrote something in his note pad.

"Okay," Chicky said, pushing down on the table to lift himself up. He grimaced with the foot pain. "Why don't we check your answering machine first and see if there is a message on it," he said. "You can use the phone at my desk. Then we'll bring you in with Phil and you can give the artist anything additional you might recall."

"What about Carl's family?" Webster asked.

"They've been contacted," Raul said. "After the autopsy, they're going to take the body back to Chicago for burial."

Webster took a deep breath and shook his head.

"This can't be happening."

"Oh, it's happening, Mr. Martin, and it happens a lot more than people know," Chicky said.

Webster nodded and then followed them to Chicky's desk. He called his answering machine and waited for the messages. There was only one, from his father.

"Sorry," he said. "She might call later."

"I don't think so," Chicky said. "But if she does, don't scare her off. Try to set up a meet with her and then call us."

They took him into another conference room where Phil sat with the police artist. Webster and Phil hugged each other and then sat exchanging their disbelief.

"I didn't want to keep calling him when he didn't pick up the phone. I figured if he had changed his mind about lunch, he would have called me, so I dropped over about the time I was supposed to pick him up," Phil explained. "He didn't answer the door, but I decided to go in and check my answering machine to see if he had called while I was en route. I used the phone in the kitchen and then I just wandered into the living room and gazed through the bedroom door. It looked like someone was still in bed.

"Carl?" I called. "No answer, so I . . . Christ, Web, when I walked in there and saw him. His eyes were wide open, glassy, staring up at the ceiling, and the blood . . ." Phil lowered his face to his hands and shook his head to drive away the image.

Webster swallowed hard and looked at Raul.

"I guess I could use that cold drink now," he said.

"No problem."

"I gave them the best description I could remember, Web," Phil said.

Webster leaned over and looked at the police artist's sketch. He shook his head.

"It looks like her, but I can't recall much detail."

"You agree she was about five six, five seven?" Chicky

asked. "Nice figure, dark brown hair, almost black, about that length."

"Yeah. Yeah, I think so."

"Might be a good idea to get a drawing of the woman you were with, Mr. Webster."

"Okay," he said. He had a very detailed memory of Shelly's face and so dictated. The artist was very good. A little more than an hour later, Webster gazed at the rendition. It put a pang of regret in his heart and tapped out a hope in his mind. Let her not be a married woman and in any way responsible for what happened to Carl, he prayed.

Chicky and Raul returned.

"None of the cab companies report a pickup at your address either late last night or early this morning," Chicky said.

"Maybe the woman Carl was with had the car and picked her up," Webster offered.

"Maybe."

"You need us anymore?" Phil asked.

"No. You guys can go. Thanks for your help. Remember, if you hear anything or think of anything else . . ."

"Right," Webster said. "You'll be the first to know."

"What are you going to do?" Phil asked him outside.

Webster squinted in the sunlight and then reached for his sunglasses. "Just go home. Maybe she'll call. Want to come over?"

"Yeah. I hate the thought of being alone right now. Anyway, maybe when we talk, we'll come up with something else that might help."

Webster nodded and the two drove back to his apartment. He finally phoned his father and told him.

"I'm always worried when you guys go to hang out at those places," Gordon Martin responded. "I see crap like this every night on the news. I'd better call Sidney and ask him if there's anything we should be doing."

"I don't need an attorney, Dad. I'm not a suspect."

"People get in trouble when they speak to the police without an attorney present," he lectured. "It always comes back to bite you somehow," his father insisted.

"I'm tired and overwrought, Dad."

"Want to come over?"

"Not right now. Phil's here. We're just going to have something light to eat and . . ." He didn't want to tell him he was waiting for his own mystery woman to call. It meant more involvement with the police and his father was sure to insist on their attorney being present. "We're going to relax, if we can."

"Well, let's all have dinner together at least. I'll take you guys to Chasens. I know this is quite a shock."

"Thanks. Yeah, maybe we'll do that, Dad." He hesitated, and then added, "Everything's fine at the site."

"Good. It's better you keep your mind working. I know what it is to lose close friends. Call me if you need anything, Webster."

"I will. Thanks, Dad."

He hung up and joined Phil in the living room. His friend was staring down at his hands in his lap and shaking his head. There was already a funereal atmosphere surrounding the two of them. They felt they had to speak in voices barely above a whisper.

"I keep going over it and over it," Phil said. "I watched you guys for a while. You were both having such a good time. After you left, I joined Carl and Kathleen for a few moments, but neither even glanced at me. You know what that feels like."

Webster didn't, but he nodded, imagining Phil had felt that way often.

"Anything she wore that you didn't tell the police about?" he asked. "Jewelry that might help identify her?"

"No. I told them about all of that and they got it in the drawing." He closed his eyes. Then he opened them quickly.

"What?" Webster asked.

"Her arm, her left arm. I remember noticing she had a black-and-blue mark, like the kind I get whenever I have a blood test, no matter how I press down afterward or how good the lab technician is."

"Black-and-blue . . . on the arm, here?" Webster pointed.

"Yeah."

"Now that you mention it, Shelly had one there, too. I recall noticing it. I asked her about it and she told me she had some routine physical lately."

"That's something. I don't know what it means, but we should call Detective Siegler and tell him, don't you think?"

"Yeah, I suppose. I'll do that," Webster said. He rose, feeling as if a marine layer of fog had seeped into his head. What the hell did all this mean?

Siegler wasn't in, but someone else took the message and promised the detective would call him.

"You want something to eat?" he asked Phil.

"Sure. I threw up breakfast. I better get something in my stomach."

"We'll just go around the corner," Webster suggested. He told him about his father's dinner invitation. Phil thought it would be fine. He liked Webster's father; the man had style and an inner strength he envied, and at this time, he liked the idea of being around such a man.

After lunch they returned to Webster's apartment and Webster noticed there was a message on the answering machine. The two waited anxiously as the machine rewound and then played the incoming. The message was from Chicky Siegler, asking them to call him at the station.

"I didn't think she would be calling you, Web. The police are probably right. Married women out on a fling, jealous husbands. Jesus, you guys just fell into it."

"Yeah, maybe," Webster said. He called the police station and asked for Chicky. Then he told him about the marks on the arms of the two girls.

"What'd he say?" Phil asked as soon as Webster cradled the receiver.

"He thanked me, but I think he thinks we're two nut cases," Webster said.

Phil nodded.

"Maybe we are."

"When they were interrogating me, and I kept saying I didn't know anything much about Shelly, I felt the width of the generation gap. That detective looked at me just the way my father sometimes looks at me when I tell him about my dates. It suddenly made me think about it, you know what I mean?"

"No. Think about what?" Phil asked.

"It's like we treat each other as if we're just things and not people. Funny thing was, I didn't want it to be that way with this woman. She was . . . exciting and different."

"How different?"

"I don't know . . . we didn't talk about anything heavy and we fooled around a lot, but she was no valley girl. She was . . ."

"What?" Phil pursued. Of the three, he was the least experienced when it came to women. He was always looking for insights to help him solve the mystery of the opposite sex and help him to become more successful. It was always on his mind, incredibly, even now.

"Wiser," he offered.

Phil shook his head. He had no clue. He blew some air through his lips and then slapped down on his knees and stood up.

"Well, I guess I'll go home for a while. Call some people. The news is going to spread fast."

"So you're definitely joining my father and me tonight?"

"Yeah, sure. What time?"

"Meet us at seven," Webster said. He saw Phil out and then he returned to the living room and sat back, dazed and tired from the events. When the phone rang, he expected it was one of the people Phil had referred to, some of their other friends who had heard the astounding news.

"Hello," he said in a tired voice.

"Webster, I'm sorry I left without saying good-bye last night, but—"

"Shelly? Damn. Shelly, this is great. Where are you? When can we meet?"

"I'm calling because my girlfriend . . . Kathleen. You remember. She was with your friend."

"Yes?" Webster said, holding his breath.

"Well, she hasn't returned and I was wondering if she was still with your friend."

"My friend was murdered this morning and Kathleen is gone, Shelly."

"What?"

"He was shot to death. The police want to talk to you and to Kathleen. Where are you?"

She was silent.

"Kathleen, you've got to help catch these killers. Who could have done this? Why? Who are you? Where do you work? Live? Are you a married woman? Is Kathleen?"

"I can't talk anymore, Webster. For your own good, don't look for us."

"Kathleen!"

He heard the click.

"Wait!" He stood there with the dead receiver in his hand for a moment and then quickly punched out Detective Siegler's number. "She just called," he told him as soon as he answered. "But she didn't tell me where she was."

"What did she say? Try to remember the exact words."

"She wanted to know if her girlfriend was still with Carl. When I told her what happened, she said, 'For your own good, don't look for us.' "

"That's it?"

"She hung up before I could ask her anything."

Chicky was silent a moment.

"That rules out her girlfriend picking her up, and if no cab had, and you drove her to your place, she either walked miles, lives nearby or . . ."

"Or what?"

"Had someone waiting for her. Someone who followed the two of you from Thunderbolt. Did you notice anyone else leave when you two left? A man? Another woman beside the woman Carl was with?"

"No. But that doesn't mean there wasn't anyone else right behind us. I just didn't notice."

"This Shelly whatever her name is," Chicky said, not hiding his annoyance. "She must really be something to look at. According to you, you never took your eyes off her."

"She was for me."

"All right. Stay in touch," Chicky said. "And Webster."

"Yeah?"

"Do what she said. Don't go looking for her," Chicky warned.

5

Of course, Shelly Dorset knew she and Webster Martin had been followed. Zack Steiner had assigned Herbie Shagan and Mike Robbins to, as he put it, look after her. When she objected to being watched, Zack gave her that oily smile and said, "It's just a service Renaissance provides. Believe me, we have no interest in spying on you, Mrs. Dorset. But Renaissance does have a lot invested in you and your well-being."

"I think I've invested a lot in Renaissance," she countered. "Like my life, my future, my money . . ."

He nodded and held that cold smile.

"Don't worry. We'll be unobtrusive. I promise; but we will be there when you need us."

It wasn't that she didn't appreciate all this attention and protection. However, Shelly Dorset was sensitive to anyone or anything that would restrict or confine her, now that she finally had what she believed was real freedom.

Shelly's husband, Thomas Nelson Dorset, one of Chicago's most successful real estate developers, had been a domineering man who actually would have smothered her if she had not found clandestine ways to breathe independently. The day after he was buried, she began to rid the house of his memory, first having all those horrible animal heads removed from the walls in his sacrosanct den. His precious art, all depictions of war from Hannibal to Vietnam, she donated to the Fine Arts Department of Roosevelt University in Chicago, and she had her financial manager sell off Thomas's gun collection. Then she proceeded to change the decor in the den, feminizing everything, as she liked to call it. The dark, brooding colors were replaced with pinks and blues. She got rid of the cold-looking nailhead-trimmed leather chairs and black leather settees, covered the hardwood floors with plush beige carpet, and changed lamps, lighting fixtures, as well as the chandeliers in the dining room.

Methodically, she paraded through their mansion, seeking out the smallest artifact that had Thomas's identity or stamp of approval on it. She replaced his Mercedes, even though it was barely six months old. Of course, she cleaned out his closets, donating everything to the Salvation Army. She worked on the house and her surroundings for weeks until finally, she could sit back and feel he was truly gone; she was liberated.

But strangely enough, this liberation didn't produce the result she had expected. All of the friends she had made, she had made because of Thomas. Those women she liked that Thomas didn't like avoided her before his death because of him and continued to do so no matter how she approached them afterward. It was as though she would always bear the onus of Thomas Nelson Dorset even though he was dead and buried. And there wasn't much chance for her to develop some sort of meaningful relationship with any one of the men she had known through her three extramarital affairs. They were all off and married themselves and living in different parts of the country.

Widowed, childless, she discovered that without Thomas she didn't even have the little social life she had once enjoyed. She tried to start over, to join charitable organizations, to make new friends, but few of these acquaintances were sincere, and the ones that had some sincerity didn't seem to last for one reason or another.

She was too young at heart to seek out other widowed women her age. She hated the senior citizen trips people proposed and found the People Without Partners dances utterly ridiculous. She had been married too young to a man who shackled her to his identity and his ego. She had walked in his shadow for so long she was blinded by the unblocked light. Depressed and disappointed, she finally retreated to her introverted life without much hope until Ben Stoddard, one of Thomas's business associates, approached her.

At first she thought it might be some sort of practical joke. She never trusted most of Thomas's male friends. Either they were uncomfortable alone with her or she was uncomfortable with them. Most of them made her feel as if she were just another one of Thomas Nelson Dorset's possessions. Rarely did they talk to her about anything substantial. It was as if they thought she was a mindless blob, had to be because Thomas wouldn't tolerate a woman with an independent mind.

But Ben Stoddard was different. He was, according to Thomas, worth ten times as much as anyone else he knew, and very powerful. He was also not one to underestimate anyone, be they a woman or a man. She listened to what Stoddard had to say, and then Dr. Harrison Woodruff himself came to see her.

She wasn't terribly impressed with him personally. He was far too cold a man for her taste, and even a bit odd, but she ascribed that to his being a scientist. What sold her was the pictures he had brought along. She sat there perusing them in disbelief and then, on the last page, there was that picture of herself fifty years younger. It was impossible to turn away from that.

"You can do this?" she asked, incredulous when it pertained to her.

"Absolutely," he promised.

Now, a few months later, she was young and carefree, full of abandon and adventure, and she would be damned if she would let the likes of Zack Steiner put a governor on her new acceleration. But every time she came out of a nightclub or left an assignation, they were there, waiting to be of service. And also, they were there to remind her how much time remained. Dr. Woodruff was very explicit about that. He wanted her back at the compound, as it was now known, on schedule for follow-up examinations.

At four in the morning, after she and Webster had collapsed in each other's arms, he passing out from the booze as much as the lovemaking, she quietly got up and went to the window to look down on Wilshire Boulevard. As she expected, they were parked, waiting. Resigned to using them, she dressed, gazed down at this beautiful young man one final time, risked kissing him on the cheek and then left the apartment.

The moment she stepped out of the front entrance, Herbie Shagan got out of the vehicle and ran around to open the rear door for her. He had that shit-eating grin she despised.

"Have a good time, Mrs. Dorset?"

"Fuck you, Herbie," she said and he laughed. She settled back and then glanced once through the rear window to look up at Webster's penthouse. Why couldn't I have met a man like that years ago? she wondered. Why did I have to jump at money and power?

She liked to blame her marriage on her mother and father, who were so eager to see her married well, they deliberately blinded themselves to Thomas's bad qualities. Whatever she complained about, her mother diminished, or rationalized. She always fell back on that stupid statement, "It's just as easy to fall in love with a rich man as a poor one." It wasn't; it was harder, if not impossible.

"Mrs. Cornwall's finishing up with a bang tonight, huh?" Mike Robbins, who was driving, asked her.

"You probably know better than I do," Shelly snapped. Then she relaxed, thinking about Kathleen Cornwall. They had grown to become fast friends back at the compound. Kathleen was almost a stage ahead of her, so she left for her furlough nearly a week before Shelly had. But they met again at the safe house in Brentwood and started going out together, shopping together, enjoying lunches on the patios in Beverly Hills and West Hollywood together.

Shelly and Kathleen had completely different reactions to the deaths of their husbands. Kathleen had had a far better marriage than Shelly. Kathleen had loved her husband, Philip Cornwall, dearly and had felt great sadness and emptiness when he passed away. She continued to cherish and dote on Philip's possessions and had turned his den into a shrine, keeping it clean and everything polished just the way he would have if he were still alive. She hadn't given away a single thing, not clothing, shoes, nothing. Everything had remained as if he were just away on one of his business trips. Kathleen confessed to Shelly that she had gotten so she almost expected one day he would come walking through the front door and say, "Dead? You thought I was dead?"

She and Philip would laugh about it and go on and on forever. That's what Kathleen had told Shelly and Shelly's eyes had filled with tears, not so much for her friend as for herself, for she realized she hadn't had a relationship with half that passion and love and time had passed her by. Almost.

Kathleen told her she almost didn't choose the opportunity at Renaissance.

"A life without Philip seemed empty no matter what the circumstances," she said. "But then I thought, maybe I could find someone like him; maybe I could start again. And what was the alternative? My house was full of ghosts and my loneliness was so deep, I couldn't sleep; I couldn't eat. I was literally pining away.

What was it Rossetti wrote: "Beauty without the beloved is like a sword through the heart?" That's how I felt about everything, Shelly. I couldn't enjoy music, art, movies, theater. I had no patience for reading and I couldn't stand listening to my friends talk about their happy-go-lucky lives. I hated them for their happiness.

"So when I heard about Renaissance and Dr. Woodruff came around to see me . . ."

"I know," Shelly said. "It's wonderful we have this opportunity, that for the time being at least, the Renaissance Corporation wants to concentrate on wealthy widows, huh?"

It was wonderful, Shelly had agreed.

But now she was very worried about Kathleen. They had decided that they would have late breakfast or brunch together before Kathleen returned to the compound. Shelly slept late. Despite her fantastic new energy, she was quite exhausted when she finally went to bed at the safe house. It was nearly noon when she opened her eyes and by the time she showered and dressed, it was close to one.

The safe house was a walled-in Spanish hacienda. Shelly wasn't sure how many rooms were in it. The grounds were beautifully maintained. There was a Mediterranean-style pool in the rear, the kind of pool where the water came to the very top, overflowed, and recirculated. The tiled patio had luxurious, thick-cushioned lounges, pink-, white- and blue-padded chairs and umbrellas. There was always music and someone to serve you margaritas. To the right of the pool were two clay tennis courts, with a tennis instructor on call.

If Shelly wanted to remain at the safe house for dinner, she could order from a menu of great variety. The one time she and Kathleen had done so, they were both very impressed with the ambience, the service and the food. They had their own recreation room with a bar and music, too. One thing was for sure: Renaissance didn't stint on anything.

And there were other safe houses in other cities, if Shelly so chose. She could have gone to Miami, Portland, Vancouver, New York, Montreal, even San Juan. She had been everywhere, but she had never really spent a great deal of time in Los Angeles, and Hollywood was still Hollywood.

She was surprised Kathleen hadn't called her room or come around, but she imagined her friend had given her last fling all she had. Shelly laughed to herself, envisioning Kathleen's pursuit of one more orgasm. She walked down the carpeted corridor, its walls hung with large, gilt-framed paintings of the Costa del Sol, and cityscapes of Madrid and Barcelona that she recognized from her own travels. She passed medieval suits of armor and shields, and huge vases and pots filled with silk plants that she had to smell or touch to determine if they were real or not.

When she arrived at Kathleen's door, she tapped lightly and waited. There was no response, so she tried the doorknob and found it still locked. Surprised, but not willing to disturb her friend, Shelly returned to her room and ordered some coffee. She decided she would give Kathleen another half hour or so. After another thirty-five minutes, she was surprised when her new friend still hadn't phoned; she knew Kathleen had a tight schedule today, so she finally rang her. Confused when there was no answer, she walked down to Kathleen's room again.

This time she knocked hard and put her ear to the door to determine if Kathleen was in the shower. She heard nothing. She knocked again, practically pounding, and waited, but there was no response.

Shelly turned from Kathleen's doorway when she heard a door close up the tile corridor and saw a maid, Flora, emerging from another bedroom. She called to her. Flora always looked nervous about speaking to any of the guests. She pretended to know little English.

"*Buenos días, señorita,*" she said, and started to turn away. Shelly seized her arm.

"Open Mrs. Cornwall's room," she ordered. "I want to see that she's all right."

Flora looked terrified of the idea.

"*Abierto!* Open it!" Shelly commanded.

The maid inserted the key and turned the lock. Shelly pushed past her and gazed into a room that hadn't been disturbed. The room was empty, the bed unused. She knew Kathleen had been told to be back before morning. Where was she?

"Have you seen Mrs. Cornwall this morning, Flora?" Shelly asked.

"*No, señorita,*" she said, shaking her head. She looked absolutely terrified.

"All right. *Gracias,*" she said and waved at the door. Flora hurried away.

Shelly thought for a moment and then marched quickly down to the grand living room with its stone fireplace, layered pink shell fountain and sprawling Southwestern furniture. The floor was composed of Mexican pavers and the decor was all blue and mauve. Usually Mike Robbins, Herbie Shagan, Tommy Murden and Satch Norris were loitering about, watching television, betting on games and fights, or playing cards. This morning, she found no one.

Growing a bit frantic, she went to the dining room. René, the waiter, was thumbing through the newspaper and leaning against the wall near the kitchen door when she entered. He looked up expectantly.

"Breakfast, *señorita?*" he asked, jumping to attention.

"Where is everyone?" she demanded. He shook his head.

"The chef is in the kitchen," he replied stupidly.

"I don't mean him. I mean . . ." She wanted to say, the goons. "I mean my drivers."

"I don't know, *señorita.* I don't see no one this morning, *señorita,*" he replied. "Would you like some juice, coffee?"

"What? No, nothing," she snapped and headed for the front entrance. When she opened the door, she shaded her eyes from the bright sunlight and squinted. She saw Herbie and Mike near the wrought-iron front gate, smoking and talking. Mike saw her first and poked Herbie. They looked her way.

"What are you doing up so early, Mrs. Dorset?" Herbie said, smiling and walking toward her, the heels of his boots clicking on the cobblestone.

"Where's Mrs. Cornwall?" she demanded. Herbie looked back at Mike Robbins, who quickly followed.

Mike and Herbie exchanged a look and then Herbie shrugged.

"Ain't she upstairs, still sleeping it off as always?" he asked.

"No. She never used her room last night."

"No kidding? Never used it, huh?" Mike said, nodding.

"Well?" she demanded. "Don't you know anything about her whereabouts? Is there something wrong?"

"Hey, she ain't our responsibility. We got our hands full with you, Mrs. Dorset. She's Satch and Tommy's."

"Well, where are they?"

"I don't know," Herbie said. "That's right, Mike. Where are they?"

He shrugged.

"Maybe they started back for Renaissance already. She was due to return today, right?"

Mike shrugged.

"That's all we know, ma'am."

"I'm sure that's not all you know," Shelly said. She started to pivot.

"Er, there is one thing, Mrs. Dorset."

"And what's that?" she asked, turning back.

"We were told to keep you here at the hacienda until Dr. Woodruff speaks with you. He'll be calling you."

"Keep me here? What is that supposed to mean?" she asked, her eyes bright with indignation.

"Just that, Mrs. Dorset. We're supposed to ask you not to go anywhere until he calls."

"This is ridiculous. I will not be held prisoner by you or anyone else," she said, but she saw the gate was locked and the two were not intimidated. They both stared at her coldly. "When is he supposed to call me?" she demanded.

"Within the hour. He's traveling," Herbie said.

She glared back at him for a moment and then she pivoted to march back to the hacienda, her heart pounding. When she reached the front door, she looked back and saw they watched her without speaking. Then they turned casually and returned to the gate.

She decided to get some breakfast. All this commotion and excitement had stirred her appetite. She felt a bit foolish sitting by herself at the grand dining room table, but she ordered one of those fantastic omelettes Henry made and some of those fabulous soft rolls with jam. While she sat there eating, she thought about Kathleen and how good a time they were both having at Thunderbolt. How excited Kathleen had gotten when Webster and his friends had arrived.

"Two fish ten o'clock high," Kathleen had said. Shelly had laughed and then set eyes on Webster. He was a catch, she thought, and then she thought about doing the forbidden: calling him to see if he knew anything about Kathleen's whereabouts. It was forbidden because during this first furlough, Dr. Woodruff had asked that she not see anyone more than once.

"Don't develop any relationships just yet," he warned.

But perhaps Kathleen had remained with Webster's friend.

She went to the front window and looked out to see if Herbie and Mike were still at the gate. They were. Then she went to the phone in the den and she made the call.

After she heard what Webster had said and she had

warned him, she walked up to her room, her heart thumping. She saw her reflection in the bathroom mirror. She was nearly milk white. The blood had drained to her feet. She was suddenly unsteady and very groggy. She expected to be somewhat sleepy after the night she had had, but this onslaught of fatigue was too fast. Her eyelids felt like they were made of lead.

"What's going on?" she wondered and settled back in the big cushioned chair. She closed her eyes for a moment, hoping she wouldn't fall asleep and thus not hear the phone ringing. She was waiting for someone to call, right? Who again? Oh yes. Dr. Woodruff.

Why hadn't he called yet?

Why was she suddenly so tired?

Why did they shoot that nice-looking young man?

Where's Kathleen?

They put something in my coffee, she thought. It was her final thought before she drifted into a deep sleep.

The phone never rang.

6

"What the hell do you make of these guys?" Chicky asked Raul. He had just spoken to Webster on the phone and related Webster's conversation to Raul, who sat across from him doodling on a long yellow pad.

"To me it sounds like he was shit-faced when he brought the woman up to his place. Now with the murder of their friend, their imaginations are running wild. They're making it sound like these women escaped from a psycho ward or something, black-and-blue marks, his girlfriend warns him not to look for her . . . no addresses or phone numbers . . ."

"Think they're into something that resulted in their buddy's early demise?"

Raul considered and shrugged.

"Hey, you know better than me, Chicky. Don't discount anything these days. Even Mother Teresa could be fronting something. I'll run some background checks on both of them."

Chicky nodded and thought for a moment.

"And Carl Slotkin, too," he said.

"Right."

"What time they say the bartenders come on at Thunderbolt?"

Raul checked his watch.

"About now, to prep."

"Let's get over there with the drawings," Chicky said and pushed down on the desk, groaning as he dropped his body weight on his feet.

"Why don't you go to a fuckin' doctor, already?"

"Soon," Chicky promised. He hobbled behind his younger counterpart, quickly turning his grimace of pain into a smile when the chief of detectives glanced up from his desk. Raul caught it.

"Kronenberg's hoping you'll retire two weeks sooner," Raul muttered. "He's salivating over the money he's going to save on your salary."

"Reduced to a line on a budget. That's what you've got to look forward to, Torres. I'm hanging on just to aggravate the bastard," he added, and Torres laughed.

Dance clubs, even fancy ones that cost millions to create and decorate, had a tired, seedy look to them in daylight. To Chicky, who had been in them only when duty required, the walls looked grateful for the respite. This younger generation that gravitated to the expensive watering holes, seemingly oblivious to the loud music and noise, confused him. What sort of romance did they hope to initiate in such settings? Was it all done with sign language these days: eye contact, a gesture, turn of the shoulders, smiles and then they were rolling around in one or the other's bed?

Yet, he recognized that there was an excitement, a high they experienced in the rhythms and beats and under the roving spotlights. The bigger, more expensive clubs had these enormous large screen monitors that projected the dancers. For a few hours, at least, they were all stars, highlighted. It was the sort of activity that stroked egos and fulfilled fantasies. But what especially made Chicky shake his head in wonder was the sight of much older men and women, dressed in the garb of their children's generation, their hair similarly styled, out there on the dance floor, pretending they were in their twenties again. Or at least, as they liked to claim, catering to a younger viewpoint, unlike their contemporaries who had surrendered to golf carts and bingo. "If you think young, you'll stay young," he was told, but his reply was, "Tell that to my aching lower back."

Thunderbolt was no different from the other upscale discos in Los Angeles. Perhaps it was more glitzy, had more lights, more gimmickry. Two men in their thirties owned the establishment, Mike Hoffman and his cousin, Dave Deutch. Their fathers, brothers, had given them the money to invest, and finally, after losing thousands of their fathers' money in other pipe dreams, they had an enterprise that was making a real profit. Their fathers had finally come to the realization, however, that neither son was much of a businessman. They hired an accounting firm, Rapp, Carn and Daniels, to ride herd over their progeny. The two owners were at the bar, reviewing the firm's analysis and instructions with a junior accountant, when Chicky and Raul entered.

They showed I.D. and explained what they wanted.

Mike Hoffman, who had been involved in a car rental agency that had gone under when it was discovered a number of the vehicles he had purchased were stolen, was more sensitive about their visit and questions.

"This isn't getting the place in the newspapers, is it?" he whined.

"No reason for that," Raul said. "Nothing illegal happened here. That we know about," he added. "Is there something you want to tell us?"

"Just let them talk to Ted and Art, will you?" Dave Deutch urged his cousin." The junior accountant whispered in Mike's ear and Mike called the bartenders.

"These are two LAPD detectives," he said. "Cooperate with them, will ya?"

Raul showed them the drawings.

"We're looking for these two women. We need addresses, phone numbers, where they worked, anything you can tell us about them."

"They look like at least a dozen women I've seen in here," Ted said. Art nodded.

"I think I did see this one," he said, pointing to Kathleen. "She's been in here a few times this month."

"Anything you remember about her, any detail?"

Art gazed at the owners who were watching and listening like two hovering hawks.

"We don't fraternize much with the clientele. It's not like your neighborhood tavern where people sit and talk to the bartender all day or night," Art said.

"Probably couldn't hear much anyway," Chicky muttered.

"What?"

"I was going to ask you about the health of your hearing."

Art glanced at the owners again and then in sotto voce said, "I wear some cotton."

"And we think we have a dangerous job," Chicky quipped. Raul nodded.

"You want to look at these pictures again?" Chicky asked Ted. The younger of the two bartenders gazed at the drawings, but shook his head.

"I don't know. Maybe they're on a tape."

"Tape!" Chicky and Raul said simultaneously and looked at Hoffman and Deutch.

"We videotape a little every once in a while and play with editing to give the clientele the feeling they'll be seen more."

"Where are these tapes?"

"We don't keep them long. All we have is tape from what, the last two weekends?" Mike asked Dave. He nodded.

"What about last night?" Chicky asked.

"Yeah, we have it."

"I'd like to have someone view it," Chicky said.

"What did these girls do?" Mike asked.

"One or maybe both might be involved in a murder," Raul said.

The two owners looked at each other and then at the junior accountant, who shook his head with concern.

"I'll get the tape," Dave said and went to the control room, which looked as elaborate and complicated as a regular network television control room. He returned with the tapes and gave them to Raul.

"If either of you think this woman has shown up again, please give me a call," Chicky said, handing his card to Art and Ted.

"What happened to your foot?" Art asked as Chicky and Raul started away. Chicky glanced at Raul before replying. His partner was smiling gleefully.

"Some heavy woman stepped on it on the dance floor at Roseland," Chicky said.

"Roseland? Where's that?"

"East," Chicky said. Raul shook his head, laughing as they left.

"I gotta go up to the hospital," Chicky told him in the car. "It's the day I have dinner with Maggie."

"No problem. I'll round up Martin and Gold and have them glued to the television monitor at the station."

"I'll come down right after," Chicky promised. At the station he got into his own car and headed for the psychiatric hospital in which his wife of nearly thirty-five years, nearly suffering a lobotomy by chemical therapy, sat staring at the television set in the recreation room. For her all the programs seemed to run together, and if she did laugh, which was rare, it was usually thirty or forty seconds after the comedy had implanted itself on her retina. The journey to her brain was that cluttered with mangled and discarded thought.

As usual when he arrived, Chicky stopped to speak to the doctor on duty. This time it was the younger man, Dr. Seligman. He was well into his mid-forties, but he was one of those people who seemed to age at a snail's pace. There wasn't a strand of gray in his dark brown. When it did come, the contrast would be sharp and quickly reveal it. His almond eyes had the glint of youth that complemented his smooth skin, soft mouth and gentle jawline. On the telephone, he sounded like a teenager. It was hard to listen to him and accept his knowledge and expertise while looking at him. This was an example of where age was an asset. Doctors, Chicky thought, should graduate from medical school looking like they were old, reliable and wise.

Chicky knocked on the office door and peeked in. Seligman was at his desk, writing. He looked up and smiled.

"Good evening, Mr. Siegler."

"How you doing? How is my wife doing?"

"Oh, she's been doing fine. We haven't had any talk of suicide or reference to it for some time. She's been more active in the recreation room and she's been reading again. I think we're closing in on the right doses.

"I had a really interesting conversation with her this afternoon," he added, sitting back.

"Oh. About what?"

"You know. How she sees herself, what bothers her. I'm preparing an article for *Psychology Today* about this subject," he said, nodding at his note pad.

"What subject?" Chicky didn't like the thought that his wife was some sort of statistic for some doctor's article.

"Depression and its causes in the modern world, to be exact," Seligman replied somewhat pedantically.

"I thought her problem was chemical."

"Oh, it is, to a large extent, but when the problem arises in people, certain things exacerbate it.

"For example, people today, especially women, because they're targeted more by the media, are obsessed with being young and looking youthful, thin, attractive. The older we get and the more age reveals itself, the more depressed we become, even without a chemical unbalance. That's normal to a certain extent of course, but there used to be something called growing old gracefully. Now, we tell people to resist, battle, exercise, eat differently, and when all else fails, see the plastic surgeon.

"Why are you limping?" he suddenly asked.

"Huh? Oh, corns I let get away."

Seligman nodded and then squinted as he suddenly focused on Chicky.

"You're close to retirement, aren't you, Detective?"

"Yeah, close."

"How do you feel about that?" he asked. He had his pen poised.

"Fucking grateful," Chicky said. "My wife in recreation?"

"Yes, she is," Doctor Seligman said with disappointment.

"Thanks," Chicky muttered and limped down the corridor.

Maggie was sitting with three other patients in the recreation room. From previous visits, he recognized them. Two of them, a young blond man with eyebrows so light they looked nonexistent over his powder-blue eyes and a thin woman suffering anorexia nervosa, looked at him and smiled in greeting. He said hello and approached Maggie. She gazed up at him.

"Hi, honey," he said.

She looked back at the television set. Then she looked up at him again as if he had been there for hours.

"Suppertime?"

"Yep," he said. She looked at the television, sighed deeply and then stood up. The emerald green hospital gown she wore looked a size too large. Although she wore a pair of thongs on her bare feet, she lumbered along as if she wore iron boots. He took her hand quickly when she reached the doorway and they walked out together.

The cafeteria was clean and brightly lit by three-foot-long fluorescent bulbs in bland fixtures; the eggshell-white walls and black tile floor had been scrubbed shiny and clean. The tables were a light gray Formica; the kitchen equipment, dazzling stainless steel. Despite the fact that it was nearly three-quarters full, the cafeteria was relatively quiet, many of the patients eating without speaking to each other. The food was halfway decent, but Chicky didn't have much of an appetite. He rarely did when he came here and only forced himself to eat to make sure Maggie was comfortable.

After they got their food and sat at a table for two, she ate slowly, mechanically. Her once vibrantly blue eyes were subdued, dim, glazed. She had her hair brushed down and tied softly just at the nape of her neck. Maggie still had a remarkably rich complexion, smooth, almost alabaster skin. Tiny blue veins were visible at her temples.

Chicky didn't understand what Dr. Seligman had just told him about depression and Maggie. If anyone had aged gracefully, it was Maggie. When people learned her age, they were convinced she had had cosmetic surgery. She always looked after herself, exercised, ate well and, long before it was emphasized, avoided excessive exposure to the sun.

I guess we never see ourselves the way others see us, Chicky thought. Maggie had been looking in the mirror and spotting the tiniest changes. She probably knew the exact number of gray strands in her light brown hair.

Maybe the kids were right: maybe he did bear some blame. He never complimented her enough; he took too much for granted. He always assumed that whenever she saw the way he looked at her, she felt his love, his admiration. Perhaps he was too much of a cop, too dedicated to the job, always bringing it home with him. How many times did he drift off while he and Maggie were supposedly having a romantic dinner?

Still, he rationalized, I wasn't any different when we first met. She knew what she was buying into when she said "I do." Maybe she thought she would change me or I would change myself. Disappointments in love and marriage grow like tumors and infect everything, if they're permitted free rein, he thought.

"You're on a new case?" she asked suddenly.

He smiled. He was doing it again, and sedated or not, Maggie knew when his mind was racing along other mental highways.

"Yep. Murder. Young man about twenty-six. Picked up a woman in a dance club. The next morning his friend finds him shot in the head and heart; the woman's disappeared."

"It's safer in here," she said. He laughed.

"Maybe I'll move in with you."

She stared at him as if he had made a possible suggestion.

"Jackie wants me to go live with her. She never stops asking."

"We all want you out of here, Maggie," he said, reaching for her hand. She didn't squeeze back. She gazed down at their two hands.

"I'm going to retire soon, you know. And then I'll be all alone."

"I've been alone a long time, Chicky. You get used to it," she said.

"Come on. You haven't been alone, honey."

She just nodded.

"It will be different," he promised.

"Different?"

"Better. I swear."

She smiled at him as if he had said a childish thing. He raised his eyebrows and smiled back.

"I mean it, Maggie. This old dog has really learned some new tricks."

She took a deep breath and then nodded slowly.

"I have thought about it," she confessed. His eyes brightened with hope. "If I could walk out of here and you and I could go back to the time before reality, when we were happily stupid in our dreams, just for a little while again, I'd trade all my remaining days of gloom."

"Hey, we can be happy again. I'm going to retire. It will be just the two of us. We'll travel, see things. Remember when I talked about getting a mobile home? I've been checking them out. I'm going to look into it, seriously. I told you I got an offer on the house," he said quickly. The excitement of such a possibility did make him feel young again.

But Maggie pulled her hand back.

"I don't want to look forward to anything," she said. "That way, I won't be disappointed."

"You won't be," he pledged.

An elderly man at a table in the corner began to laugh aloud. There was no one with him, so he was laughing at his own thoughts. His laughter grew so intense, he started to cough and choke on his food. The attendant had to rush to him and help him swallow some water. He calmed down, but he was too weak to continue eating and the attendant took him out of the cafeteria. It sent a cold shiver up Chicky's spine. It felt like a hand made of ice had seized the back of his neck and his hair stood up.

He reached for Maggie again.

"I love you, Maggie," he said. "I really need you."

"Do you?" she asked with surprise.

"Yes," he insisted.

She looked down at her food and then up at him again, her eyes tearful.

"Give me a little more time, Chicky."

He sat back. That was something. That was an improvement. She saw a possibility.

But he wondered if she was right not wanting anything so she wouldn't be disappointed. And suddenly he realized if we didn't have hope, we wouldn't have fear, because fear was only the threat of disappointment. She meant it when she said she was safer in here. In here she expected nothing. There were no risks.

But loving someone was built on hope. Sure it was filled with risk and with disappointment, but it was still something that gave your life greater meaning. Nothing worth anything was easy. He just had to convince Maggie that loving him was worth it again.

How do I do that? he wondered.

The answer came as simply as the question. He had to show her that he really did need her. He had chosen a profession that required him to be macho. He had to radiate self-confidence and never show weakness. It could be fatal. He had been so good at being strong, he couldn't relax. He couldn't let down his guard, even with her and their own children. The job had consumed him. He resembled an actor who had gotten into his role so well, he was no longer acting. He had become the character.

But now that he was seriously thinking of retiring, he could come to her and say, "You know what? I'm afraid of disappointment, too."

He could cry. He could cling. And maybe, finally, they would be man and wife.

7

Zack Steiner was waiting at the Palm Springs airport when Dr. Harrison Woodruff arrived on the American Eagle shuttle. Like two bookends, Satch Norris and Tommy Murden stood stiffly beside him.

At fifty-five, Zack was still a very fit man whose lethal capabilities had not diminished one iota, but he harbored the fear that if he wasn't used for what he was trained to be, he would lose the edge. Few CIA operatives enjoyed the work as much as Zack had, and in fact, it was that unabashed pride in the successful kill that troubled his immediate supervisor who eventually recommended him for transfer to a desk job.

Zack opted for early retirement. He had made enough contacts to get himself a position in the private sector working corporate security. Now that the Cold War had ended, industrial espionage had taken the front seat. He had qualities that were of inestimable value to some business executives. One of these qualities was his loyalty to whoever employed him.

He rarely questioned orders and only did so from a technical standpoint, if he did. Zack's allegiance, however, wasn't motivated by the monetary rewards. His fidelity was to the process, to the legalization or, in corporate activity, the rationalization of the violence he committed. It was like bringing a compulsive vandal to an old building and saying, "Go ahead, throw rocks through the windows. It's okay. We want you to do it. No one will blame you or take you to task."

They even put the rock in his hand.

But loyalty was truly his one admirable quality. Once he was given a command, he would follow it as gospel. He was as dependable as anyone could be without being robotic. He wasn't happy about this particular assignment; actually, he had grown to the point where he hated it, but it was an assignment Ben Stoddard had personally asked him to assume, and Ben Stoddard was a man who appeared to have almost as much power as some executives in the CIA.

"It won't be forever," Stoddard promised when Zack expressed some reluctance after he heard he would be baby sitting some scientist doing research in Palm Springs, California. It sounded too simple, too sedentary. "I need a good man to handle the security and associated matters from the start. After we're well under way, I'll replace you and get you an assignment more to your liking, if you want. For now, Zack, you're going to have to be something of an administrator. I'm even going to expect written reports," he said smiling.

"Who am I working for?" he asked.

"The Renaissance Corporation. It's real. I formed it myself. I'll introduce you to the head of research and development, Dr. Woodruff. Hopefully, you two will get along well enough to keep everything running smoothly."

Zack didn't like Harrison Woodruff from the moment he set eyes on him. Not only was Woodruff too soft a man for Zack's liking, he was condescending, making Zack feel as if he were some plumber here to fix the toilets. Zack sensed that in Woodruff's eyes the work Zack did was too dirty, below him. But this type of man was helpless without his wallet, Zack thought. He had no survival skills unless you wanted to consider balancing a checkbook a survival skill.

However, people in high places were supporting Harrison Woodruff and his Renaissance Project. Zack was intrigued with the wand of power he wielded under the umbrella of the Renaissance Corporation. There wasn't a police agency, a government agency, anything or anyone remotely connected to the power structure, that couldn't be used or manipulated if need be. Agencies, organizations and individuals who were normally in some conflict were suddenly eager to be cooperative. The way the Renaissance Corporation was given the highest priorities, he felt as if he were still in the CIA.

"There he is," Tommy said.

"I can see," Zack snapped.

Harrison acknowledged them with a nod. Despite their size and their downright vicious nature, both of Zack Steiner's men looked meek and polite whenever they were in his presence. To Harrison it seemed they were always anticipating Zack's explosion of anger. Steiner looked harder than his cohorts, his face cut from granite. Physically he was in far superior shape, and there was a look in his eyes that told of his ability to distribute death wantonly, indiscriminately, casually, if necessary, without a hint of conscience.

Harrison found it ironic that Steiner was a snappy dresser. Always in style, his ties were the current fashionable width, as were his jacket lapels. His shoes had a military shine, his hair was neatly brushed. He looked like he shaved with a scalpel, not a fugitive hair visible on his neck or his chin or cheeks. He had a collection of expensive watches—Piagets, Movados and Rolexes—and wore whichever matched his outfit. Today, he wore the Movado.

"Get his bag," he snapped and Tommy rushed forward to take Harrison's carry-on. Harrison was going to protest; it was just a carry-on, but he decided not to counter one of Steiner's commands.

"What's going on?" Harrison asked immediately. Zack glanced at some of the tourists moving toward the metal detector, turned and marched just a step faster, forcing Harrison to speed up as well.

"Wait until we're in the car," he replied sharply.

Harrison understood that Steiner had been waiting at the gate just for drama. Ordinarily, he would be in the car listening to his Gregorian chants and smoking those long, thin brown cigarettes he imported from Italy.

The black Mercedes limousine with the heavily tinted side and rear windows was at the curb where parking was expressly forbidden, but no one ticketed the car or even came looking for the driver. Satch moved forward quickly to open the door for Zack and Harrison. Zack stood back to let him get in first, which was not a polite gesture, but an instinct. Zack always paused at his car to gaze around quickly to see if anyone were watching.

Satch got behind the wheel and Tommy, after he put Harrison's carry-on into the trunk, got into the front quickly. A moment later they were headed for Renaissance.

"Well?" Harrison said firmly. "You've succeeded in getting my full attention, Mr. Steiner."

"Finally," Zack muttered. "I told you how I felt about these furloughs, as you called them, when you first told me what you were planning to do."

"And I thought I explained why it is important to keep my subjects emotionally happy. Stress has an impact on my results. Besides, the whole purpose of this is to reintroduce them to the outside and see if they can readjust, function, live normal lives again," Harrison lectured.

Zack lit one of his long, thin cigarettes and blew the smoke into the ceiling. Then, he gazed out the window for a moment. No one uttered a sound.

"Mrs. Cornwall resisted retrieval," Zack finally said.

"Resisted retrieval?" Harrison grimaced. "I'm not sure I understand."

At times Zack Steiner did seem to speak a different language. Words and phrases were chosen for their euphemistic value. People weren't killed anymore; they were terminated. No one was kidnapped; he was impounded.

Zack turned, the right corner of his upper lip lifted into his cheek.

"She wouldn't stop fucking the man she picked up at

the disco. She didn't come out when she was supposed to. My men were patient, nevertheless. They waited until morning and then they tried to call her, but no one answered the phone."

"Really?"

"Yes, really. According to the schedule, she was supposed to be out by two A.M., three at the latest. She could sleep late into the morning. You gave her permission to leave the safe house by midafternoon," Zack added. "She was even scheduled to have brunch with Mrs. Dorset." Steiner described the social schedule as if every event was a bitter pill he had to swallow.

"I know the details of her schedule," Harrison said. He hated repetition and thought redundancy was the Eighth Deadly Sin. "And I was very clear about the time, adamant about it."

"Not adamant enough; not clear enough, apparently. It put pressure on my men; they had to make a decision on the spot, in the field."

"What did they do?" Harrison asked, looking toward the front of the vehicle. Both Satch and Tommy kept their faces forward, their heads and shoulders so stiff, they looked like manikins.

"They went up to get her, and . . ." Zack said and blew some more smoke.

"Yes, and?" Harrison asked, annoyed at Zack's deliberate hesitation.

"They found she was her old self."

"What?" Satch turned and smiled at Zack. "I don't understand and I don't appreciate having to pull teeth here, Mr. Steiner."

"You don't have to pull teeth. They all fell out."

Tommy laughed.

"Mrs. Cornwall has had, what you doctors would call, a relapse."

"Relapse?" Harrison grimaced. "You mean, aged?"

"I'm afraid that's the way to put it," Zack said.

Harrison felt a heaviness in his chest. Suddenly the air-conditioned automobile was stifling. He swallowed.

"What happened?"

"Well, since they found she had already started to regress in front of the man she was with, they had no choice. They terminated him and packed her up."

"Terminated him?"

"You should have seen how stupid she looked in that dress," Satch added. "Right, Tommy?"

"Really stupid, Zack," Tommy echoed.

"You had the man killed?"

"It was necessary," Zack said sharply, "or it wouldn't have been done."

"Where is Mrs. Cornwall now?"

"In the lab at the compound. Miss Kleindeist isolated her."

"But what about this . . . termination?"

"What about it?"

"Won't it create other problems?"

"Everything's been taken care of for now, Doctor. I've given orders to keep Mrs. Dorset at the safe house. My suggestion is you retrieve her before something else occurs. Obviously, the process you thought was perfected, is not, and we can't be everywhere every moment with them, you know."

Harrison said nothing. He sat back, the disappointment draining him of energy.

What had gone wrong? He had thought he had succeeded. Everything looked fine. If anything, they were growing healthier, sharper, stronger. Regression was eliminated. He thought he had waited long enough before sending them out to see how they would function in a normal setting.

"Well?" Zack pursued.

"Well what?"

"Should we retrieve Mrs. Dorset?"

"She's been out only a little more than a week," Harrison said, hating himself for sounding like he was whining. He should have more confidence and authority in Steiner's presence. Steiner worked for him. It wasn't the other way around.

"You want to take another chance in light of this situation?"

"Let me think about it," Harrison said.

"Yeah, think about it."

Zack sucked on his cigarette and blew the smoke straight into the back of Tommy's head.

Harrison wasn't looking forward to what he would find at the compound. After recruiting what he considered one of his best candidates in New Orleans, he was upbeat and optimistic. Now, a cloud of gloom hovered above the entire project. It colored the way he viewed the world, even here in the normally beautiful desert twilight. The descending sun's rays painted streaks of turquoise and pink across the nearly cloudless sky. Deep shadows poured over the San Jacinto and San Andreas mountains. But for Harrison, it was all stark gray and gloomy.

As soon as they drove up to the clubhouse, he hurried out of the car.

"Take your time, Doctor. She ain't going anywhere," Zack called after him. He heard the three laugh behind him as he pushed open the door and marched over the tiled lobby to the corridor on the left. The lighting was deliberately dim, but at the end of the corridor, the nurse's station was well illuminated. Sandra Kleindeist lifted her gaze from the papers on her desk and saw him approaching. She rose quickly.

"How is she?"

"Fading fast," she replied. "The progeria is acute. She's in number four."

Harrison turned to the doorway of the room, his heart thumping from a mixture of fear and anger. It was as if Nature were punishing him for toying with Her. The irony was so sharp. He could almost hear Her whispering in his ear. "Trying to stop the natural aging process? I'll show you what that gets you . . . an accelerated aging process. How do you like those apples?"

Harrison paused just inside the door and gazed at the once attractive, elderly lady he had promised renewal. He recalled how lonely she was and how his project held up a glimmer of hope, a reason to go on. Now, she was shriveling right before his eyes.

Sandra Kleindeist had placed the now sixty- or sixty-five-pound woman in bed with the sides up. It looked like a large cradle. From the cradle to the cradle and then to the grave, Harrison thought sadly. Kathleen was curled in a fetal position. The skin on her face, her hands, legs and arms was thin, folded in dry ridges. Her hair was nearly all gone and the chalky surface of her small skull was completely visible. Her eyes were already sewn tight, the lids in tiny folds, and a thin, yellow line along her sunken cheeks emanated from the corners of those eyes.

Usually, the strange and rare disease of progeria affected young people. Infants with progeria appeared normal at birth but within a few years began to look old, developing a relatively large head and beaked nose. Their skin became thin, hair was lost and accelerated atherosclerosis developed. Heart attacks became common by the age of ten or so and their life span was often no longer than fifteen years.

Many scientists had long held the theory that longevity was determined by the ability of the cells to divide and replace themselves. The DNA in the original fertilized egg cell held the entire set of genetic instructions that preprogrammed the course of an organism's life. Triggering substances, often hormones, switched on genes to transmit their essential instructions at the proper time.

Of course science knew that normal cells do not live forever. Under certain circumstances, cells were in fact programmed to die. Human embryos start with paddles for hands, for example, and it is cell death that gives them fingers. Dr. Woodruff knew from his research on cancer cells that they were cells that seemed to have forgotten how to die. He concentrated his attention on the why. He knew that healthy cells apparently had a precise system for ensuring their mortality; short strips of DNA known as telomeres appeared to provide a molecular clock. When a cell was young, it had more than a thousand telomeres strung along the ends of chromosomes like beads in a necklace. Each time the cell divided, ten to twenty telomeres were lost and the necklace grew shorter. Eventually, after many cell divisions, the necklace became so short that the cell failed an internal healthy check designed to keep old, possibly damaged cells from reproducing. The result was a cessation of cell division; the cell began to age rapidly.

Most of the time nine to ten trillion cells in the average human body had the capacity to replace themselves as they wore out or died. In humans the cell division was about fifty, but in the Galapagos tortoise, for example, the cells would undergo ninety to one hundred and twenty-five doublings. People afflicted with progeria, on the other hand, were limited to around ten. Even if the cells were put into a deep freeze for a period of years and then thawed and put back into the culture, the cells "remembered" and went through only the limited multiplications and ceased.

Cell division longevity, therefore, apparently was predetermined. Nevertheless, Dr. Woodruff began with the theory that age was a disease. The symptom, loss of cells, showed itself through what was known as the aging process. There was a decline in height, shrinkage of muscle, thinning and graying of hair and wrinkling of skin. Internally, and more significant, there was the progressive loss of cells in the brain, kidneys and other vital organs.

While working at the Gerontology Research Center, a branch of the National Institute on Aging in Bethesda,

Maryland, he had experimented with the theory that cells that have lost the capacity to reproduce themselves could be taught to do it again. He discovered hormones that triggered the reproductive process and then proceeded to create an artificial virus made of perfectly copied DNA molecules. Once transfused into the subject, it revitalized the cell's failing powers and reproduced the telomeres, thus rejuvenating the subject. He had succeeded with pigs first and then, after he had left the Institute and had had his own research unit created by the Renaissance Corporation, without any government agency limiting his experimentation, moved to human subjects.

The experimentation had begun with the homeless. The results in the early days were dramatic but always fatal. It was why he had this unreasonable and admittedly unscientific fear that Nature was punishing the subjects for his toying with the process. These early subjects developed accelerated progeria after only a few days of rejuvenation and degenerated in a matter of days.

As he improved and the rejuvenation lasted longer and longer, he began to interest the right people in his project and he got more cooperation and more money. It also provided him with a network of support, ranging from the security system Zack Steiner oversaw to the influence Harrison enjoyed with other government agencies.

It was Harrison's idea that they experiment on wealthy elderly people who would also contribute financially to the project. He recalled when he had first proposed they stop using homeless old people and carefully select wealthy widows and widowers instead. Ben Stoddard, the chairman of the Renaissance Corporation, didn't see why they should suddenly involve the project in so much effort to get subjects for experimentation. They had an endless, safe source. Who really cared about the homeless?

Of course, the homeless wouldn't be missed, Harrison agreed, but they were without hope now and they wouldn't have any afterward. Why rejuvenate people who wouldn't appreciate it or benefit from it? What was even more important was they would only provide half the study results.

"I need to know how the subject behaves in rejuvenation, too. I need subjects who have the will and the desire to go back, to have a second chance. Homeless people, for the most part, are deranged mentally. We won't be able to trace their genealogy. They won't have the same commitment to the project. And we can get the wealthy to commit money, too," Harrison added.

Stoddard nodded slowly and widened his eyes.

"You're right," he said. "We'll do it your way with only one codicil: use only wealthy widows." Stoddard smiled. "After you've perfected the process, I want to be the first male rejuvenated. Besides," he added not without some bitterness, "women usually outlive their husbands. There are more of them for experimentation; they're more expendable."

Stoddard, ironically, had outlived his own wife. Harrison knew from the well-subdued whispering that Stoddard had young women brought to him. However, unlike most wealthy, older men, he didn't flaunt the beautiful women by having them at his arm when he attended shows and balls, nor was he often seen with a young woman at any of the restaurants. Stoddard thought his elderly friends looked absolutely ridiculous beside women less than half their ages. Out of fear their associates pretended they believed the women really admired these men, but of course, they were there only because of the money and power.

Stoddard, on the other hand, was fascinated with Harrison's work at Renaissance, because if he did succeed and Stoddard could be rejuvenated, he would win the love of one of his beautiful women and have a second chance at a real romance. Who wouldn't want another opportunity if he could carry his wisdom and experience back with him for the new start?

And so, the second phase involving only wealthy widows began. Harrison had no problem promising his wealthy female candidates he could rejuvenate them forever. After all, he believed he was continually on the verge of the breakthroughs that would make that true. He recognized the risks, of course, but, he reasoned, these wealthy women had little or no future anyway. What time he gave them was still a precious gift and they were contributing through their funds and their bodies toward the ultimate goal, weren't they?

Still, when he gazed at Kathleen Cornwall, one of, he thought, his better subjects, he felt some remorse. He recalled the way she glowed as the reversal began to take effect. Every day he came into her room, he found her staring at her image in the mirror.

"I can't believe it," she said. "Look at my skin. Feel how smooth. Look at how thick my hair is again. And, Doctor, watch this!"

She squatted with her hands on her hips, kicked out her right foot and then her left like a Cossack dancer. Harrison Woodruff laughed.

"I used to do that all the time," she said. "I must admit," she confessed when she stood up, "I was skeptical, very skeptical."

"Who wouldn't be? I appreciate your trust and faith," he said. She was positively radiant.

"I can't wait to try out this new body," she said. "I want to dance again, eat spicy foods, buy the latest fashions, go to the theater, flirt, flirt and then make love the way I used to with Philip. Of course, I won't just throw myself at anyone," she added. Harrison laughed. It was wonderful how, despite her mental age, she was young at heart again, adventurous, impulsive, exciting. "What about it?" she asked, and then they talked about her furlough. She resembled a schoolgirl learning what her first trip away from home would be like, hanging on his every word, her eyes bright with expectation.

Now look at her, he thought. Her thin frame shuddered. The skin on the backs of her hands flaked and the odor of decomposing flesh rose to his nostrils.

Sandra Kleindeist came up beside him.

"She's going faster than the other two," she said. No one except him and Sandra Kleindeist knew about the two other recent failures. He nodded sadly. He was convinced he had solved the problem; he really was.

"Mr. Stoddard called."

Harrison turned.

"Oh?"

"He's at the Ritz in Rancho Mirage. He wants you to

join him for a late dinner tonight. I assumed it would be all right."

"Of course. Did he inquire about Mrs. Cornwall?" he asked, assuming Zack Steiner had already made a report to Ben Stoddard.

"No." She smirked. "But that doesn't mean he doesn't know," she added. Harrison nodded.

Then they both turned abruptly because Zack Steiner appeared in the doorway as if he sensed they were thinking about him.

"Now that you've seen her, have you thought about Mrs. Dorset?" Zack demanded. Harrison gazed at Kathleen Cornwall again and then turned back to him.

"Okay. Bring her back. Retrieve her," he said sharply. Zack smiled.

"Very wise, Doctor," he said. Zack started to turn away.

"Mr. Steiner."

"Doctor?"

"Don't frighten her and don't harm her."

"Why, Dr. Woodruff, I'm surprised at you. Don't you have any confidence in me?" He put a new thin cigarette into his mouth and gazed with ice in his eyes.

Harrison turned away. Kathleen Cornwall was beginning to sound her death rattle. It would be only a matter of a few more minutes.

Somewhere in the back of his mind was the annoying thought that Nature had deliberately waited for his arrival so he could witness the death.

8

You never know how stupid people look out there until you see them when you're sober," Webster commented as he and Phil viewed the videotape from Thunderbolt.

"There are a few women out there who don't look so bad," Phil said.

Raul grunted his agreement and smiled. The three of them were in a conference room at the station, Raul standing and leaning against the wall, Webster and Phil seated before the monitor. It was five-thirty. Webster told Raul he and Phil could view the tape until six-thirty. Whatever they had left to look at, they would look at to-morrow. He didn't want to postpone the dinner with his father, especially by telling him they were down at the police station, participating in the murder investigation.

"No chance you two guys knew these women from somewhere before, huh?" Raul suddenly asked.

Webster glanced up at him and saw how keenly the

detective was waiting for their response, studying their reactions to his question.

"I think we'd know if we did," Webster replied sharply. Raul nodded.

"I just thought they might have seen you, you might have seen them, even for a few minutes someplace else," he fished.

"If I saw this woman someplace before, I'd know a lot more about her by now. Besides, how could we . . . why would we keep something like that secret? What are you suggesting?"

"Hey, I gotta ask questions. Sometimes, it stimulates memories and we all benefit," Raul protested.

Webster smirked and glanced at Phil, who closed and opened his eyes. They both squirmed in their chairs.

"This doesn't look like the night I was there," Webster said, now irritable. "Maybe they gave you the wrong tape."

"The owners said that was from last night."

"Maybe they taped before we arrived or . . ." Webster leaned toward the set. "Wait a minute. Wind it back."

Raul jumped to do so.

"I'll run it slow motion," he said. Webster studied the screen. Between two dancers, he could see himself and then, he saw Shelly.

"That's Shelly!"

Raul froze the frame. Webster got up and pointed her out on the screen.

"Okay. That's good. Look for Carl," Raul said. He noted the number on the counter and started the tape. Webster was glued to the screen.

"Isn't that him, Web?" Phil said. "In the right corner?"

"Yeah. I think so. Damn, they moved the camera."

"Maybe they'll go back," Raul said. After five more minutes, the camera did pan left and Carl came into view, only he was blocking the woman he was with. Just as it looked like the camera was moving away again, he stepped to the left and she came into view.

"It's her!" both Webster and Phil cried. Raul marked the counter.

"That's great. We'll make something of those shots."

"What are you going to do?" Phil asked.

"We'll freeze the picture and blow it up into a still. Thanks a lot. You've been a great help," Raul said.

Webster and Phil rose, but Webster turned at the door.

"Will you tell me if you find her?" he asked.

"Sure. We'll need a personal identification from both of you," Raul replied. He watched them leave and then took out the tape to bring to the lab. Afterward, he left word with the dispatcher that he was going home to have dinner.

"Tell Chicky I have an I.D. from the tapes and I'm having them blown up into stills. I'll be back in two hours," Raul said.

Two hours and ten minutes later, Chicky was at his desk waiting for him when Raul returned. One look at Chicky's face told Raul Chicky didn't have as good a time at dinner as he had had.

"Because I hurried through dinner and rushed back here, Tina thinks I'm turning into you," Raul said as he sat down. It wasn't until he had done so that Chicky realized Raul was there. He looked up, surprised, and shook his head.

"Don't do that, Torres. Whatever you do, don't turn into me."

"It was bad?" Raul asked, assuming Chicky's visit to his wife was the reason he was so down.

"I don't know. I don't know how we got to this point, how all this was going on while I was out stalking vampires. I used to think Maggie was secretly very proud of me, you know. Every time we brought one in, she seemed to strut about the house. I guess I was just hoping or imagining it all," he said, shaking his head.

"One time, not so long ago, when we had an argument, she told me I was nothing but a different sort of garbage man. Maybe that's true," Chicky muttered. Raul thought his mentor suddenly looked terribly old. It put a cold chill in his heart.

"What do the doctors say?"

Chicky shrugged.

"That she's not talking suicide anymore. They think they have her medicine adjusted right."

"So, she's getting better. You have to look for the break in the clouds, Chicky. Don't concentrate on the overcast."

Chicky raised his eyebrows and looked at Raul.

"What are you, a weatherman now?" Chicky laughed and then turned serious. "What happened with the video? Pete said something about positive I.D.'s."

"It paid off. They spotted the two women. I brought the tape to the lab. They should have the pictures isolated and blown up for us by now," Raul said.

"That's good news."

"Yeah. I did the background checks on these guys. Motherhood and apple pie."

"Straight?"

"Looks like it. Webster Martin is a hardworking young man. He and his father have built up quite a construction outfit. Phil Gold has an impeccable reputation and is an up-and-comer in the insurance game. Slotkin was doing well, too. Not making a fortune, but respectable."

"Impeccable? You're improving your vocabulary, Torres."

"That correspondence course Tina made me take," he replied. "No record of anything, not even a speeding ticket."

"Anything on the water glass?"

"There were two clear prints, but so far, nothing."

"What else do we have?"

"All the blood found belonged to Slotkin. Powder stains on the rug put the shooter at the door. Forensics says the pubic hair sample was gray, Caucasian."

"Gray? You mean like in old?"

"It wasn't dyed gray, and yes, quite old, dead strands." Chicky smirked.

"There were some gray strands on the pillow next to Carl Slotkin, too."

"Didn't Phil Gold tell us she had dark brown hair?"

"Yeah, and the young woman they picked out of the video has dark brown hair."

"I guess she's just turning prematurely gray or something."

"Pubic?"

"Maybe does all her worrying down there first. How do I know?" Chicky looked at his watch. "Okay, let's pick up the pictures and go dancing. Chances are these two hit some of the other hot spots. Maybe the bartenders in these other places can help."

Although the pictures were grainy, the faces were clear enough for an identification. Chicky and Raul hit two places in West Hollywood and one in West L.A. before they found, not a waiter or bartender, but a bouncer who recalled Kathleen. It was at a dance club called the Greek House on Pico Boulevard. The bouncer was a stocky man in his late twenties with long, slicked back dark brown hair and a face that resembled a rubber mask because of the way his thick lips and wide nostrils twisted and curled while he gazed at the pictures. Chicky thought they hired him for his bad looks and thick fingers that formed fists like mallets.

"Yeah, I remember her. She came here a few times this month. I used to kid her because she walked in, paraded around, had a drink and left pretty soon after. After the first time, I said, what's the matter, you don't see anything you like?

"She turns to me and says, no, I'm afraid I don't. She was real sincere like, you know. So I says, what'cha lookin' for, Mr. Right?

" 'Of course,' she says." The bouncer laughed, which was only a twitch in his cheeks and a rumble in his rubbery lips. "I said, how about Mr. Left? Then she asked me lots of questions."

"What sort of questions?" Chicky asked.

"Stuff like how I got the job, why I wanted to do this. Don't I want to do something better with my life? Tell you the truth," he said, "she looked great, maybe in her late twenties, but she sounded like my mother after a while. I started to kid her, call her Ma. She thought that was funny."

"She tell you anything about herself?" Raul asked.

He shrugged and then thought of something.

"Yeah. I asked her what *she* was doin' here if it wasn't the place for me. She thought a minute and says, I'm trying to find my way back."

"Back? Back where?" Chicky asked.

He shrugged again.

"I don't know. I asked her but she only smiled. She must have money, though."

"Why do you say that?" Raul wondered.

"When she left, I seen her get into this black Lincoln Continental. Two suits were waiting on her. They looked like bodyguards, know what I mean?"

"You remember anything else about the car?" Chicky asked.

"Late model, maybe this year's. Like I said, black. Didn't see the plate, if that's what you mean."

"She always came here alone?" Raul asked.

"Whenever I saw her. I haven't seen her since the weekend before last."

"If you see her again, will you call us?" Raul said, handing him his card.

"Sure. What she do?"

"Maybe nothing, but she might have been a witness to a murder," Chicky replied.

The bouncer blew some air through his thick lips and put the card into his pocket.

"Women who get driven around in nice cars and are escorted by bodyguards," Raul said as they walked away.

"Maybe you're right. Maybe they're married to rich old guys, one of whom had his young wife tailed and then taught her a lesson by shooting the guy she picked up."

"We got pictures, we got descriptions, first names and an approximate idea of age. Let's let Niles work miracles on his computer with the Department of Motor Vehicles. Maybe these women have California driver's licenses," Chicky said.

Back at the station, they gave the information and copies of the pictures to Niles Grossman, a curly haired blond man with a dry wit to match the dry work he did in records and statistics. Chicky thought Niles always had that far-off, distant look in his beady blue eyes. It was as if he were still seeing the rolls and rolls of data scrolling over his computer monitor, even when he was away from it. He was the new breed of cop, the plugged-in, networking, electronic age policeman who, working only with a blood sample, could not only identify a suspect through DNA, but the suspect's entire bloodline.

Chicky had the feeling Niles saw it all as just another computer game. After all, Niles never confronted a suspect in the flesh, never questioned an alleged perpetrator, never walked a beat, rode in a patrol car or visited a crime scene in real life. All his crime scenes were reenactments on a television monitor. But he did wonders and so had to be tolerated, even respected.

"Why don't you just bring me a haystack and a copy of the needle?" he asked when they presented him with what they had.

Chicky pretended to be disappointed. He knew how to get at Niles's ego.

"Not enough to try?"

"Yeah, sure it's enough. It's just going to take a while. I'll start with this one," he said, looking at Kathleen's picture and information. "And isolate all the dark-brown-haired, blue-eyed women in the twenty to thirty age range with first name Kathleen. The computer will punch out a list and I'll call up each for a look at the photo. No idea how long the list will be. I've got a backlog of other stuff."

"Will you keep us informed?"

"Yeah. Just don't nag."

"What? Me, nag?" Chicky said.

"No, I'm talking to the two hundred and fifty other nags standing in here," Niles replied and turned back to his monitor as his fingers danced over the keyboard and brought up a search program.

Chicky watched him for a moment and then nodded to Raul. They left Niles's office and returned to their desks. The dispatcher was waiting for them.

"Kronenberg wants to see you two," he told them.

"The chief is still here this late?" Chicky quipped. The dispatcher glanced toward the chief's office to be sure the door was closed before replying.

"He left, but came back, and he didn't look happy when he returned."

"Maybe it's just indigestion again," Chicky said. Raul smiled.

They knocked on the door and entered the office. Walter Kronenberg was a rather small man for a police officer. He was barely five feet five and one hundred and forty pounds, balding, with diminutive, almost feminine facial features. However, for one of those cryptic reasons that lay buried under the wall of bureaucratic mystery, Kronenberg was promoted with firm rapidity until he became chief of the division's detective unit. Some ventured to say he was the bastard son of a former city police chief; some thought a former mayor. Whatever, he definitely knew the right people and was often invited to top brass functions and frequently hobnobbed with state and federal officials.

Kronenberg was an efficient bureaucrat, the type who got the trains to run on time, but who had little feeling or consideration for the soldiers in the field. He was impersonal, abrupt and usually uncompromising. Around the division and even elsewhere, Kronenberg was called Little Napoleon, the Little added to denigrate him further. No one liked him, some respected him, all feared him.

He always wore a suit and tie, no matter how hot and humid. Chicky swore the man's sweat glands had been removed, because he always looked cool. Like all bureaucratic demigods, he sat before a desk twice the size he needed and struck out with his telephone and intercom, preferring, whenever posssible, to snap commands over wires rather than face-to-face.

When Chicky and Raul entered, Kronenberg was on the phone. With his right forefinger, the nail manicured to a shine, he pointed to the chairs in front of his desk and continued to listen to the other party.

"Just do it the way I told you to do it," he concluded and cradled the receiver without saying good-bye. "This new case you two are on . . ."

"Murder of a young man named Carl Slotkin," Raul

said, nodding. "We're trying to locate the woman who was with him either right before or during the killing. Chicky here thinks . . ."

"Find something else to do," Kronenberg said abruptly.

"Excuse me?"

"It belongs to the feds. I got a call on it a few hours ago."

"The feds? Why?" Chicky asked. "It's a murder in our jurisdiction and—"

"The feds are on it," he said sharply. Chicky just stared. "It's not like we haven't other things to do around here. When another agency wants to pick up on our load, it frees us to get to other matters."

"Well, who's in charge of the federal investigation? Doesn't he want what we have?"

"Just bring your file in here and leave it on my desk," Kronenberg said. "I'll handle the transfer of information personally."

"Feds? Doesn't make sense," Chicky insisted.

Kronenberg's bald head reddened.

"Are we talking about the F.B.I.? The B.A.T.F.? The D.E.A.?" Chicky continued.

There was a deep moment of silence. Raul cleared his throat. Kronenberg leaned forward on his forearms. His eyebrows jerked upward as his forehead developed folds.

"You know," he began with a slow deliberateness, "when you retire, you will have plenty of time to waste. But right now," he continued, raising his voice, "neither I nor you nor Raul here have that luxury. You can forget this current investigation and move on to other things.

Why? How? Where? What? These are not your concern, and to tell you the truth, they're not mine either." He looked at his watch pointedly and then looked up, his eyebrows hoisted again.

"Doesn't make sense," Chicky muttered.

"Okay," Raul said, rising, but Chicky didn't move.

"We ran a background on these guys. They're clean. They're not involved with drugs; they're not smuggling in immigrants or secretly brewing whiskey and beer. Some jealous rich old fuck either offed the kid or had one of his goons do it. It's cut and dried. If the feds called you, it's because someone got to someone," Chicky concluded.

Kronenberg's crimson head turned dark cherry and the blood dropped down through his narrow cheeks.

"Well, they didn't get to me. I follow orders. It's that simple. You should have learned how before you retire, which, I assume, will be on schedule."

"You know what they say about assuming. It only makes an ass of u and me," Chicky quipped. Raul didn't laugh. Kronenberg just glared. "Yeah, I'm on schedule." He rose, turned and limped to the door.

"Why don't you consider some sick leave, Siegler? In your case it's justified. I'm assigning Raul a new partner first thing next week, anyway," Kronenberg added.

"I'm not complaining, Chief," Raul said.

"I know that, but it's too dangerous for you to have to carry someone and do your job, too."

"Carry someone!" Chicky spun around.

"Let's go, Chicky," Raul said, turning him toward the door. "It's all right. It ain't worth it."

Chicky twisted around to face Kronenberg.

"You know, Kronenberg, you were sure born in the wrong place too late. There was a house painter in Germany who could have used the likes of you."

Kronenberg didn't respond. He stared and then he started to flip through some papers. Raul put more pressure on Chicky's shoulder and turned him toward the door again.

"Do you believe that little bastard?" Chicky muttered after they had stepped out of the office. "Carry me?"

"No sense arguing with him, Chick. It's a waste of time and energy."

"Why is that little fuck behind that desk? How can the system be so screwed up? I should do just what he said, take sick leave up to my retirement and forget the whole thing."

"Probably should."

Chicky looked at Raul for a moment and then went to his desk and sat.

"This smells, you know. The feds?"

"What do you want to do? You got your own problems. Just worry about Maggie now and think about that mobile home," Raul advised. "First thing tomorrow, go to the doctor with that foot, too, will ya?"

Chicky nodded.

"I don't know who to feel more sorry for, Torres, you or me. You got to continue working under the likes of him."

"Simple, then," Torres said. "Feel more sorry for me."

Chicky looked up at him and nodded.

"I do," he said. "I really do."

9

Shelly Dorset woke in the back of the limousine. Her eyelids fluttered and opened, closed and then opened to give her a full view of the back of Herbie Shagan's head. The car slowed as they approached East Los Angeles and the different freeway entrances on the 10 Los Angeles. Drivers had to get into the correct lanes for their various highways.

"Stupid sons of bitches never know which lane to get into," Mike Robbins said as a white van cut into his lane and then out again. Shelly turned her head and focused on Robbins for a moment. Then she groaned and pulled herself into a straighter and firmer sitting position.

"What's going on?" she finally asked.

Robbins turned, but Shagan kept muttering about the traffic.

"Hello, Mrs. Dorset. We're on the way back to Renaissance. Dr. Woodruff's orders."

"What happened to me?" she demanded as her

strength returned. Robbins shook his head with a look of innocence painted over his face. "How did I get into this car?"

"Oh, we helped you do that, Mrs. Dorset," Robbins said casually. He started to turn around when Shagan cursed a driver cutting in front of them.

"Look at that old bastard. She didn't even signal."

"But how did I . . ." Shelly rubbed her cheeks vigorously and took a deep breath. The last thing she could recall was sitting down in the overstuffed chair in her room and closing her eyes. "I passed out," she cried when the realization occurred to her. Robbins turned around again.

"Yeah. That's why Dr. Woodruff thought we should bring you right back, Mrs. Dorset. You haven't been well."

"I was fine. I was . . ." It all came rushing back to her. "What happened to Kathleen Cornwall?"

"Don't know, Mrs. Dorset. Why don't you just sit back and relax. We're in for a little bit longer ride than usual because of the damn early rush hour here. Nobody works a full day in Los Angeles, huh, Herbie?"

"I don't know why they bother going in. An hour later, they're on their way home just to beat the rush hour, so they create an earlier rush hour."

"Yeah, that's right," Robbins said, laughing. "What do you think, Mrs. Dorset?"

"I don't understand. I was supposed to have more time. What happened to Kathleen?" she asked.

Robbins smirked and shook his head.

"You're not thinking straight, Mrs. Dorset. Just relax,

close your eyes and leave the driving and thinking to us," he said. Herbie laughed.

Shelly fought hard for clear thoughts. When she had called the young man she had met the night before to see if he knew anything about Kathleen, he had said his friend had been murdered and the police were looking for her and for Kathleen. Something had obviously gone terribly wrong. She raised her eyes and looked from Shagan to Robbins. What sort of men had Dr. Woodruff employed? What had they done to Kathleen? Why wouldn't she have called or contacted me? Shelly wondered.

"Where's my purse?" she suddenly demanded. Robbins turned slowly, his head moving as if it took all his strength to do so.

"What is it now, Mrs. Dorset?"

"My purse, my things."

"Your purse is in your suitcase in the trunk. You don't need it now, so don't worry about it," he added.

"How do you know what I need and what I don't need?" she snapped back.

Robbins glared at her and then just turned away.

"Maybe I should hop on the sixty," Shagan said.

"Naw, it'll only be bottled up around Riverside. Stay where you are. Once we get past San Bernardino . . ."

"Thanks for the optimistic traffic news," Shagan said. Robbins chuckled and leaned forward to turn on the radio.

"I had things in my room I wanted to bring back with me," Shelly said. Neither man responded. "I don't like this. I was supposed to hear from Dr. Woodruff."

"Mrs. Dorset," Robbins said, turning sharply this time,

"you were asleep when Dr. Woodruff called and gave us the order to bring you back to Renaissance. Now what the hell are you carrying on about, huh? Why can't you just close your eyes and enjoy the ride?"

Shelly tried to swallow. Her throat felt like someone had painted stucco up and down the inside of it and the roof of her mouth actually ached from the dryness.

"I need a drink," she said. "Something cold. Please," she pleaded.

"Now?" Robbins moaned.

"I'm so thirsty, it's painful. Dr. Woodruff wouldn't want you to let me suffer," she warned. Shagan turned to Robbins and Robbins shrugged.

"Wait until we get to West Covina, Mrs. Dorset. We'll pull into the mall and Mike will run in to get you a cold drink, okay?" Shagan said. "Jesus."

"Yes, thank you," she replied.

Her mind was racing. Kathleen might have fled the scene last night. She might be wandering the city. They could be lying. She didn't just fall asleep back there; she wasn't that stupid. They had put something into her coffee. It had to be. She wasn't getting straight answers. Why hadn't Dr. Woodruff called?

Shelly took deep breaths and extended her arms. She exercised her legs by pushing them down with all her might and then relaxing. The dynamic tension pumped the blood around her body and she began to feel somewhat more revived. The two men didn't look back, didn't notice what she was doing. They continued to talk about the traffic and the ride and kept their faces forward. The traffic was heavy and Shagan couldn't take his eyes off the road for more than an instant. It was too much stop and go.

Shelly waited and thought. She knew instinctively that something was very wrong and that she didn't want to just be taken back to Renaissance, not without knowing more and certainly not without talking to Dr. Woodruff. Maybe he didn't know what was happening. Maybe these men were doing something without his knowledge or permission. For all she knew, they weren't really heading back to Renaissance anyway. Dr. Woodruff didn't strike her as the sort of man who would order a murder.

She plotted and she waited.

"I'm very thirsty," she whined. "Can't you just pull into a roadside stand or something?"

"For Christ's sake, Mrs. Dorset, this is the freeway, not some side road," Shagan wailed.

"We're almost to the exit for the mall, Mrs. Dorset," Robbins said. "Hold your water."

Nearly a half hour later, Shagan reluctantly turned off and they drove up to the mall's main entrance.

"What'dya want, a Coke?" Robbins asked.

"No. I'd like something like Evian water or Perrier."

"Sure. What else would you want?" Robbins said, smirking. "Herbie?"

"Get me a fucking Coke with ice."

"Right," Robbins said. He got out and hurried to the front entrance.

"I want to stretch my legs," Shelly said. She tried the door but it was locked. "I just want to walk around the car, for God's sake!"

Reluctantly, Herbie Shagan hit the button to unlock the doors. Shelly stepped out and stretched. Then she started around the back of the vehicle.

"Don't go far, Mrs. Dorset," Herbie said, sticking his head out the window.

"What am I, a three-year-old?" she replied.

"Just don't go far," he warned.

She stayed close to the vehicle and walked around the front. He brought his head back and relaxed, watching her cross and come down his side. She seemed to be heading for the door to get back in, but when she reached it, she sped up and continued around the rear of the car, walking quickly toward the entrance to the mall.

"What the fuck—"

Herbie stuck his head out again.

"Mrs. Dorset, Mike's getting the drinks. Stay here!" he cried. She kept walking.

"Fucking spoiled bitch," he muttered and opened the door. Just as he did, Shelly sped up and ran to the front entrance. Shagan's eyes nearly popped. "What are you doing?" he cried, and headed for the door.

The entryway was a long, tiled corridor. Shelly hurried down and went to her right, gazing back to see Shagan jogging after her. She moved faster until she reached the entrance to a department store and hurried down the aisle toward women's clothing.

"Mrs. Dorset!" Shagan called.

She moved faster, turned around a display and then ran toward the rear of the store. She saw the escalator and stepped on it just as Shagan came around the display. He saw her, shook his head and charged forward.

Shelly stepped past an elderly lady and then, taking two steps at a time, rushed up the escalator, pushing past other customers, who complained.

Upstairs, she gazed quickly right and left and chose the left to go toward housewares. Shagan had jostled past the people on the escalator, too, and when he reached the top, he broke into a run. Shelly saw him closing and without hesitation, when he reached the aisle she had entered, she deliberately swept her left arm through a display of glasses and bowls, sending the dishware crashing to the tile floor behind her and between Shagan and herself. The pieces shattered around Shagan, who stopped in disbelief as a salesman came rushing to the scene.

"What happened?" he cried.

Shelly Dorset made another turn and then broke into a run across the housewares section and into appliances. She saw a door marked Exit and shot toward it. Without looking back, she rushed through and down the metal steps. The door had set off an alarm, which caused more commotion behind her.

At the bottom of the stairway, she lunged through the door and onto the first floor of the mall. She kept herself at a fast walk, heading for a crowd of customers who had gathered at the front window of the pet shop to watch the puppies and kittens play. Pushing through them, she spotted the wall signs for rest rooms and went in that direction. When she turned the corner, she looked back to see if Shagan was behind her. He wasn't, so she stepped into the ladies' room. At the moment there was no one else there.

She recalled a scene in a film where a teenage boy, fleeing pursuers in a similar setting, went into a rest room stall, locked the door, but stepped up on the toilet so his feet weren't visible under the door. Without hesitation, she did the same thing, sitting on the top of the commode's tank, her feet on the seat, and waited.

Her forethought was not in vain. Less than ten minutes later, after she heard some teenage girls come in, she heard the door open hard and Robbins and Shagan muttering. The teenage girls smoking at the sink spun around and screamed.

"We're just looking for someone," Shagan said. "Cool it."

"There's no one else here," one of the girls said. "So get the hell out or we'll call the cops. Pervert."

Shelly smiled and waited. Shagan and Robbins studied the rest room for a moment longer.

"Where the fuck is the bitch?" Robbins moaned. Then they left.

Shelly listened to the teenage girls talk about them. One girl said it was just the sort of thing her sister warned her about at malls.

"They pretend to be looking for someone, but they hope to catch a girl with her pants down."

"We should still tell the cops," the other girl said. "We should."

They left. Shelly waited. Her heart was pounding, but she felt all right and rather proud of herself. Two months ago, she couldn't have walked quickly enough from that car, much less stride and jog away. Of course, two months ago, she wouldn't have had any reason to be in the car with those goons, either.

She knew they weren't about to give up. They would
be out there waiting, watching, searching. What do I do
now? she wondered.

Slowly, cautiously, she emerged from the stall and
went to the bathroom door. She opened it a crack and
peered out. The immediate corridor looked safe, no sign
of either of them. She envisioned them waiting just
around the corner, however. Trembling, she stepped out
of the rest room and waited. People gazed at her, but not
with any extra curiosity. She turned to her right and just
walked down the corridor. She paused at a furniture outlet and entered.

The two salesmen were busy with customers, so she
just wandered around the living room displays and
stepped into the bedroom area. It was very quiet, only
one other customer, a woman in her fifties perhaps,
looking at a vanity table. Shelly saw a door marked Employees Only and headed for it. Maybe she would just
hide out for a few hours and they would think she had
gotten away.

The stockroom was dark, cool and long, but down to
the right she saw a door open to the rear of the mall and
a burly man, about forty, carrying in a carton that contained a kitchen chair. He set it next to a half dozen others and went out. She hurried to the entrance and gazed
through, seeing the man jotting something on a clipboard next to his truck. There was another, taller, thinner
man, a younger man, perhaps about thirty, beside him.

Shelly stepped out and looked up and down the rear of
the mall. There were no customers here, no cars, just another delivery truck about a thousand yards to her left.

The tall man took the sheet from the truck driver and turned to go back into the furniture outlet.

"Can I help you?" he asked, surprised to see her.

"No. I guess I'm just a little lost, but it's all right. I needed the fresh air," she said. He didn't smile.

"What do you mean, you're lost? Where do you want to go?"

"Los Angeles," she quipped. He laughed.

"Well, this isn't the way to Los Angeles. There's a doorway down right about a hundred yards, see it?" Shelly nodded. "That will take you right through the mall and out to the customer parking."

"Thank you," she said. He nodded and entered the outlet. The truck driver who had been watching smiled at her and reached up for his door handle.

"Excuse me," she said. He hesitated and she approached him.

"Actually, I've lost a ride. Can I get one with you?"

"What?" He smiled with confusion and amusement.

"Where are you going?"

"Sherman Oaks," he said. She nodded.

"That would be fine."

"I can't take riders, ma'am. Sorry." He started to get into his truck.

"Wait a minute," she said. She thought quickly and pulled off her watch. "These are real diamond chips," she said. "The watch is worth a minimum of two thousand dollars. It's yours if you'll give me a ride."

"Huh?" He gazed at the watch. "What's the story?"

"I'm trying to get away from someone unpleasant."

"That unpleasant?" he said, gazing at the watch again.

"Yes, that unpleasant. It's no big deal. You just take me along, drop me off anywhere and this is yours to either sell or impress your wife with."

"My wife ain't going to believe me," he said, raising his left eyebrow.

"So, just sell it and buy her something nice. Buy yourself something nice." She pushed the watch at him. He took it and looked at it closely.

"I bet these aren't real diamond chips, but it's a nice looking watch."

"They are real," she insisted.

He looked at her again. She didn't appear to be a fugitive from justice.

"Why don't you just go to the mall security?" he asked.

"It's more complicated. That's why I'm offering such a valuable watch."

"I don't know . . ." He shook his head, but when he saw her look of disappointment, he softened. "All right. Get in. I'll probably regret it," he muttered.

"Thank you." She hurried around and got into the truck.

"My name's Randy," he said.

"I'm Shelly. Do you mind if I slump down as we pull around the mall?" she asked.

"Slump? Sure. Slump," he said, laughing, and started the engine. He watched her with some amusement as he drove to the exit and pulled onto the side street that would take them to the 10 Freeway West. She lowered herself until her head was below the window. He shook his head in disbelief, but sped up. When they were away from the mall, he looked down at her.

"It's all clear," he said. "The bad guys won't see you now."

"Thank you," she said.

"You wanna tell me about this?"

She thought for a moment.

"My husband," she said, "had me followed."

"Oooh," Randy said and smiled. "Now it makes sense."

Shelly laughed.

"I'm glad," she said, and sat back as he shifted down and sped up to enter the freeway and take her back toward Los Angeles, where she knew not what she would do, for she had no money and she certainly didn't want to return to the safe house.

As they drove on, she continued to spin this fabrication about her affair with a younger man. Randy listened, intrigued.

He asked her why she just didn't get a divorce and she explained that she was a religious Catholic.

"But you're having an extramarital affair, ain't cha?" he said. "That ain't bein' a good Catholic."

"I confess every Tuesday," she replied and Randy roared.

Actually, he enjoyed having her along. They discussed religion and politics for a while and then he talked about his own marriage and his children.

"You sound like a very wise woman for someone your age," he said. "I bet you'll figure a way out of your predicament."

"I hope so."

When they reached Ventura Boulevard, he asked her where she wanted to get off. She gazed around and said anywhere would be fine. As he came to a stop for a red light, she thanked him.

"I really don't have to keep your watch," he said.

"It's all right. A deal's a deal. But I'll tell you what . . . lend me a couple of dollars. It really is a valuable watch."

He laughed and reached into his pocket.

"How's a ten sound?"

"Very generous," she said. She opened the door. "So long, Randy."

"Good luck," he called. She stepped away from the truck, the light turned green and he was gone. For a moment she just stood there watching the traffic whiz by. Then she turned and walked down the street until she found a pay phone. She went into a convenience store and bought some gum to get change. She was surprised at how much it cost to get telephone information, but she realized she rarely, if ever, used a public phone.

"What city, please?"

"Rancho Mirage, Palm Springs area."

"Yes?"

"Renaissance Homes."

"Thank you." After a pause she heard, "Sorry, I have no listing for Renaissance Homes."

"No listing? Well, how about just Renaissance?"

"No, nothing with that name. Sorry."

"Wait. Try Woodruff, Harrison, a doctor."

After a pause. "Sorry."

"But—" There was a click and her change was returned.

She stood there, bewildered. Perhaps she shouldn't have been so impulsive. What was she going to do now?

She knew only one other number in Los Angeles. She gazed around. The cars continued to fly by, the drivers indifferent to her plight. She had dropped herself into a sea of strangers, into a world of insensibility, and she could easily drown.

"I have no choice," she muttered. "I can't just stand here."

She put the money in and tapped out Webster Martin's number. It rang and rang and then the answering machine came on. She hesitated.

"I . . ."

She didn't know what message to leave, so she just hung up.

Confused and desperate, she turned and started walking down the street. What would she do? She certainly couldn't return to her old life, call anyone from the past, not now. When and if they saw her, they wouldn't believe it was she. She felt like someone trapped in limbo. Maybe this is purgatory, she thought. I'm on my way to hell for what I've done.

What have I done?

She paused before a storefront and gazed at her image in the window. Her mind told her one thing, but her eyes another. It was as if she had the power to look back through time, but when she closed and then opened her eyes, she expected she would find herself in the present, her true self.

She blinked. Nothing had changed. She was still adrift, like a balloon caught in the wind with no power to control where she would be taken.

She turned around and saw a Sizzlers that advertised a chicken dinner for five ninety-five. She might as well eat something, she thought, and started for the crosswalk. As she went toward the Sizzlers, she laughed. She hadn't eaten in one of these places for years, but she imagined at the moment it was going to be one of the best meals she'd ever had. Afterward, afterward . . .

She had no idea about afterward, no idea at all.

"What am I doing?" she asked herself aloud when she reached the front of the Sizzlers. She didn't know the answer. She knew only that she was afraid and needed someone who she thought would treat her with kindness.

10

Webster and his father were already seated at their table having cocktails when Phil arrived at Chasens. The upscale, old Hollywood restaurant was filling up quickly with business people and wealthy looking couples in their fifties and sixties. There was an air of excitement. Some movie actors were having a private party in the rear.

"Sorry I'm late," Phil said. He looked tired and drawn, as if the tragedy had begun to shrink him.

"Sit down, Phil," Gordon Martin ordered. He signaled to the waiter. "What do you want to drink?"

"Absolut vodka and tonic, please, with a twist of lime."

"Very good, sir," the waiter said.

Phil gazed at Webster. The two looked at each other as if the other was hoping to hear this was all a bad dream.

"How are you doing?" Gordon asked.

Phil shook his head.

"I was doing all right until I went home and people

started to call from the office. It's a big city, but news travels as fast as it does in a small hamlet when it's bad news," Phil remarked. Gordon Martin nodded.

He was a burly man with heavy eyebrows and a full head of stark white hair. His eyes were bluer than Webster's and he had sharper bone structure with a hard, square jaw and thicker lips. Still very muscular and virile in his fifties, Gordon Martin looked like an ex-prize fighter. He hovered over his glass of straight rye whiskey, his large hands wrapped around it so it was practically invisible. He wore a plain gold wedding band and on his right hand a gentleman's Victorian sapphire pinkie ring set in gold. On his thick left wrist he still wore his trusty Timex, a subject of endless joking between himself and Webster, who wore a gold Pulsar. "Time is just time," Gordon would respond. "No sense dressing it up to be more than it is."

"I was just telling Webster," Gordon said, "that in today's world, you can't be too careful. It pays to be distrustful and not worried whether or not people will accuse you of being paranoid. I know you young people hop into bed ten minutes after you're introduced nowadays, but still, when beautiful women are too easy to pick up, you got to be suspicious."

Phil nodded.

"What the hell are you agreeing with him for?" Webster asked, smiling. "A ten-ton truck couldn't have held you back if one of them would have smiled first at you."

Phil smiled and shrugged.

"He's right about that, sir. It would have been pretty hard to resist either of the two."

"Yeah, well, you got to think with the head that's on your neck, not the one that dangles between your legs," Gordon quipped. Webster and Phil laughed. It felt good. Phil's drink came and he took a fast, long sip.

"Needed that more than I thought." He looked at Webster. "Before I forget, Marilyn Myers wanted me to tell you to call her. She wants to organize a memorial service with just Carl's fellow employees and close friends."

Webster shook his head and took on that dazed look again. Phil sipped his drink and looked away when the tears came into his eyes.

"Let's get some good hot food in your stomachs. You guys need some intestinal fortitude," Gordon said, looking at the menu. They all ordered and Gordon then ordered another round of drinks. Phil hurried to catch up.

"It's so damn unfair," he said between gulps. "If it was a jealous husband, why didn't he shoot his wife? How the hell was Carl supposed to know she was married?"

"Maybe he did shoot her, too, or did something worse to her," Gordon replied. Phil thought and nodded.

"Could be why her friend called you looking for her," he said to Webster. Webster closed his eyes sharply, resembling a man who had just suffered a pain shooting through his head. Gordon Martin spun in his chair.

"What'dya mean? The woman called you?" he demanded.

"She called but she didn't give me any new information. She just hung up when I told her about Carl," Webster said.

"When was this?"

"In the afternoon after Phil had left my place. I told him to keep it quiet," he added, raising his eyebrows and clenching his teeth.

"Did you tell the police?"

"Of course, but there wasn't anything to tell them." His father stared at him. "Really, Dad, no big deal."

"I don't like it," Gordon said. "Next time she calls, just hang up. They're probably married to organized-crime bosses. You have to be very diligent for the next few weeks, Webster, especially around the job sites. You know we deal with some shady characters from time to time."

"I know, Dad. Don't worry."

"I don't think you guys should go wandering around late at night for a while, either," Gordon said.

"We don't wander around, Dad."

Webster flashed Phil another look of reprimand and Phil gazed down at his glass and hors d'oeuvres.

"Maybe you oughta go visit your aunt Dottie in Florida for a while."

"Dad, will you cut it out. No one's coming after me."

"How do you know that? We should probably ask the police for some protection."

"Will you stop? If you don't stop, I'm getting up from this table right now. I mean it, Dad," Webster threatened.

Gordon Martin saw the determination in his son's eyes and relaxed.

"I'm just trying to help."

"Just forget it. That's what we came here to do, wasn't it?"

"Yeah."

"All right, then. I think we oughta think about a new electrical contractor. Crawford is putting us behind schedule. I know he's too stretched out and I think . . ."

Phil listened politely as Webster skillfully steered the discussion from the murder of their friend to the various projects the Martins were developing. He changed the topic quickly to a discussion of cars, knowing the purchase of foreign cars was one of his father's favorite pet peeves.

Before their meal ended, they saw Tony Bennett walking through the restaurant and Gordon called to him. The legendary singer stopped at their table and made some small talk with Gordon about music not being the same anymore.

"You keep going, Tony," Gordon said. "There are still people who like to hear the words."

The laughter spiked the mood and after coffee and chocolate soufflés, they were stuffed and truly upbeat. Phil thanked Gordon.

"It was real nice of you, sir," he said.

"Never mind. You two just watch your rear ends, hear?"

"Yes, sir, I do, and we will," he promised, gazing at Webster.

"Good night, Dad," Webster said. They hugged at the door. Gordon's 1989 Ford Thunderbird was brought up first. It was in mint condition.

"Now this is a car," he said as he got in. Webster shook his head and smiled.

They watched him drive away and then Webster let

out a lungful of tight air and jabbed Phil in the shoulder.

"Thanks for talking about the phone call."

"How the hell did I know you didn't tell him, Web?"

"Yeah, well, Dad's like the IRS. The best thing to do when around him is say as little as possible."

Phil laughed.

"Going right home?" he asked suspiciously.

"No."

"What are you plotting, Web?"

"I thought I'd just look in at Thunderbolt."

"Ah, they'd never go back there, Web. And if they did, the owners would call the police, right?"

"Maybe. People, especially people in business, have a way of looking the other way when it comes to controversy and trouble. Besides, I don't think I could go home and just hang out tonight. Coming along?"

"I don't think so," Phil said. "I'm feeling a good buzz. I want to take it to bed. At least I know that's safe."

Webster laughed. His Mercedes was brought up and he embraced Phil quickly and then got in.

"Be careful, will ya, Web?"

"Sure, Dad," Webster quipped and got into the car. Phil watched him drive off and then hurried to his own vehicle, afraid the dark thoughts would come back and drive away the pleasant respite from grief.

A few moments after Webster entered Thunderbolt, he thought Phil had been right. First, the vivid memory of him, Phil and Carl coming here the night before came rushing back and with it, the terrible sense of sadness and shock. He could close his eyes, open them, and see

Carl leaning against that bar, excitedly talking to the beautiful young woman. Every once in a while until Webster had left, Carl would flash him that look, that beaming face full of pleasure.

Webster shook his head to rid himself of the image. Then he perused the present crowd of revelers. Everyone was happy, vibrant, completely unaware that his friend had been murdered after spending the same sort of delirious time here last night. The owners certainly wouldn't tell anyone. No negative imagery; it's bad for business, bad for having fun.

Webster suddenly hated the upbeat sound, the glitzy lights, the laughter and shrill cries. He despised them for their energy and their smiles. After he felt confident he had looked the whole place over carefully and not seen either of the two women, he spun around and practically ran from the dance club. In his car he found he had to sit for a while to catch his breath and slow his pounding, furious heart.

Dad's right, he thought. Lay low. He started the engine and drove away. The sky looked overcast tonight, barely a star visible, and the street traffic was lighter than usual at this time of night. The atmosphere appeared to have been created for his mood.

The garage under his apartment building had a wrought-iron black gate that rattled its way slowly over the tracking to open after he pressed the transmitter. He had signed a petition with most of the other condo owners to have the association replace the gate with a faster opening and closing door, but nothing had been done yet. Bureaucracy, no matter how small, was still bureaucracy. The directors had taken the petition, assigned the problem to committee and awaited the result of research and study.

When the gate opened, a set of lights illuminated the entrance. He pulled in quickly and found his spot near the rear of the garage. Then he locked the car doors, set the alarm and walked to the elevator. As he walked, he thought he heard additional footsteps. He paused to listen and all he heard was a dripping from a water pipe at the right rear end of the structure, so he continued toward the elevator.

The elevator required a key. It was another step in security. Anyone could get into the garage by rushing in behind a car, perhaps, especially with the slow closing gate, but unless he or she had an elevator key, he or she still couldn't get into the building.

Webster gazed up at the display and saw that the elevator was coming from the penthouse floor. There were a half dozen units up there, his being one of the two larger apartments. Just before the elevator arrived, Webster turned to gaze around the dimly lit garage again. He saw no one, but when he turned around as the elevator doors opened, he found himself facing two rather stocky men in suits. They both smiled at him. He waited for them to step out, but they remained standing there, staring out at him. Finally, the curly haired man on the left spoke.

"Step right in, Mr. Martin. We've been waiting for you," he said.

"Who are you? Police?"

"Yes sir. Please step in, sir," he said.

Webster hesitated. They stared.

"You have I.D.?" he asked.

The man on the right smiled.

"Absolutely," he said. He reached into his jacket and produced an identification wallet. When he opened it, Webster stepped forward and gazed at the picture and the paper badge. It read Herbert J. Shagan, Special Agent, Federal Bureau of Investigation.

The man on the right flashed his I.D., too. Michael R. Robbins, Special Agent, F.B.I.

"F.B.I.?" Webster said. Shagan nodded. "How come?"

"This just doesn't involve the murder of your friend. It involves kidnapping. Going up?"

"What? Oh. Yeah," Webster said, nodding. He stepped into the elevator and Shagan pushed the button for Penthouse.

"I told the police everything I know," Webster said.

"We understand and we appreciate your cooperation. Have you had any more contact with the woman you were with last night? Has she phoned or did you just see her by any chance?"

"See her? Hell no. If I had, I would have brought her to the police myself," Webster said. The doors opened and they followed him out. "I did hear from her earlier, but I called Detective Siegler and told him. She didn't say much."

"What did she say?" Shagan asked. They all paused in the hallway.

"She wanted to know if I knew where her girlfriend was and I told her about Carl's murder. Didn't Siegler tell you guys?"

"He told us, but we always like to reconfirm. It's the way the F.B.I. operates," Shagan said. Robbins smiled when Webster looked at him. "What else did she say?"

"Nothing much. She told me not to look for her. She sounded terrified."

"No shit?"

"Yeah. Anyway, that's it. My only other contact," Webster said. They didn't budge.

"We'd still like to go over things again with you, if that's all right. We won't stay long," Shagan said.

"Fine," Webster replied. He led them to his door and opened it.

"Nice place," Mike said.

"Yeah," Herbie Shagan agreed, gazing around.

"Thanks. Can I get you something to drink, soda, juice, coffee . . ."

"Nothing for me, thanks. Mike?"

"Naw, I'm fine. Thanks."

"Let me check my answering machine. You guys can make yourselves comfortable," he added, nodding toward the living room.

"We'll check the machine with you," Herbie said.

"Yeah," Robbins agreed. "Lead the way, Mr. Martin."

Webster stared at them for a moment and then walked into the kitchen. The machine did indicate a number of calls. The first three were from friends of his and Carl who were calling to offer condolences and find out if there was anything they could do. Marilyn Myers had called about the memorial service.

"Terrible thing," Mike Robbins said. "Ain't it, Herbie? I mean, Agent Shagan?"

"Makes me sick," Herbie Shagan said, glaring at Robbins.

The last message wasn't really a message. They heard whoever it was pause and then they heard, "I . . ."

"What was that?" Herbie Shagan asked Webster.

"I don't know. It sounded like . . . like her," he said.

"Mrs. Dorset?"

"Was that her name? Dorset?" Webster asked quickly. Mike Robbins looked at Herbie Shagan, who smirked. "How did you find out? You know about these women?"

Neither replied.

"Play it again, Sam," Herbie said, smiling. "Please."

Webster moved slowly but did so. They heard the "I . . ." once more.

"Sounds like her," Mike said to Herbie, who nodded. "She was trying to leave you a message, but thought again, obviously. I think she might call back," he added.

"We'll just have to wait and see," Herbie agreed.

"Dorset? How did you know her name?" Webster inquired.

"It's a complicated case, Mr. Martin."

"Maybe I will have that drink. You got any Coke?" Mike Robbins asked.

"Coke? Yeah, at the bar," Webster said. They followed him to the living room.

"Great view from here at night," Mike said, gazing out the French doors.

"Yes," Webster said. He went behind the bar and opened the small refrigerator. "Ice?" he asked Herbie.

"Please," he said. Webster started to pour the Coke.

"So can't you tell me how you found out her name?" he asked.

"We've been after these two women for a while now, Mr. Martin," Herbie said. "They're crazy as hell. Nymphomaniacs. They fuck the brains out of every guy they meet."

"But why does that involve the F.B.I.?"

"We told you, kidnapping," Mike Robbins said.

"I don't understand. Why kidnapping?" Webster asked.

"When they were in Illinois, they picked up some poor asshole at a disco and took him at gunpoint along for a ride West," Herbie said.

"Why?"

"To fuck while they were on the road. But that's still kidnapping," Herbie said, "even if the victim's enjoying himself most of the time."

Mike Robbins laughed.

Webster shook his head.

"Shelly didn't seem like that sort of woman," he said.

"They're good at what they do," Mike Robbins said and smiled. Then he gulped some Coke.

"But why did they have to kill Carl?"

"I don't know. Why did they have to kill Carl, Herbie?" Mike Robbins asked him.

"If a man is unsatisfactory, they kill him," Herbie said. "They dumped the guy from Illinois on a highway two days later. He was fucked out."

Webster stared at them for a moment. He had seen their identification, but there was something crude about them and he had the definite feeling they were making things up as they went along. He thought they were more like some sick comedy team, black comedy. He made up his mind he would check them out after they left.

The phone rang.

The two stared at him. It rang again.

"Pick it up, Mr. Martin. It could be her again," Herbie ordered.

Slowly, Webster did so.

"Hello,"

"Webster," Shelly said. "I need your help. I can't explain anything over the phone, but I need you to promise you won't call the police. I'll explain everything to you and even tell you who killed your friend. Will you come meet me?" she recited without taking a breath.

Herbie moved closer.

Webster made an instinctive decision.

"Look, Phil, I know how you feel. How the hell do you think I feel, but I'm tired."

"Someone's there?"

"Yes."

"Is it two men, one with dark curly hair?"

"Yes."

"Don't trust them, Webster. They are part of who killed Carl."

"All right. I'll meet you for a quick one, but I don't want to stay out late, you hear? Where?"

She told him the corner she was on in Sherman Oaks.

"I know it. See you in twenty-five minutes," he said and hung up. "My friend Phil who was with us last night. He's having a pretty bad time with it. I gotta go spend a little time with him."

Herbie stared and then he looked at Mike Robbins.

"Well, we can check back later," he said.

"Huh?" Mike Robbins said.

"Later, we'll call and see if Mr. Martin has heard anything new, understand?"

"Oh. Right," Mike Robbins said. He put the glass down.

"We'll go down with you, Mr. Martin."

"Okay," Webster said. They left the apartment and went to the elevator.

"Where are you meeting your friend?" Herbie asked.

"He lives in Encino. I'll just hop on the 405. Freeway's fast this time of night."

"Right."

The elevator doors opened.

"How did you guys get into the building?" Webster asked casually as they stepped into the garage.

"Hey, Mr. Martin. We're the F.B.I. We get into any building we need to get into," Mike Robbins said.

"Yeah, right. I forgot. Oh," Webster said, turning back to them. "How do I get in touch with you guys if she should call?"

"Don't worry. We'll get in touch with you," Herbie said.

"Are you going to put a tap on my phone or something?"

"We might do that, yes. Do you mind?" Herbie asked.

"No. Not in this case."

"Good. You be careful now, Mr. Webster. These women are very dangerous. Don't do something stupid like agree to meet them alone, hear?"

"Right," Webster said.

He walked to his car. When he turned around at the car door, they were nowhere in sight. He got in, started the engine and drove out, pausing at the sidewalk to look in the rearview mirror. Where the hell were they? They hadn't gotten into a car and pulled up behind him. He thought for a moment and then drove on. When he reached the corner, he looked in the rearview mirror again.

Maybe they were the F.B.I. Maybe Shelly knew what these agents looked like. Maybe he was riding into some sort of trap. Maybe they were psychotic women. Did he make a wrong choice, instinctively?

He drove on, but tentatively, his foot barely touching the accelerator. When he reached the entrance to the freeway, he paused. There were lots of cars behind him now. Any one of them could contain those two men. As he turned toward the ramp, he dug into his jacket pocket and produced the card the L.A. detectives had given him. He read off the number and then began to punch it out on his car phone.

"I need to speak to either Detective Siegler or Detective Torres immediately, please. My name is Webster Martin," he told the dispatcher.

"Neither are here now. Can I take a message?" the dispatcher asked.

"It's an emergency."

"All right. What's your number? I'll have one of them contact you as soon as possible."

"I'm on a car phone," Webster explained and gave the number. He drove on. Just before the turnoff to the 101 East, his car phone rang. It was Chicky Siegler. He sounded very tired, maybe even drunk because he slurred his words.

"What can I do for you, Mr. Martin?"

Webster quickly explained why he had called and how he was suspicious of the two men.

"One's name was Shagan and the other was Robbins," he said.

"Don't be suspicious, Mr. Martin. Raul and I were taken off the case today."

"What? Why?"

"We were told the feds were on it. Just cooperate with them," Chicky said, his voice thick with fatigue.

"They knew her name and they told me the two women were from Illinois, I think. They said they had kidnapped and killed a man."

"I bet," Chicky said. "We had a computer genius working on tracing them to California drivers' licenses and he hasn't come up with anything yet. Probably are out of state. If you learn anything else, call them."

"That's just it; they didn't give me a card. They said they would be in contact with me. Don't you think that's strange?"

Chicky was silent for a moment.

"Then they told me to be sure and not agree to meet with her alone. But if she called and asked me to do so, how would I let them know? They haven't tapped my phone yet."

"How do you know?"

"I asked. They said they were going to. But what if she reached me someplace else? How do I reach them? They didn't even tell me to call you and why wouldn't they want me to call them if they were the F.B.I.?"

"I don't know. They have their ways and we have ours, I guess. Just cooperate with them," Chicky said. "Okay?"

Webster held the receiver and thought.

"No, it's not okay," he said.

"What do you mean, Mr. Martin?"

"I might have made a big mistake. She called me and asked me to pick her up."

"Called you? When?"

"Just now, while they were in my apartment questioning me. I pretended it was Phil. I'm on my way to Sherman Oaks to meet her," he confessed.

"And you didn't tell them?"

"I just . . . had a bad feeling about them."

"Where are you supposed to pick her up?" Chicky asked.

Webster gave him the address.

"All right. Try to wait there. I'll call a friend of mine at the L.A. F.B.I. office and have him patch in the information."

"I thought they might be following me."

"Maybe they are. You shouldn't have taken on this sort of responsibility, Mr. Martin. You're in too deep with people who are violent. Leave the police work to the law enforcement people who you and your fellow citizens pay all those good tax dollars to train," Chicky concluded.

Webster hung up. He was approaching the exit he had to take.

These people were violent. Why did he agree to do this? What was this really all about? He wasn't sure about the police and he certainly wasn't sure about Shelly.

He turned off the exit, feeling like someone who had swum out a little too far to turn back.

11

Zack Steiner always knocked first on Harrison's office door before entering, but he never waited for Harrison to say, "Come in." Knocking wasn't a request to enter; it was a warning he was coming.

There were all these little annoyances right from the beginning of their relationship. Steiner would never ask permission before lighting up one of his smelly skinny cigarettes in the office, and if there wasn't an ashtray, he would flick the ashes into his open palm and then casually deposit them on a corner of the desk. Soon, Harrison was providing an ashtray.

It didn't matter if Harrison was on the phone when Steiner barged into the office, either. Zack would stand over him, waiting, intimidating, until Harrison would tell whomever he was speaking to that he would call him or her back shortly. If he said something to Steiner like you should knock first, Steiner would say he had and he hadn't time to wait around either. His time was just as crucial.

Zack Steiner always looked like he was ready to go to the mat over a dispute, no matter how small. Harrison imagined Steiner could just as easily kill a man for stepping in front of him in an elevator or on an escalator as he could kill him for anything else.

Consequently, Harrison rarely challenged him head-on. If he disagreed, he did so and retreated or looked the other way. But he felt certain that whenever Steiner had his psychotic fantasies, killing Harrison in exquisite ways was an integral part of them.

"I have some interesting news for you," Steiner said as soon as he entered Harrison's office. Harrison was bent over his paperwork, logging in Emma Forsch and logging out Kathleen Cornwall. The disappointment he felt in the pit of his stomach made him irritable, even, with great risk, in Steiner's presence.

"Please close the door," he said.

Steiner stood there, tottering on the tightrope, the glint in his eyes brightening with anger for a moment and then cooling. He closed the door and smiled icily.

"What do you think you have around here, spies, Doctor?"

"I like the little privacy I enjoy," Harrison said. He sat back. "What is the interesting news?"

Steiner took his time now. He reached into his top pocket and produced one of his cigarettes. He lit it and then sat in the chair just to the right of Harrison's desk. It had become Steiner's chair, in Harrison's mind anyway, and it was on that corner of the desk that he had relented and placed an ashtray.

Harrison's office was kept immaculate and well organized. Despite the size of the dark walnut desk, he kept little on it: a holder for pens, pencils and a ruler, a desk clock and a calculator, the telephone and answering machine, and whatever papers he was working on at the time. Piles of paperwork were never left there. They were always placed in their proper file in the wall of matching walnut cabinets behind him.

The office had no windows, just a large air-conditioning duct. The room was lit with efficient incandescent bulbs in rather plain fixtures. The eggshell Sheetrock walls bore no plaques, no framed diplomas. There was a cryptic-looking chart on the wall in the corner to the left of the cabinets and alongside it were the bookcases filled with reference materials dealing with genetics and studies in gerontology. Except for a small, dark gray area rug in front of the desk, the floor of the office was white ceramic tile. There was a small gray vinyl settee and two metal frame, black-cushioned chairs, but no tables, no standing lamps.

Steiner leaned back and blew his smoke straight at the ceiling. Then he fixed his cold gray eyes on Harrison and smiled again.

"Mrs. Dorset has escaped," he said coolly.

"Escaped? What do you mean?"

Steiner shrugged.

"Escaped means got away, ran off, left the scene."

Harrison shook his head and sat forward.

"I don't understand. Mr. Shagan and Mr. Robbins were bringing her back to Renaissance, correct?"

"Retrieving her, yes."

"So?"

"So on the way she asked for a cold drink, whined until they agreed to pull over at the mall in Covina. While Mike was getting her a drink, she stepped out of the car to stretch her legs and ran into the mall. Herbie chased after her, but she disappeared into a store. He got Mike and they searched and searched, until they located a manager in a furniture store who had seen her out back. They think she got a ride with a truck driver and returned to the Los Angeles area."

"Back to Los Angeles? To where? Where would she go? She must still be hiding out in the mall."

"They're certain she left."

"Did you call the safe house?"

"Of course. She hasn't appeared there. Why would she if she wants to get away from us?" Zack said. He took another drag on his cigarette and this time blew the smoke toward Harrison.

"What are you doing about it? We can't let her wander around out there."

"I thought you might come to that conclusion. I sent Shagan and Robbins to stake out the apartment of the man she was with last."

"Why?" Harrison wasn't as curious about Zack's strategy as he was about Shelly Dorset's.

"I found out she called him earlier, and besides, as you so aptly put it: Where is she going to go? She can't go home again. She's dead and how would she convince her old friends who she was now, anyway?" Zack said as if the answer was obvious.

"What made her run away?" Harrison asked. It was a question for himself, more than it was a question for Zack.

"She and Mrs. Cornwall were supposed to have a late lunch together before Mrs. Cornwall returned to Renaissance. She kept asking questions about her. Herbie said she was very agitated when he told her she couldn't go wandering off until she had heard from you."

"Yes, but—"

"She was upset about being drugged and carted off, too," Zack Steiner casually added.

"Drugged? You had her drugged?"

"I wasn't going to take any chances, Doctor."

"You can't give my people any medications without my knowing," Harrison chastised. Zack glared back and Harrison softened his tone. "There could be physiological complications of which you couldn't be aware."

"That wasn't the problem," Zack said.

"What was it, then?"

"Let's just say she was losing confidence in us. Especially in you, I suppose," he added with some glee.

"Have your men seen her at this man's apartment yet?"

"Not yet, but they'll find her. She had no money when she ran off."

Kathleen Dorset didn't strike Harrison as someone who would be so rebellious. Perhaps the metamorphosis was creating some sort of mental aberration. He envisioned her wandering on the city streets, babbling, aging, until she died in an alley and was thought to be just another poor, deranged homeless soul.

Steiner crushed his cigarette roughly in the ashtray and then looked up sharply, his face granite-hard.

"When we locate her," he said, "we should terminate her on the spot."

"What? You can't do that. You have no idea of the amount of research and effort that has gone into her. I expect to learn a great deal from this rejuvenation. I need her back here, healthy and whole," Harrison insisted. "There is no debate about this."

"No debate, huh? What happens if she continues to resist retrieval?"

Now it was Harrison's turn to smile coolly. He leaned back, confident.

"You don't mean to tell me, Mr. Steiner, that a woman in her seventies can outsmart you and your people. She's no trained government spy, no soldier, no policewoman. What sort of competition could she possibly be?"

Zack stared. The man showed his anger only in his eyes. His lips held that half smile.

"I wasn't thinking so much about what she could do herself, but if she enlists allies, talks, gets this guy interested, for example, the problem grows, understand, Doctor? It spreads and I have to do more to solve the problem, more to cover up the fuck-up, get it, Doctor?"

Harrison swallowed. This on top of a spectacular new failure with Kathleen Cornwall, all in one day. He felt as if the walls around him were starting to crumble.

"I'm sure you will do what has to be done, Mr. Steiner," he replied. It was the closest he could come to giving the man a compliment. Steiner appreciated it nevertheless and sat back with some satisfaction.

"You can be sure of that, Doctor. However, I think we

should all discuss this program of what you call furloughs, don't you?"

"We'll reevaluate, yes," Harrison said reluctantly.
Steiner enjoyed watching the superior mind eat crow. He
smiled.

None of this made any sense to Zack Steiner or held
any great value, anyway. It wasn't like stealing the plans
to a superior weapon or taking out an undercover agent.
It wasn't even industrial spying, for Christ's sake. He
didn't appreciate Harrison Woodruff's work; research
like this and laboratories were too mystical. It was
voodoo magic. He suspected Harrison Woodruff was a
charlatan of sorts, pulling the wool over the eyes of men
in power, men who couldn't see as clearly as he could see
being out in the field. Whatever wonders Harrison was
supposed to be creating out here looked like shit. All
Zack had helped do since he was given this assignment
was make it possible for some old ladies to lose their iden-
tities. That and supervising the guarding and escorting
of the nymphomaniacs Harrison Woodruff created.

"Will you let me know as soon as you've relocated
Mrs. Dorset?" Harrison asked. "And will you do all that
you can to bring her back in good enough condition for
me to evaluate?"

"Sure, Doc," Zack said. He stood up. "Oh," he added at
the door, turning, "I guess I'll drive us up to the Ritz
tonight."

"Pardon?"

"The Ritz, late dinner with Mr. Stoddard? Didn't your
trusty sidekick tell you?"

"Oh, yes."

"He wants me there, too. I guess he wants to talk about whether or not we should go ahead with your new candidate. In light of what's been happening, I suppose," Zack added with a smile. "Huh?"

Harrison stared at him.

"I have a suspicion you know the answer to your own question, Mr. Steiner."

Zack laughed.

"You mean you have a theory, don't you, Doc?" He laughed again and then his smile evaporated quickly. "I'll let you know about Mrs. Dorset," he said.

When he closed the door behind him, Harrison felt as if a chilling draft had just been sucked out of his office. It left him in a sweat, the heat centering around his heart.

He should have spoken directly to Shelly Dorset the moment he heard there had been a problem with Kathleen. He knew they had become friends. He should have reassured her himself, but how could he at the time? He didn't know exactly what had happened. Damn that Steiner for not giving him all the details on the telephone. That excuse about not being specific on an uncleared line was just subterfuge. Zack Steiner is deliberately sabotaging Renaissance, Harrison thought. He made up his mind he had to rid the project of the man. Surely, he thought, they could provide me with someone who has expertise in security and yet someone who was not psychotic.

He took a deep breath and thought about Shelly Dorset again. Thumbing through the file, he studied her numbers, and thought about her time clock in light of what had occurred with Kathleen Cornwall. He needed at least two weeks with Shelly back here, he concluded. The body's predesignated, genetic longevity was reestablishing itself with a vengeance, resembling an armada of white blood cells fighting an infection. In this case, overkill. Why? How?

Despite the care he was taking in perfecting what he now called his "youth virus" from the molecules of the subject's own cells, there was still an eventual rejection. He had to solve that problem soon.

There was another knock on his door, but this time the individual waited for his response. It was Miss Kleindeist.

"I have Mrs. Cornwall prepared," she said. He nodded, pushed back his chair and rose to go do the autopsy. He needed the cell samples from the brain, some nerves and, of course, the heart.

Miss Kleindeist smiled at him encouragingly. She was thirty-eight years old herself, but she had the mature look of a woman closer to fifty. Her brown eyes always looked wet, dull under those large black-framed, thick glasses. She had a bony nose that had a small rise in the bridge, just where the glasses sat. Her ears were too large and too long for her small round face, but she kept them hidden under her dark brunet hair, usually swept down and pinned.

Harrison had brought her with him from the National Institute. He had, for the most part, kept their relationship professional, but he sensed that she had an affection for him that was growing in intensity. He took advantage of that affection, giving her the feeling that he was confiding in her because he liked her. She was as loyal to him as anyone could possibly be, and very protective. They hadn't discussed it in any great detail, but he knew she despised Zack Steiner as much as he did.

When Harrison took the time to look at her as a woman, he found himself revolted. She did nothing to complement the little femininity she exhibited. She never wore any makeup, even a trace of lipstick, and she never bothered to pluck the small hairs that grew wildly under her chin. Her teeth, although healthy, were always yellow and she had tiny warts along her collarbone.

Small-framed and thin, she looked utterly devoid of womanly curves. It was as if her formulating genes had been genuinely confused as to their purpose and direction. Some started in one course and others in the exact opposite. The result was a woman in physiology who lacked the intrinsic feminine softness. She was almost unisex.

Yet he did sense her carnal craving from time to time. He would catch her gazing at him with longing and whenever their bodies happened to touch, graze each other in passing, she would close her eyes just a little as if the mere contact caused an orgasm. In some ways she reminded him of an adolescent who would scribble his initials on note pads. Without ever discussing her personal history, he felt certain she was a virgin and had never had any sort of romantic relationship.

"You can't let yourself get discouraged, Dr. Woodruff," she said. He smiled gratefully.

"I know, Miss Kleindeist."

"You're so close. I know you will solve the problems

soon and make the breakthrough. Then they'll appreciate you. Everyone, even Mr. Steiner," she emphasized.

He nodded, but she didn't move. She wanted to squeeze his hand to offer reassurance. He let her do so and then he nodded and mouthed "Thank you." She took a deep breath and turned to lead him out and to the autopsy room where Kathleen Cornwall's corpse lay.

Despite the fact that Kathleen Cornwall was not dead very long, and despite the air conditioning, the room reeked with a putrid stench. Harrison Woodruff and Sandra Kleindeist had to put on their masks immediately. Harrison glanced at Sandra Kleindeist. He saw only her eyes, but remarkably, he saw her smile.

Wasn't love an amazing thing? he thought from a scientific viewpoint. Even under these horrendous conditions, she enjoys being beside me, working with me. He was intrigued, but again, like a scientist, he wished he could somehow dissect the emotion and discover its power, rather than like a man, mourning his own inability to feel as strongly about anyone.

He pulled the sheet off Kathleen Cornwall and stepped back in shock. The skin around her rib cage had already decomposed and the organs exposed were crumbling right before his eyes, flaking and dropping into dust. It was as if some creature were gobbling her up from within.

Miss Kleindeist, stepping up beside him, gasped and seized his arm as if she were about to topple.

"Steady," he said.

"Why is this happening so rapidly this time?" she asked.

"I don't know. Something . . . quickly," he said, "hand me the scalpel. I must get some of these cells frozen."

He worked as rapidly as he could. By the time they were finished, most of Kathleen Cornwall's skin had decomposed as well as most of the organs. Her skeleton was beginning to flake. Harrison covered what remained of the body quickly and shoved it into the zipper bag. He felt it crumble like thin china and then he carried it from the laboratory as he would carry a small bag of garbage and brought it to the incinerator. After he cast it in, he shut the door and lowered his mask. When he turned in the corridor, he saw Miss Kleindeist standing there, her mask down, her arms around herself. She was trembling.

"That was . . . the worst . . ." she said, her lips quivering. "It was as if she had been dipped in some horrible acid."

"There, there now, Miss Kleindeist. It's quite understandable once we consider the enzymes and the accelerated decomposition. Don't lose perspective," he advised. "There's nothing supernatural here. It's all explainable." He smiled, but she shook her head.

"When you think of her the way she was, the way you had made her, and then, what she became . . . I feel so cold suddenly," she said and shivered.

Harrison thought about it for a moment and then he walked over and embraced her, rubbing her bony shoulders and back with the palm of his hand.

Even though he did it perfunctorily, she moaned and clung to him, taking the opportunity to wrap her arms around his waist and put her head on his shoulder.

"Come along, now," he said, patting her lightly on the top of her head. "Let's have a cup of tea. We've earned it," he said, and actually had to push her away; but he did it gently, still holding a comforting smile.

She pulled back her shoulders and nodded. As they walked down the corridor, he drew farther away from her until he was a step ahead as usual, but as usual she was following obediently.

12

Webster cruised Ventura Boulevard, glancing up at his rearview mirror periodically. He still had not caught a glimpse of the two men who had identified themselves as F.B.I. agents, but he assumed that if they had followed him, they would be good enough at it to keep him from knowing they were doing it.

When he reached the corner at which Shelly Dorset was supposedly waiting, he slowed and pulled to the curb just a few yards before the valet parking for the Pussycat Lounge. He gazed around, twisting in his seat to look behind the car. She was nowhere in sight. The valet looked at him and then looked back at the doorway of the lounge. A moment later he sauntered over to Webster. He was a Mexican who looked like he had grown a mustache to pass for twenty-one.

"Park your vehicle, sir?"

"No, I'm not going into the lounge. I was just waiting for someone."

"Named Shelly?" the valet asked cautiously.

Webster looked up sharply.

"Yeah. Where is she?"

The valet didn't respond. He walked back to the lounge entrance, nodded, and then returned to Webster's car, opening the passenger door as Shelly came hurrying out. She handed him all the money she had left and got into the vehicle.

"What the hell was all that about?" Webster asked with a nervous half smile.

"Please, just drive away," she said.

He put the car in drive and started to pull away from the curb just as a black Lincoln cut in front of him and came to a stop, blocking his forward movement.

"Oh no!" Shelly cried.

Herbie Shagan and Mike Robbins got out of the car and casually strolled back to Webster's Mercedes.

"Lock the doors! Back up and pull out!" Shelly screamed. Webster didn't move.

"Well, well, Mr. Martin. Looks like your sad friend's changed sex, huh?" Herbie said.

Mike Robbins laughed and came around to Shelly's door. She slapped down the door lock.

"Just get out of the car, Mrs. Dorset," Herbie Shagan said, stepping back.

"Please, Webster," Shelly pleaded, squeezing his arm, "don't let them take me."

"They're F.B.I.," Webster said.

"No, they're not. They work for the Renaissance Corporation. I'll explain everything. Get us away."

"You had better get out, too, Mr. Webster," Herbie said

firmly and reached under his jacket for his pistol. "Now!" he commanded, waving the gun.

"Why?"

"You lied to us," Herbie said, grimacing angrily. "Now you're aiding and abetting a known felon. If you don't cooperate quickly, we'll place you under arrest, too."

Mike Robbins tapped on Shelly's window with the barrel of his pistol.

"Get out, Mrs. Dorset. Come on now, be nice."

"Webster, use your car phone. Make them tell you what F.B.I. office they're from and call that office. You'll see," Shelly said as Webster started to unbuckle his seat belt. "Go ahead, ask them."

Webster studied her desperate face for a moment and then turned to Herbie.

"What office are you out of, L.A.?"

"Just get the fuck out of the car, Mr. Martin. We're through talking to you. You lied to us."

"Make them tell you, Webster. Why should they be afraid?"

"Let me see your I.D. again," Webster demanded. Herbie reached for the door handle just as Shelly hit the button for auto lock. His reaction was immediate and furious. He reached through the window and seized Webster at the throat, squeezing with lethal power.

"Open the fucking door and get out. Now!"

Webster gagged, tried to push his hand away, and then, his eyes bulging with the effort, made another instinctive decision and slapped the car into reverse. He hit the accelerator. The car shot back, the window jamb slamming Herbie's forearm and spinning him around.

Mike Robbins, taken by surprise himself, stood watching for a moment.

"Stop them!" Herbie shouted, holding his bruised arm against his chest.

Robbins raised his pistol.

Shelly screamed and Webster cut the wheel and threw the transmission into drive. Robbins fired; the bullet shattered the window on Shelly's side, showering glass over her and Webster, but miraculously, neither was cut. Webster accelerated and they shot into the street, cutting off a pickup truck. The driver swerved to avoid them and ran smack into the rear of the black Lincoln because it was still sticking out on the street.

His heart pumping, nearly in shock, Webster wove around another vehicle and sped up. He turned sharply down a side street and accelerated again.

"Who are those guys? What is this all about?" he cried.

As carefully as she could, Shelly brushed the shards of glass from her shoulders and lap. She pulled some out of her hair.

"Are you all right?" he asked her.

"Drive," she said. "Just drive, Webster."

"Who are they?"

"They're security men for the Renaissance Corporation. They're not F.B.I. agents, as you just saw." She brushed some glass off his leg. "I don't think I'm bleeding anywhere. How about you?"

"I'm all right."

He looked up at the rearview mirror. Two headlights were coming fast.

"They're after us!" he said and pressed down on the accelerator to turn and go up a hill. They were heading for Beverly Glen, a route from the valley into West L.A. The road was narrow at times and there was still moderate traffic. He passed the car in front of him, cutting in a little too close. The driver pounded his horn.

"What's the Renaissance Corporation? Who are you? Who's Kathleen? Why did they kill Carl?" he demanded.

"Let's get someplace where we can talk calmly, Webster. You're not going to believe anything I say right now."

"No shit?" he said. He looked into the mirror again. His pursuers had not only passed the car behind him; they had driven it off the road. Neither he nor Shelly heard the gunshot, but another bullet crashed into the car, shattering the rear window. Again, glass rained down; this time a piece cut him on the back of his neck. It stung and he howled.

"Webster!"

"I'm all right. Keep your head down!"

His own head was barely up high enough to see over the steering wheel.

They careened around a turn and started on the descent into Westwood and Sunset Boulevard. It was a heart-stopping flight, tires squealing, near misses with vehicles in front of them, vehicles pulling onto the road, and vehicles parked. At times, the Lincoln looked like it would run right over them, and then Webster would accelerate, pass a car on a turn, risking their lives and the lives of people in an oncoming vehicle; however, he was able to put some distance between them and the pursuers.

They bounced over a hump; he nearly lost control, but

he caught the wheel in time to turn and speed up at an intersection. When they arrived at the streetlight on Sunset, it was red. Webster laid his hand on his horn and shot in front of a car anyway. The driver hit his brakes, which caused the car behind him to slam into his rear. Other vehicles spun, some shot to the right, one almost went head-on into an oncoming Land Rover. The mix-up blocked the intersection and Shagan and Robbins got caught behind them in the mess.

Webster opted to remain on Sunset. They headed for Pacific Palisades. When he reached the small city, he slowed down and took a left turn behind a mall. He drove around until he found a fairly deserted parking lot and pulled into it. For a long moment after he stopped, neither of them spoke. Webster's wrists actually ached from the intensity with which he had been gripping the steering wheel. After a moment more, he got out of the car and carefully brushed his clothing free of any glass. She did the same.

"I'm sorry," she said. "I should have known they would figure out that I would call you and then they would follow you to find me."

"You should have known?" He stood there, gazing around at the dark windows and the quiet street. The sea breeze lifted strands of his hair. Above them the stars peeked in and out of wispy clouds. "Okay, who are you? Who's Kathleen? Who killed Carl and why?" he demanded.

She looked down the street in the direction from which they had come as if she still expected Shagan and Robbins to appear at any moment.

"We lost them," he said. "It's time to talk and to tell the truth, Shelly."

She nodded.

"My full name's Shelly Dorset."

"I know that now. They told me," he said, jabbing his forefinger toward the east.

She came around the front of the car and leaned against the left side of the hood. For a moment she just combed her fingers through her hair.

"What else did they tell you?"

"That you and Kathleen were nymphomaniacs. That you kidnapped a guy and dumped him somewhere after you screwed his brains out. That you were dangerous."

She laughed.

"That was the best fiction they could create?"

"Well, what's the truth, then?"

"I'm from Chicago. I'm what you would call a volunteer in a research project, I guess. Only I had to pay for the privilege."

"What research project?"

"Renaissance. You never heard of it. It's just a name the head of the project chose."

"What sort of a project is it?"

She looked up at him. In the pale glow of the parking lot light, her face looked smooth and shiny, her eyes luminous. It was the face that had mesmerized him the night before, the face he took into his dreams and expected he would see when he had opened his eyes in the morning.

"Rejuvenation," she said.

"Rejuvenation? You mean like . . . making people younger?"

"Exactly."

Webster shook his head.

"Wait a minute," he said. "Just a holy, fucking minute." He paused and looked from his shattered Mercedes to a Honda Accord that had turned down the street. It went by the parking lot, the driver not even looking their way. "What is this, like some kind of beauty program or something? Like those spas in the desert?"

"No, Webster, it's a highly financed, well-organized research project run by an expert in genetics. Its purpose is to reverse the aging process. Kathleen and I are volunteers. We submitted ourselves to the procedure."

He stared at her.

"Yeah? And it worked, I suppose."

"Yes, it has."

"And how old are you then, Shelly?"

"I'm seventy-four," she said.

He smiled.

"Seventy-four?"

"Yes."

"Years old?"

"Yes."

"And Kathleen?"

"She was only seventy-two."

"Only seventy-two? A kid," he said.

"I told you that you would have trouble believing me. It wasn't the kind of thing I could tell you about. We were forbidden to discuss the project when we were on furlough."

"Furlough? What the hell is that?"

"We were permitted to go back to population when Dr. Woodruff, the head of the project, determined our rejuvenation was complete. He wanted us to try to live as normally as we could and then return to the research center for evaluation. We were given a specific number of weeks on the outside. Kathleen was ahead of me in treatment, so she was out longer than I was. She was supposed to go back today, but only after she and I had had lunch together. When she never came home last night, I called you and that was when I learned your friend had been killed."

"So why was he killed?"

"I don't know," she said. "And Kathleen was taken back to the center before we could meet. Then, when I tried to find out what had happened—"

"What?"

"They drugged me and put me in a car to take me back. I woke up in the car and escaped. That's when I called you. I don't know what's going on anymore and I was afraid. The head doctor never spoke to me and these people . . . well, you've seen what they're like."

Webster said nothing. He took a few steps away and stood with his back to her, his hands on his hips.

"You expect me to believe this story?" he finally asked.

She approached him. Despite all that had happened, he couldn't help how he felt when he looked at her. It wasn't just that she was beautiful; he had been with attractive women before. There was something between them, some chemical reaction that triggered a longing deeper than any he had felt for any woman lately. It was like first love, that all encompassing, overwhelming initial crush that overtook him, that filled him with an excitement for life, for awakening, for hurrying out to see her, to be with her, to hear her voice, that seemingly silly desire to write her name or just say it, even when he was alone.

"I was hoping you would," she said softly.

"Why me? Why call me if you're in trouble? You and I hardly know each other. You wouldn't even tell me your full name, right? You wouldn't tell me anything much about yourself."

"Now you see why."

"No, I don't."

"How could I tell you the truth then? What would your reaction have been? And . . ."

"And what?"

"I never expected to see you again. I wanted to," she added quickly, "but it was specifically forbidden for me to develop any sort of relationship, at least during the furlough."

"So why me now? Why didn't you call one of your old friends, or are they all in rest homes?" he asked with a mocking smile.

"You're not far from the truth. The problem, however, is that I'm dead."

"Huh? Wait a minute. You're not only fifty years older than you look, you're also dead?"

"Not literally. I had to die, to have my death arranged before I could go to Renaissance."

"Why is that?"

"They're not ready to have their subjects return to

their lives fifty years younger. They're not ready to reveal what they're doing yet. At least, that was what I was told. I'm thinking now that the powers behind it want to dole out the rejuvenation very selectively and obviously tap into the lucrative potential."

"And exactly who are these powers?" Webster asked, still with a skeptical tone.

"I don't know exactly. My husband had friends in high places, government officials, wealthy businessmen. They contacted me originally. Some of them apparently have formed a quiet alliance to oversee the project and they have been able to get the cooperation of whatever agency they needed at the time. My death was no problem for them, for instance. It was all official, legitimate. I even saw the signed death certificate and read my own obituary. I had a decent funeral, too," she added, almost wistfully.

Webster grimaced.

"Your husband?"

"My husband, Thomas Nelson Dorset. He's been dead almost four years. He was a very successful real estate developer in Chicago. Maybe, because you're in that line, you've heard of him."

Webster thought for a moment. He had heard the name. Dorset had developed those large-scale luxury stores on Chicago's Magnificent Mile.

"Now that I think about it," she said, smiling, "it's kind of ironic that I started an affair with another real estate developer."

"An affair? One night? You call that an affair?"

"I'm on dead time, Webster. One night is like a month to me."

He shook his head. Rejuvenation. Dead time. Renaissance. Maybe they were just overzealous F.B.I. agents and she was mad as a hatter. It occurred to him that he was now a fugitive if they were legitimate, and if they were not and her mad story had any validity, their pursuers could have enough power and influence to make him a fugitive anyway. What was it Detective Siegler had said, he and his partner had been taken off the case? It had been turned over to the feds. People in high places were already taking action, so either way, he was screwed.

"I'm going to call the police again," he said.

"I don't know as you can trust them," she replied.

"I have no choice," he said dryly and returned to the car. He reached in and got the car phone.

"Wait," she said. "Before you do that, let me prove that I'm telling you the truth."

"And how do you propose to do that?"

She thought a moment.

"If you give me twenty-four hours, I think I can do it. Please," she pleaded and reached for his hand.

He stood gazing into her eyes.

Maybe she was some kind of a witch who could throw a spell over him. He certainly didn't feel like turning her over to anyone, police or mental institution authorities. What he wanted to do most of all right now was embrace her, hold her. He tried to overcome the feeling.

"I don't know. Look at my car," he said for want of anything else.

"It's fixable, Webster. One thing I've learned over the years, don't cry over things that can be replaced or repaired. Shed tears only for what's really lost and gone forever."

"Wisdom of old age, huh?"

"Something like that," she said, smiling. What if she were telling the truth? he thought. He was in love with a seventy-four-year-old woman? She's older than his mother would have been. Christ, she could be his grand-mother.

"You know I hope you're just crazy. I know I'm not ready to share Geritol cocktails."

"Do I look like I need Geritol?" she replied.

"Hardly."

"So? Let's go someplace where we can get some rest and think. I'll tell you more and after a while, you'll see I'm not crazy." She hooked his arm and spun the magic of those eyes on him.

He recalled Phil remembering that both she and Kath-leen had those bruises on their arms, the kind that re-sulted from blood tests. She did say she and Kathleen had undergone some sort of treatments. He shook his head. Could this be possible?

"Maybe I'm the one who's crazy," he said. "Get in the car."

She leaned forward and kissed him softly on the lips.

"I'm glad," she said. "Glad we're together again."

He watched her go around, brush off the seat and get into the vehicle. Then he looked toward the east. They could still be roving around back there, searching for him.

He got into the car, took some side streets and brought them out onto Pacific Coast Highway. Then he headed for Venice Beach and a small hotel he knew between Venice and Marina del Rey. On the way they passed a patrol car, but the policemen within didn't take any special note of them, despite the shattered windows. Such a sight, even for a Mercedes, was not rare in the City of Angels these days.

Webster half expected the black Lincoln to pop out of a side street and come after them, but their ride to the hotel was uneventful. Neither of them had spoken for a while, but when she saw where he was going, she reached over to squeeze his hand. He turned to her.

"Thanks for trusting me a little," she said. "I guess I do have some wisdom. I chose the right handsome young man last night."

Webster shook his head.

"Lucky for me," he said and pulled into the hotel parking lot. She laughed, but he wasn't sure whether he should laugh or cry.

13

Satch Norris shifted the limousine into low as he made the turn off Highway 111 in Rancho Mirage and started up the steep incline. The Hyatt was one of the more elegant properties in the desert, but the classic hotel with its rich decor had another advantage. It was situated high up on a hillside, providing spectacular views of the Coachella Valley, especially at night when the lights in the desert communities dazzled, resembling a scattering of diamonds, rubies and emeralds.

Harrison Woodruff sat in the rear, uncomfortable. Zack Steiner smoked, of course, but he was also silent, smiling coldly whenever he turned to Harrison and Harrison could see his face in the glow of streetlights.

The doorman and the valet rushed out to greet them as they pulled up to the entrance. Harrison stepped out quickly, eager to get this dinner meeting finished. Steiner caught up with him in the lobby.

"Full of vim and vigor tonight, huh, Doc?"

"What? Oh. Sorry. I'm just in deep thought."

"I know you're in something deep," Zack said and laughed. Harrison ignored him. They walked down the corridor to the restaurant and paused at the entrance.

"We're meeting a Mr. Stoddard," Zack told the host.

"Yes, sir. Right this way," he said, snapping to attention. He led them through the restaurant toward a rear table where Ben Stoddard sat gnawing on a piece of bread, his glass of heavily peppered tomato juice before him.

Ben Stoddard was seventy-eight years old, but looked like a man in his early sixties at the most. The personification of the self-made multimillionaire, he radiated strength and independence. He always appeared disinterested, gazing everywhere but at the speaker when he was in a conversation, but he had a built-in bullshit detector and when his patience ran out, he would cut right to the quick, the heart of the argument, with ruthless speed. The first time Harrison met him, he thought the man had more than vision; he had perception, microscopic eyes, a mind so nimble, it was futile to avoid confessing mistakes or dressing up an argument. He was merciless when he knew he was being lied to or, worse, not told the whole truth.

Harrison understood that Stoddard made his fortune in oil speculation. He was very close with the Saudis and the Kuwaitis and had some vague but influential connection to the Venezuelan oil industry. Presidents relied on him for advice and he was a heavy contributor toward the campaigns of senators and congressmen. It was rumored that he even had influence with two or three justices of the Supreme Court.

On the surface, he looked like the quintessential grandfather and in truth, he did have eleven grandchildren, as well as four great-grandchildren. Whenever Harrison had seen him, he found him robust, his cheeks flushed, his dark eyes clear. He stood only about five feet six and he was soft in the stomach and round-shouldered, but Stoddard was one of those men who looked naturally powerful. It was all in his quiet, superior demeanor. When he did finally rivet his eyes on someone, he or she would stop talking and wait for his judgment. Would he compliment or condemn?

Harrison knew that Stoddard had at least half a dozen homes in some of the world's most desirable locales. In America he had houses in Aspen, Westport and Palm Beach. He had a London apartment near Harrods, a house in Portugal and a villa on Corfu. Yet he wasn't a man who flaunted his wealth and he always treated servants well. He commanded loyalty with his generosity, but he demanded excellence.

Harrison thought it was fortunate he had this sort of man on his side, that he wanted Harrison to succeed more than he wanted anything he had ever pursued in his life. For now, or up to now, Harrison was Ben Stoddard's fair-haired boy, and that meant carte blanche whenever it was needed.

"Mr. Stoddard," Harrison said, extending his hand. Ben Stoddard took it quickly and nodded toward the seat on his right.

"Hello, Mr. Stoddard," Zack said without offering his hand. He sat directly across from him.

"Order something," Stoddard said, his eyes glancing at the menus. Each man picked his up and perused it.

"Can I get anyone a cocktail?" the waiter asked.

"They're going to order now," Stoddard said sharply.

Harrison chose the range hen and Zack ordered a New York strip steak, rare. Neither wanted anything but water. As soon as the waiter left, Stoddard leaned forward and swirled the juice in his glass. He drank some and then took a deep breath.

"Tell me about Mrs. Cornwall," he said.

Harrison gazed at Zack, who looked stoic, detached from the conversation, but after working with the man for as long as Harrison had, he noted the small wrinkle in his lips, the tiny smile of satisfaction.

"Well," Harrison began, "this is a good example of why I need to continue the furlough program. There are psychological problems to understand and we can't even begin to scratch the surface of them if the subjects are kept imprisoned on the compound.

"In this case," he continued quickly, "our subject suffered some sort of mental breakdown and didn't follow the procedure. I'm even considering the possibility she was suicidal, given what she knew was happening to her," he added.

Even Zack's tiny smile evaporated. He glanced quickly at Mr. Stoddard to see if he was buying Harrison's spin on the events.

Stoddard cleared his throat and gazed around the restaurant.

"As I understand it, she had already begun to regress," he finally said.

"Yes, that's true. It was unexpected. I felt confident I had solved the problem, but there is apparently one more thing to do."

"What's that's supposed to mean . . . one more thing to do?"

"I have a technical problem," Harrison admitted. He waited as the waiter brought the salads. Stoddard and Steiner began to eat theirs. "There appears to be a correlation between the speed with which the rejuvenation is effectuated and the length of it. Simply put, the faster, the shorter. I'm not sure why just yet, but I will be," Harrison began. He was about to get into the specific scientific detail when Zack grunted.

Stoddard's eyes rose and then returned to the salad he was devouring. Harrison couldn't recall anyone Stoddard's age with as voracious an appetite. He was not a very neat eater, either. Usually his lips and chin were wet with some part of his meal at all times throughout the dinner, but no one had the nerve to tell him there was a particle of spinach on his face or a piece of angel hair at the side of his mouth.

"How long before you will be sure?" Stoddard asked.

"A month, maybe. Maybe six weeks."

"Maybe a year," Zack muttered.

Harrison felt his face flush.

"Hardly a year, Mr. Steiner. I think in light of the progress I've made over a year, I can safely say I should pinpoint a problem in far less time."

Zack patted his mouth with his napkin and sat back, his eyes on fire.

"We had to put down someone because of what happened with Mrs. Cornwall," he reminded Stoddard. Ben Stoddard didn't like being reminded of anything.

"What do you think, Mr. Steiner, I forgot in a matter of hours? Do I look like a man suffering with Alzheimer's disease?"

"No, but—"

"Is that the best contribution you can make to this discussion? Repetition?"

"I'm just trying to emphasize the danger of continuing this stupid furlough program. I'm going to need an army out there, soon. Mrs. Dorset," he added quickly, "is still not retrieved."

"What's the update on that situation?"

"I'm awaiting a call from my associates in the field," he said. "We'll have her back, but as you know, we had to involve some lower level agencies. That's never good."

Stoddard turned to Harrison.

"What about Mrs. Dorset?"

"The retrieval wasn't handled well," Harrison said. "I never gave the order for her to be drugged while she was at the safe house. She's not stupid. She realized what had been done to her and she panicked when she was being dragged back. I've always prided myself on the painstaking effort I make to win their confidence. In a matter of minutes, literally, weeks and months of building that confidence were erased."

Ben Stoddard nodded. Harrison felt the tension lessen in his chest. The waiter began to serve the entrees. Stoddard, who had ordered grilled swordfish, dug right in, cutting himself pieces almost as large as his mouth. He chewed vigorously, his eyes bulging, his jawbone working so hard the veins along his cheeks became embossed. When he swallowed, his Adam's apple writhed like a snake beneath his skin. He sipped some water. Harrison and Zack ate quietly, their eyes moving surreptitiously from each other to Stoddard.

"Dr. Woodruff has got to be the final authority on all this. No dramatic actions should ever be taken without first clearing it through him," Stoddard said.

"He was en route from New Orleans at the time," Zack began.

"There are phones on planes nowadays. You, of all people, Mr. Steiner, know that communication is never a problem. If you wanted to, you could contact someone in the African jungle right now. Am I correct? Am I?"

"Of course."

"Then that wasn't the issue."

"I didn't think it was prudent to discuss these matters on lines not cleared."

"You have access to clear lines when you need them," Stoddard reminded him.

"I did what I thought had to be done. I was assigned to head security . . ."

"Not in a vacuum. You have to realize this is a more delicate project, different from anything you've done before, I would imagine."

"That it is," Zack said dryly.

Harrison suddenly realized that Ben Stoddard hadn't wanted Zack Steiner at the table with them for the reasons Steiner had thought. It wasn't going to be a dressing-down of Harrison with Steiner confirming the problems. Obviously, Stoddard had his own sources of information and wasn't dependent on Steiner's reports. He already had known every detail Harrison was going to describe. He wanted only to confirm it and to make his point.

"There are many other researchers seeking to extend longevity and find the so-called secret of life, but what makes Dr. Woodruff's project unique and of great interest to me and to my associates," Stoddard continued, "is that his really follows the motto on the masthead of the *Journal of Gerontology:* To add life to years, and not just years to life.

"Suppose I could live another twenty years. What would it buy me? A longer dotage, employment for caretakers, profits for pharmaceutical companies? No, Mr. Steiner, but to live and not to age, to return to vigor and keep a quick intellect, to be able to say with Rabbi Ben Ezra, 'Grow old along with me!/ The best is yet to be.' Ah, there's the dream.

"And Dr. Woodruff's work provides the first real possibility of that dream becoming a reality.

"And this isn't just a selfish hope," Ben Stoddard continued, cutting up the last of his grilled swordfish as he spoke. "Just think what a tragedy aging really is for mankind. Just when we arrive at wisdom and that wisdom makes it possible for us to do something significant for humanity, just at this point, our energies diminish and we began to deteriorate, some so rapidly it's pathetic."

He put the piece into his mouth and started to chew, the juices running down the side of his jaw.

"No wonder George Bernard Shaw said youth was wasted on the young, huh?"

Stoddard laughed. Zack offered a reluctant smile and chewed on his own meal. Harrison beamed.

Suddenly, Stoddard turned on him.

"But you have to be more aware of the real world too, Dr. Woodruff. You are working in a protected, isolated environment. However, you are sending your subjects back to reality, as it were. You have to anticipate problems, prepare better for them. We can't be chasing old women around Los Angeles, now, can we? Although, when I look at Mrs. Dorset's pictures, she certainly doesn't look very old," he added with a cold smile.

Zack Steiner smirked with glee.

"Yes, well, I did promise Mr. Steiner that I would reevaluate the program."

"And listen to his advice, take some of his suggestions. He has an expertise we wanted and an expertise we're paying highly for, correct?"

"Yes," Harrison said.

"Now, we come to the next subject. You've already interviewed her, and Mr. Steiner, you've already set some of the groundwork for bringing her in?"

"Yes, I have, Mr. Stoddard, but I thought in light of what's going on—"

"Don't you think you'll have this situation under control very soon?"

Zack stared at Stoddard.

"Yes, I do," he said confidently.

"Then, what would be the problem?" Stoddard waited. "Is there anything different about this one that will make it more difficult?" Before Zack could reply, Stoddard continued. "I thought the data and the research we were provided illustrated an ideal Woodruff subject. I knew her husband, of course, but most of the reconnaissance came from your people, Mr. Steiner."

"No, I don't have any special problems," Zack said. "I just thought we should put things on hold until we all reevaluate this furlough thing and—"

"On hold? Time is the most valuable commodity we have. It can't be replaced and there are no substitutes," Stoddard emphasized. "I'm not a spring chicken," he added.

"Well, at least I thought in light of what's happened, we should reconsider what we're doing with these furloughs," Steiner insisted.

"And you are going to, but if Dr. Woodruff thinks it is necessary, we've got to do the best we can to make it work. I'm sure Dr. Woodruff will compromise with anything you suggest to make it work," Stoddard concluded, glaring at Harrison.

Harrison finished eating his meal quickly. He hadn't enjoyed one bite, anyway. He was under too much tension. He drank some water and then Stoddard signaled the waiter.

"I have to make some international phone calls," he said. "I'm going to leave you two to your own just deserts."

He laughed at his pun.

"Put this plus twenty percent on my hotel bill," he told the waiter.

"Very good, sir."

"Gentlemen." Stoddard rose. He looked at Steiner. "I'll hear from you in a day or so. And Dr. Woodruff, continue to give me a blow-by-blow update on your progress. Remember, Doctor, the clock ticks and I'm selfish enough to want to turn it back soon. You won't disappoint me, will you?"

"I'll try not to, Mr. Stoddard."

"Try harder, Doctor. If that's possible, of course," he added with a smile.

They watched him leave.

"You want any dessert, Doc?"

"No, I'm fine," Harrison said.

"Good. Let's get the hell out of here. I've got more to do than I anticipated," Zack said.

They rose and went out to the front of the hotel. Satch, who was talking to the valet, moved quickly to get the limousine when he saw them coming. In moments they were heading down the hill, the elegant hotel falling behind them into the darkness. Neither spoke because neither trusted the other with any comment he would make concerning Ben Stoddard.

The phone rang. Zack leaned forward and lifted the receiver.

"Steiner," he said. He listened. Even in the darkness, Harrison saw him redden.

"You know where he lives and where he works," he said sharply. "Get that staked out. Contact our connection at LAPD and get whatever help he can provide. Stay in constant touch. And Herbie, I don't want to hear about another fuck-up," he said. He returned the receiver to its cradle and sat back to light one of his cigarettes.

"Was that about Mrs. Dorset?" Harrison asked after a long moment of expectation.

"Yeah, that was Mike and Herbie."

"And?"

"Her lover boy from the night before helped her get away."

"What?"

"He lied to Herbie and Mike and picked her up. They lost them in a pursuit."

"Oh, no. What are we going to do?"

"We? We are going to find them and bring her back."

"You're not proposing to kill another young man so soon after the first, are you?" Harrison asked softly. "It would surely bring more undesired attention to our project."

"I don't think I need you to tell me how to do my job, Doctor."

"I'm just saying—"

"Worry about your test tubes and microscopes," he said in the tone of a warning.

Harrison sat back. Somehow, it was all going bad. No matter what he did, he couldn't stop it.

Indigestion set in. He had eaten too fast and was too nervous. He gazed at Zack Steiner. Nothing seemed to bother him. The man was cool, cold.

One thing was for sure, Harrison thought. If he had any control of this afterward, a man like Zack Steiner would never be given the opportunity to go around a second time.

Something deep down inside him told Harrison Woodruff he wouldn't have the power to make those decisions.

And that made him sadder still.

14

Chicky Siegler sobered up quickly and snapped on the night table lamp as he sat up with the receiver in his hand. After he had spoken to Webster Martin, he was bothered by the fear in the young man's tone of voice and the impression the young man had had of the F.B.I. agents interrogating him. The way Kronenberg had taken him and Raul off the case without even arranging for a meeting between them and the feds gnawed at him ever since he had left the station. Unable to fall asleep anyway, he decided to call a good friend at the F.B.I. office, Bill Johnstone.

In the early days, Chicky and Bill had cooperated on a number of investigations, but their relationship soon became more than a mere professional one. Chicky was at Bill's side when Bill's wife succumbed to her second heart attack five years ago. They had attended each other's children's weddings and Chicky had gone to both of Bill's grandchildren's christenings. Bill was four years younger and physically in far better shape. He was always after Chicky to lose weight and exercise. Chicky had even joined the same gym and worked out with Bill on two occasions, before letting that drift away. Bill lectured, cajoled, mocked and even threatened before giving up.

"What the fuck are you saying, Bill?" Chicky asked.

"I'm telling you no one in the local bureau office knows anything about this. We have no agents named Shagan and Robbins in L.A. either. Are you sure about the names?"

"That's what I was told."

"They showed I.D.?"

"Yeah. You're sure about this, huh? You're not holding back on me for some internal security reason, are you?"

"Who are you talking to, Chicky?"

"I'm sorry, I'm just . . . confused."

"What's new about that? How's Maggie?"

"She's improving. I might be taking her home soon."

"That's great. And your retirement . . . on schedule?"

"Maybe sooner," Chicky said.

"Good," Bill responded. "No one deserves it or needs it more."

"Thanks, I think."

Bill laughed.

"You're sure this phone call wasn't just some stupid practical joke arranged by some of your fellow officers?"

"Kronenberg pulled Torres and me off the case and said it was in the hands of the feds. Kronenberg doesn't joke. The last time that man laughed was at his mother's funeral."

"Maybe it's not the F.B.I., Chicky. There are other feds, you know. As difficult as it is for some people to believe," Bill kidded.

"Yeah. My boy did say F.B.I., though."

"People look at badges quickly. It could have been D.E.A., B.A.T.F., maybe even the Secret Service."

"I know. Think you can track them for me, too? See if they're involved in this or if there are agents named Shagan and Robbins in L.A.?"

"This is going to cost you."

"Dinner at Toscana again?"

Chicky had taken Bill there when he lost the bet on the Lakers.

"Might be someplace more expensive. Now that you're selling your house at a good profit, you can afford me. I'll let you know."

"Thanks."

After Chicky cradled the receiver, he gazed around his empty bedroom. As a gesture of hope more than for his own need, he had Sophie, the cleaning girl, come in twice a week even if he hardly used the house. The bedroom was neat, the furniture dusted and polished. All of his clothing was properly hung, too. He was behaving better than he had when Maggie was home, he thought. Every time he left a dirty dish or spilled something, he felt the enormous weight of guilt increase. Because of that, he ate out for nearly all his meals.

No room in his house intensified his deep loneliness as much as did his empty bedroom. When Maggie was here, he could feel her presence in rooms even if she wasn't in them at the time. This was especially true for the bedroom, where her perfumes and bath powder scents lingered. He loved smelling them; it reinforced her and in a warm, loving way, gave him comfort and respite from the wild, deranged world in which he lived and worked. Just a little thing like a single rose or a vase filled with gardenias reinforced her existence. The house no longer reeked with the aromas of the food she was cooking. He didn't hear her moving about, cleaning, rearranging things he had moved or misplaced. The silence was deep, cutting, devastating. He was happy he had found a potential buyer. The house he and Maggie had shared for so long had become a living tomb, echoing with memories made more painful by her absence.

He sighed and then returned his thoughts to his conversations with Webster Martin and Bill Johnstone. Something weird was occurring. He considered Torres's advice: worry about himself and Maggie and forget law enforcement. He was just about out of it anyway. Kronenberg had taken them off the case, right? His retirement was around the corner.

He lay back and started to reach for his glass of straight bourbon again, but stopped.

Webster Martin had a point when he questioned why the agents wouldn't tell him where he could reach them. It sounded strange. They questioned him and then he left the apartment. Chances were they were setting him up to follow him. But why handle it that way? What was going on here?

What are my choices? Chicky thought. Lie here and toss and turn all night in the grips of my usual insomnia, or check out this situation. He sat up again and reached for the phone to punch out Raul Torres's home number. His wife answered and, once she heard it was Chicky, dropped her pleasant tone of voice.

"Yeah, he's here," she said reluctantly. "Are you as surprised as I am?"

"Sorry," Chicky said as soon as Raul got on the phone.

"I'm still hearing it about rushing dinner and shooting off. Maybe cops shouldn't get married or if they do, maybe they should marry other cops."

"If I had it to do over again—"

"Yeah?"

"I'd probably repeat every fucking mistake," Chicky admitted. Raul laughed.

"What's up?"

Chicky described his phone call with Webster Martin and his follow-up with Bill Johnstone.

"Maybe Johnstone is right. The guy read the badges wrong. It's a different agency. Kronenberg never answered when you asked, remember?"

"I thought if you called Kronenberg and asked him, he might tell you. He and I have fallen out of love."

"I'm not crazy about the idea."

"It's just a phone call. I'll stay awake better," Chicky added. Raul laughed.

"All right. Let me think of a reason or a way to put it to him."

"Call me as soon as you find out, will ya?"

"Sure."

After he hung up, Chicky switched on the television set and flipped the channels until he caught a news program. The report on the possibility that margarine might be worse for you than butter nearly defeated his insomnia, but immediately after the scientific mumbo-jumbo from the program's health expert, the anchor announced reports of a shooting in Sherman Oaks.

"No one was injured. Police are investigating the possibility that it was gang related."

Chicky sat up. Sherman Oaks? Webster Martin said he was heading for Sherman Oaks.

The phone rang.

"Yeah?"

"He wasn't happy I bothered him at home. Why sugar coat it," Torres inserted. "He nearly bit my head off. But he calmed down when I told him I felt a responsibility to give the feds the videotapes. He said I should just drop them on his desk in the morning and he'd give it to the F.B.I. himself."

"F.B.I.? He definitely said F.B.I.?"

"That's what he said."

"But Bill tells me otherwise."

"Maybe he has to, Chicky."

"Naw, not Bill. Doesn't sound kosher."

"So what are you going to do?"

"There was just a report of a shooting up at Sherman Oaks. That's where Webster Martin was heading. I'll get the details, and either head up there or shoot over to Webster's apartment on Wilshire."

"You're kidding, right?"

"I got a bad feeling about this. I think the kid was sucked into something. We might have a couple of vengeful cuckolds on our hands and a second poor shnook about to be offed for wagging his pecker places it don't belong."

"Jesus, Chicky. Kronenberg said we're to step away."

"Who said anything about we? Talk to you later," he said and hung up quickly. The phone started to ring seconds later. He knew it was Raul, but he didn't answer it. He got dressed again and headed out. In the car, he called dispatch and asked for details on the Sherman Oaks shooting. They gave him the exact location and he realized that it was where Webster was supposedly meeting the woman named Shelly.

A very light rain had started, just a misting, really, but it was enough to make the freeways slick and cause a couple of fender-benders. What should have taken Chicky twenty minutes took him nearly forty. He pulled in front of the Pussycat Lounge where a black-and-white remained. Under the illumination of the streetlights and because of the precipitation, the shards of glass from Webster's car window and from the headlights of the truck that had smacked into the rear of the black Lincoln glittered on the street. It probably wouldn't be cleaned up until morning, Chicky thought.

When he stepped out of his car, he recognized the two patrolmen in the black-and-white, Buzz Sussman and Tony Gibson. They were comfortably ensconced in their car, pulling the easy assignment to just stay there and keep their eye on things for the rest of their watch.

"Hey, Siegler, what are you doing out this late?" Buzzy quipped.

"You know the old story. You never know how good you have it until you get promoted to more responsibility," Chicky said. They both laughed. "Was the shooting gang related?" Chicky asked them quickly.

Neither patrolman responded immediately. Chicky raised his eyebrows.

"Tough question?"

"I don't know for sure," Sussman said. Chicky caught their exchanged glances. "Time we got here, it was all over, the witness tucked in."

"Who was here?"

"We don't know for sure. Why? What's going on?" Tony asked him.

"Don't know who covered the shooting?"

"We got our orders from dispatch and here we are, baby-sitting the scene of the crime," Buzzy said.

"Only thing we do know is the witness was that valet at the Pussycat, but he's already been questioned," Tony said. "How come you're here?"

"They need an expert," Chicky said. The two patrolmen laughed. He started toward the lounge, cursing the pain that shot up from his foot to his thigh. The valet was talking animatedly to another young Mexican man and a waitress from the lounge, dressed only in an abbreviated skirt and a mesh top, underneath which she wore tassels over her nipples.

"Excuse me," Chicky said. He held up his I.D. "I need to ask some questions."

"More questions?" the waitress said excitedly.

"Did you see the shooting, too?" Chicky asked her.

"No."

"Could you step aside a moment?" he asked the valet. He looked terribly nervous, agitated. "What's your name?"

"Ricardo. I told everything I know. They said I don't

need to be in court. They said I could just forget about it. I don't want to get into no trouble."

"Easy, easy. No one's getting you into any trouble. I just got to go over this with you one more time, Ricardo. It'll be quick. You told your story to who before?"

"Who?" He gazed at the patrol car. Chicky looked back too and saw the two uniformed policemen watching him and the witness. Sussman suddenly picked up his radio and began talking into it.

"Yeah, who?" Chicky pursued.

"Policemen," Ricardo said, shrugging.

"Uniformed or in plainclothes?"

"Like those two," he said, nodding toward the black-and-white.

"Oh. Okay. Well, I'm a detective so I got to follow up. Tell me about the shooting as if you were telling it for the first time, okay?"

He nodded, swallowed hard, and started.

"Two men in suits drove in front of the man's car."

"What kind of car was the man driving?"

"Mercedes."

"You remember the model?" He nodded.

"*Sí*. I parked ones like it before. 500SL. *Mucho dinero*," he said. "I park cars for twice my life and not make enough to buy one." Chicky smiled.

"What color was it?"

"Black."

"Uh-huh. Can you describe the driver a little?"

"A man maybe thirty, thirty-five."

"Maybe younger?"

"*Sí*, maybe."

"Do you remember the color of his hair, anything else?"

Ricardo shook his head.

"I just went over to him quick when he pull up. He said he was waiting for someone and I asked him if it was Shelly."

"Shelly? Why?"

"She told me to. She waiting over there in the shadows," he said, nodding.

"Go ahead."

"He said yes and I went back and told her. She got in the car, but before they could drive away a black Lincoln cut in front of them and two men jumped out. They started yelling at them and the man backed away the Mercedes quick. They shot at him. Before they could get into their car, a truck smacked into the rear of it, but they don't stay to talk to the driver. They jumped in their car and shot off after the Mercedes. That's when we call the police."

"How the hell does that sound gang related?" Chicky muttered.

"What?"

"Nothing. Do you remember anything about the two men? What they looked like?"

"Very little. They were both *grande,*" he said, holding his hands out to indicate wide shoulders. "Once the shouting and the shooting started, I ran back to the lounge."

"Good move. You gave all this information to uniformed patrolmen?"

"*Sí.*"

Chicky thought for a moment.

"Okay, thanks," he said and turned toward his car just as Raul pulled up behind it. Still hobbling to avoid putting too much pressure on his foot, Chicky greeted him as he stepped out. "What the hell are you doing here?"

"Nothing good on television," Raul said. "So? What you find out?"

"Black-and-white, not the boys here now," he added quickly, nodding toward Sussman and Gibson, "took the information from the young wetback over there. From what he just told me, there's no doubt it was Webster Martin. He came to pick up his Shelly. Two suits, probably the two who presented themselves as F.B.I. agents, followed him and tried to cut him off. He put it in reverse and hightailed it and they shot at him. How the hell that gets reported as a possibly gang-related shooting is a bigger mystery."

"I was listening to the radio on the way up here. There were half a dozen accidents along Beverly Glen and one smack-a-roo on Sunset where Beverly Glen joins. The car chase got that far. I called Willy Petersen and he said a black Mercedes that fits the description of Webster Martin's was reported as shooting out into traffic and causing the pile-up."

"What happened to the Mercedes?"

"Went west on Sunset."

"Anything about a late-model black Lincoln?"

"Not that I heard."

"Let's get Webster Martin's license number and put out an APB on him and his car," he said.

"You really want to get involved in this?"

"I'm doing it all on my own time. I just want to do something extra for the department for all the wonderful things it's done for me over the years. Just to show my appreciation," Chicky said. Raul laughed. Chicky reached into his car and took the radio mike to call in Webster's automobile. After thirty seconds, the dispatcher came back.

"That APB is already issued, Detective."

"What? Who issued it?"

"Came out of your station," she said. Chicky looked at Raul.

"What the hell is going on here? I thought we were out of it. What'd he do, lie to us and put someone else on the case?"

Raul shrugged and shook his head.

"Kronenberg might not like it, but he's going to talk to me tomorrow," Chicky said. "He lied about it being F.B.I. and he's obviously cooperating with someone."

"He don't have to talk to you, Chicky."

"He will or—"

"Or what?"

"I'll threaten not to retire," Chicky said. Raul laughed. "Let's get a hot chocolate. I know a place two blocks east."

"And call Webster Martin's apartment. Just in case he went home."

"Doubt it."

"Me too. Maybe we should go see his buddy. He could go there."

"Gold?" Chicky nodded. Raul pulled out his note pad

and flipped the pages. "I got his address. It's in Brent-wood."

"Let's just head down there, then. We'll swing over and give Webster's place a look-see before turning in."

"Yeah, by then you should be tired enough to let everyone else get some sleep," Raul said.

"Don't bet on it," Chicky muttered.

15

Phil Gold woke with a start. He realized he had fallen asleep in the living room watching television. David Letterman was over. He had slept through practically the whole show. Too many drinks, he thought, and stretched. He reached for the remote and flipped off the set just as the doorbell sounded. For a moment he just stared at the door. It opened right on the living room, which was the way it did in most of the condos in the building.

His uncle Leon, his mother's older brother, owned a few properties on the Westside, one of which was this two-bedroom, ground-floor condo on Montana, just east of Barrington Avenue in Brentwood. It was in one of the older buildings on the street, but rents in Brentwood were always sky high, no matter how small the unit or how old the building. However, his uncle gave him a sufficient bargain for him to live here. His parents, who never liked the fact that he had moved from what they considered the far more secure Paramus, New Jersey, to the infamous Los Angeles environment, were at least placated by Uncle Leon's assurance that Brentwood was upscale and safe.

Like Webster, Phil was an only child, but unlike Webster, he was very sensitive, early on in his life, to the accusation that because he was an only child, he was pampered and spoiled from cry one. Always an overachiever, he graduated valedictorian of his class and decided he wanted to go to college in California. He majored in business, but graduated at the time jobs were scarce. He took the insurance position mainly to maintain his independence and remain on the West Coast, but he soon got to like his work and the people with whom he worked. He was promoted quickly and given a larger geographical area. Now, he was actually making good money. His parents reluctantly accepted the fact that he wouldn't return and start a life close to them. They were even considering retiring in California, maybe Palm Springs. If they should as much as hear a vague rumor about Carl's murder, they would be hysterical, nagging him to death, he thought. He was certainly not going to mention it.

Phil hesitated when the doorbell sounded again. This time whoever it was pressed the button repeatedly. It was probably Webster, he thought. He should have done what I did and just gone home. Traipsing over the city looking for these women was surely futile and emotionally debilitating. He'll probably want to sleep over, Phil concluded and hurried to the door.

Normally, maybe because of the paranoia his mother

had instilled in him, he would look through the peephole to see who it was before unlocking the door, but this time, positive it had to be Webster, he thrust it open to confront Satch Norris and Tom Murden. He thought they looked like wall-to-wall brute.

Never did he feel the smallness of his own size as acutely as he did at this moment. Dressed in his dark blue silk robe with matching slippers, a birthday present his mother and father sent him last month, and his light blue pajamas, he gaped in surprise. A slight trickle of fear began in the base of his neck and quickened his heartbeat.

Satch held out his F.B.I. identification.

"Mr. Gold, sorry to bother you at this hour."

Phil looked at the I.D. and then at Tom Murden's.

"F.B.I.?"

"Yes, sir."

Phil relaxed. It made sense that the F.B.I. would hire men of this size.

"May we come in and talk to you for a few moments?" Satch asked politely.

"What's this about?"

"The murder of your friend and the disappearance of your other friend," Satch said.

"Disappearance? Who? What other friend?"

"Webster Martin."

"Webster's disappeared? Can't be. We just had dinner with his father tonight."

"We know that, sir. May we come in?" Satch asked.

"Oh. Sure," Phil said, stepping back. "Sorry. I was just taken by surprise. F.B.I.?"

Tom Murden laughed as he closed the door behind them.

"It's no big deal," he said. "We're just cops, too." Satch threw him a look of reprimand and then turned back to Phil.

"You say you had dinner with Mr. Martin and his father earlier tonight?"

"Yes, at Chasens."

"Well, that's what he did tell us when we saw him earlier," Satch said to Tommy. Tommy nodded.

"I don't understand. What do you mean, Webster's disappeared?"

"We were supposed to meet up an hour ago and when he didn't show, we thought he might have come here."

Tom Murden was already looking around. He poked his head into the kitchen and then smiled at Phil.

"You're welcome to look," Phil said. Murden nodded and opened the door of the second bedroom. He gazed back at Satch and shook his head.

"Has he called you this evening since dinner?" Satch asked.

"No. What's this about? Why were you going to meet with Webster? He never told me anything about this."

"As I said, we met him after you saw him earlier. The F.B.I. is on the case now," Satch said. "We told Webster we needed him to confront a witness. We think she was one of the women. Our meeting was all arranged, but Webster failed to show."

"Webster wouldn't fail to show," Phil said.

"That's what surprised us. We're a bit worried about him now."

"Worried?" Phil shook his head. "How come the F.B.I. is involved?" he asked.

"There was a kidnapping across state lines and other things," Satch said. Tom Murden returned, standing just to the right of Phil, his shoulder about even with Phil's jawline.

"Oh. Did you try Webster's apartment?"

"Just came from it."

"How about his car phone? Have you tried calling him?"

Murden and Norris exchanged glances and then Satch smiled.

"No, we didn't. Good idea, though. Can you try it for us?"

"Sure," Phil said. He lifted the receiver off the pearl phone cradle on the table by the sofa and punched out Webster's car phone number.

After two rings, the mechanical operator came on to say, "The party you're trying to reach is away from his or her cellular phone."

"He's not picking up," Phil said.

"That's too bad," Tom Murden said. Satch nodded.

"Yeah, too bad. Well, then, Mr. Gold. Where do you think your friend might be at this hour? Does he have other friends who he might go to see?"

"Sure." Phil paused. "But why wouldn't he meet with you guys if he was supposed to?"

"That's the twenty-four-thousand-dollar question, isn't it?" Satch said.

"Make it twenty-four million, Satch," Tom Murden said.

Phil grimaced. Now that he had spoken to them, although they were physically impressive, these two didn't exactly fit his image of F.B.I. agents, neither as smooth as Efrem Zimbalist, Jr.

"So, who would he go to see?" Satch asked, a little more of a note of demand in his voice.

"Well, maybe Dick Berber?"

"And where might Mr. Berber live?"

"Santa Monica. He has an ocean-view condo on Ocean Drive. He's an attorney," Phil added, as if to explain why.

"An attorney, huh? Yeah, he might just head for him."

"Why?" Phil asked.

"People always get nervous when they have to involve themselves in legal things," Satch said.

"Yeah, that's true," Tom Murden said.

"Not Web. He was very anxious to get involved. He told me he was going back to the dance club to see if he could find the women again. That's why I think it's peculiar he didn't meet up with you," Phil added. He frowned. "What time did you see him tonight?"

"About ten-thirty, right, Tommy?"

"Yeah."

"Ten-thirty? Where?"

"His apartment."

"But then . . . I guess he didn't stay at the dance club long. What time were you supposed to meet him again tonight? It's . . ." Phil looked at the miniature grandfather clock on the shelf by the television set. "It's nearly twelve-thirty. Why didn't he just go with you?"

Satch hesitated just enough to start that trickle of fear

down the back of Phil's neck again. Only this time, it exploded in the pit of his stomach, giving him a weak feeling. Who were these guys?

"Can I see your I.D. again?" he asked. It was the wrong question and he knew it instantly.

"Are you sure Mr. Martin hasn't called you this evening?" Satch asked instead of taking out his I.D.

"Of course, I'm sure."

"We'd like you to call this attorney and see if he's there or if he's heard from him."

"Now? Look at the time."

"Hey, Mr. Gold, we're the F.B.I. We work around the clock to protect Americans from criminals," Tommy said.

"Please, just call him," Satch said. He nodded at the phone.

Phil felt his hand shake as he reached for the receiver. He punched out Dick Berber's number and waited. It rang four times before an answering machine picked up.

"Answering machine," he said and held the receiver out so they could hear. Neither man moved. They glanced at each other again. "He probably doesn't answer the phone this late. Checks his messages in the morning. A lot of people do that."

"What's the exact address?" Satch demanded. Phil told him.

"You're positive he hasn't called you tonight since you saw him?" Satch asked.

Phil shook his head and swallowed.

"Webster hasn't phoned me."

"What's that car phone number?"

"It's 555-8612," Phil replied. Satch nodded at Tommy, who went to the phone and punched it out. He waited and then shook his head. Satch Norris's face reddened with frustration.

"Zack ain't gonna like this," Tommy muttered. Satch widened his eyes. Phil caught the gesture and quickly looked down.

"He coulda easily rolled down to Santa Monica before," Tommy said. "Maybe that's why the guy's not answering his phone."

"Maybe." Satch gazed at Phil, who tried to avoid his eyes. "Is that a real possibility, Mr. Gold?"

"What? No. I told you probably why Dick's machine came on."

"But how does Mr. Berber know it's not an emergency? He could have an emergency phone call, couldn't he?" Satch pursued.

"I don't know. That's the way he is," Phil said and shrugged.

"Have you ever called him this late before?"

"I don't think so. No."

"So how do you know that's the reason?"

Phil didn't respond.

"Did Mr. Martin call you from Mr. Berber's home?"

"No. Look, why would he be running from the F.B.I.?"

Satch glanced at Tommy and then smiled.

"He's just confused, that's all, Mr. Gold. If he does call you, will you tell him we'll meet him at his apartment tomorrow and rearrange everything?"

"Sure," Phil said. He rose and looked at Tommy, who

was staring at him coldly. Then he turned back to Satch, who smiled and started for the front door. Phil sighed with relief and followed behind. Satch reached for the door knob.

"Sorry we had to bother you this late, but this is a very important case."

Phil nodded. He was about to say, "It's all right," but Tommy had taken out his pistol and, with it placed flatly against his right palm, brought it around to slap Phil sharply on the right temple. The blow blew the lights out. His body seemed to turn liquid as it poured down toward the floor, his silk birthday present floating around him.

"Let's see if the APB has brought up anything and then head over to this Santa Monica address," Satch said, gazing at the folded body at his feet.

"Right, Agent Norris."

"Fuck off. You probably made him suspicious with your stupid remarks," Satch said. Tommy shrugged.

"He didn't hear this one," he said and laughed.

As they left the apartment and walked through the short corridor to the building's front entrance, Chicky and Raul pulled up to the curb in their respective cars.

"You know what amazes me about L.A.," Chicky said as they joined up on the sidewalk and he gazed down the empty street, "how quiet it gets after ten-thirty, eleven P.M. It really is an early town. People can come out and walk their dogs safely," he added, seeing a man doing just that at the end of the block.

"Just watch where you step," Raul advised. Chicky laughed and they headed toward the entrance of Phil

Gold's building. Satch Norris and Tommy Murden emerged and turned right. Chicky and Raul watched them go down the sidewalk. When they stopped to get into a black Lincoln, Chicky put his hand on Raul's arm and they paused.

"You think?"

Raul nodded slowly.

"Maybe."

"Excuse me!" Chicky called after them. Satch and Tommy turned, Satch now at the driver's door. Chicky limped toward them as quickly as he could, Raul a step to the left and ahead of him. Chicky had his I.D. out and flashed the badge when he reached the pool of illumination cast by the streetlight.

"What's the problem?" Satch asked.

Chicky paused and gazed at the smashed right rear of the car. The light was shattered and the trunk door was jammed with the center of it pushed up. He looked at Raul.

"How did this happen?" Chicky asked.

"We don't know. It happened in a parking lot," Satch said.

"When?"

"Last week."

"Last week, huh? Not tonight in Sherman Oaks, maybe?"

"No, not tonight in Sherman Oaks," Satch said. Tommy still had his hand on the door handle.

Chicky, still staring at the damage, nodded.

"Do you live here?" he asked.

"What are we doing, playing twenty questions? We got places to go."

"Kinda late, isn't it?"

"So go to sleep," Satch said and opened the car door.

"Hold it," Raul said. Satch turned to him slowly.

"Why?"

"It's against the law to drive a car without stop lights, you know," Chicky said.

"We're on our way to get it fixed," Satch said.

"At this hour?"

"We know an all-night body shop. The guy's a vampire."

"I think we're going to have to ask you to wait right here. Would you move to the sidewalk, please," Chicky said, nodding toward the walk. Satch stared at him a moment.

"What's this about?"

"Maybe nothing. It will take only a minute to find out. Please move away from your car and stand on the sidewalk."

Tommy looked at Satch, who nodded slowly, and Tommy stepped back. His hand moved slowly toward the inside of his jacket.

"Please keep your hands where I can see them," Chicky said. He looked at Satch, who stepped away from the car and walked around to the sidewalk. Tommy stood beside him. Chicky turned to Raul.

"Check it out," he said, nodding toward the plates. Raul hurried back to his car. Satch and Tommy continued to glare at Chicky.

"Who do you know in that building?" Chicky asked them.

"What building?" Satch said.

"The building you just came out of."

"Nobody. We went to the wrong address," Satch replied.

"Oh. Too bad. How about both of you slowly putting some identification on the roof of the car there," Chicky said. He unbuttoned his jacket and then unbuckled his pistol holster.

"What the hell is going on here? What is this, some of that famous police abuse we read about and see on television?" Tommy asked.

"We're not abusing anyone. Yet," Chicky said. "Some identification, please."

Satch looked at Tommy and then started to reach inside his jacket.

"Slowly," Chicky warned. He put his hand on the handle of his pistol.

Satch produced a wallet and held it up. Then he leaned forward to place it on the roof of the car, only he missed and it fell to the gutter.

"Oops," he said and bent over to pick it up just as Raul started to return from his car. When Satch stood up again, he had his pistol in hand.

"GUN!" Chicky shouted and pulled out his own, moving to the side of the BMW station wagon parked behind him at the same time.

But Satch got off his first shot, hitting Raul in the shoulder. The bullet spun him around and sent him face forward to the sidewalk.

Tommy cracked off two shots at Chicky, one slamming into the hood of the BMW and one ricocheting off the street, shattering the dark window of a third-floor apartment across the street. Someone started screaming. Dogs barked. Chicky moved as quickly as he could behind the rear of the station wagon, but Satch and Tommy got into their car before he came around the other side. Tommy fired twice, one bullet shattering the wagon's windshield, the other whizzing past and into the small lawn in front of Phil Gold's apartment building. Chicky turned and saw Raul writhing on the sidewalk. As soon as the Lincoln began to pull away, he stepped out and got off two shots, but Satch spun his wheels and the car shot away.

Chicky holstered his weapon and ran, ignoring the foot pain, to Raul's side. The bullet had gone clear through, but the bleeding was profuse.

"Shit," Chicky said, turning him over as gently as he could and then opening his shirt to put a handkerchief against the wound. He put Raul's left hand over the handkerchief. "Keep this pressed down until I get back," he said.

"Easier said than done," Raul moaned. Chicky went to his radio and called for help. The shots had brought people to the windows and a few to the doors of their apartment and condo buildings. Chicky returned to Raul's side.

"Paramedics on the way. Lucky we're right near UCLA. Good place to get shot."

"Thanks. But tell me something, smartass?"

"Anything. I'm Mr. Know-it-all tonight, as you see."

"How the hell are we going to explain this to Kronenberg?"

"Simple. We thought the F.B.I. was in trouble and came to their assistance. Did you get a make on the plates?"

"Yeah. The car's registered to a business, the Renaissance Corporation out of Palm Springs, only guess what, Mr. Know-it-all?"

"What?"

"It was reported stolen earlier tonight, just about the time of the shooting in Sherman Oaks." Raul groaned. "My wife is gonna fucking kill me if I live. No, check that. She's going to kill you."

"From the looks of things, she'll have to get in line," Chicky said.

After the paramedics arrived and began to treat Raul, Chicky went into Phil Gold's building with two of the uniformed policemen who had arrived at the scene. He rang the buzzer and waited at the door. After two more attempts, he looked at the patrolmen with concern. The commotion had brought a few of the other residents out. They located the tenant-manager, a short, balding man in his fifties who had thrown on a pair of jeans and a sweatshirt.

"I have reason to believe the occupant is injured," Chicky told him. "Got a key?"

The tenant-manager went back to his apartment for it and returned quickly. Chicky opened the door and they confronted Phil Gold's unconscious body.

"Get another ambulance, STAT," he told the uniformed policemen. One hurried out to do so as Chicky leaned over Phil Gold's body and felt for a pulse. He couldn't find one.

"Jesus," he said, looking off as if he could see through walls. "Who the fuck *are* those guys?"

16

Webster flipped the light switch after he opened the door, and the small hotel room was illuminated by two standing lamps, one in each corner, and a bleached-blue ceramic table lamp on the small desk by the one window. Unfortunately, the window faced the rear of the hotel instead of the ocean and provided only a view of the back of another building.

Nevertheless, the room had the salty, worn look common to older resorts at seaside. The light blue rug was worn through in spots and faded so that only blotches here and there revealed its original color. The Sheetrock walls were painted a dark tan, the molding mahogany brown. There was a watercolor seascape in a dark frame over the bed and another beach view over the narrow dresser. The ceiling had a dead fixture that looked like it hadn't been dusted since the gold rush. Draped across the one window was a limp, eggshell-white cotton curtain. The window looked painted shut.

The furnishings were vintage thrift shop, the desk and chair not really matching the two small night tables and the queen-size, dark maple bed and dresser. The plain black phone was on the desk beside a note pad and a pencil. There was a bathtub with a shower in the bathroom, yellow rings around the bathtub drains and the sink drains. The cabinet no longer had a door. The maid had forgotten to remove a package of razor blades and it looked like something had been gnawing on the linoleum in the corners of the bathroom floor.

Shelly gazed around and then plopped down on the soft mattress, her hands in her lap. Her body bounced and she laughed.

"This is the first water bed I've been on that has no water," she quipped.

"Sorry," Webster said. "Last time I stayed in this place must have been longer than I remember. Probably when it was first built."

"I had a garage that was a palace compared to this, but any port in a storm," she said. He raised his eyebrows.

"Garage that was a palace, huh?" He loosened his tie and sat on the one chair by the desk. "Okay, you've got my full attention. Just stay somewhere between unbelievable and fantastic."

She smiled and shook her head. Then she looked away and closed her eyes, rubbing her temples with her forefinger and thumb.

"Headache?"

"Among other things," she said. She put her right

palm against her lower back and straightened her shoulders, groaning. "That was some roller coaster."

"I would rather have skipped it. It wasn't on my evening plans tonight."

She looked at him softly, her eyes warm and tender.

"Thank you, Webster. Thanks for trusting me when I needed you to back there."

"It was an investment of faith, faith in what, I can't tell. Can I get some return?" he asked. She smiled.

"Okay." She pulled herself back over the bed and after fixing the pillow for her back, leaned against the headboard. "As I told you, about two and a half months ago, one of my husband's business associates called me. He was in Chicago, he said, and he would like to come to see me. I couldn't imagine why. I had this much to do with Thomas's business," she said, holding up her thumb and forefinger. "I still don't understand where all the money is located. I have a business manager to do that sort of thing. Had, I should say. That life ended."

"Which is why you said you died?"

"Yes."

"Go on."

"This is going to take a while, Webster."

"I'm not going anywhere for the next few hours. At least, I don't think I am," he said, settling back in the chair. She took a deep breath and licked her lips.

"I'm dying of thirst, Webster. My tongue feels like an emery board." She looked toward the bathroom. "But I'm not crazy about drinking the water."

He nodded.

"All right. There's a soda machine outside and supposedly an ice machine next door. Why don't you get comfortable and I'll get us something."

"Thanks. Good idea," she said, rising to unbutton her blouse. She smiled at him. Even he was surprised at his sexual interest after what they had just experienced, but he was interested. He smiled back and hurried out to get the cold drinks and ice.

The parking lot was dimly lighted, but now that he looked more carefully, he realized his car was in full view of the street. The shattered rear window would be like a waving flag to anyone looking for this car, he thought, and gazed around the lot. He saw a space in the far right corner where his car would be better hidden from sight. He moved it and then went to get the sodas and ice. By the time he returned to the room, he found Shelly in bed, her eyes closed.

He gazed at her for a moment. She didn't open her eyes. Her breasts lifted and fell with her rhythmic breathing beneath the thin sheet. He waited, expecting her to wake, but she didn't. Quietly, he put the ice on the table and then broke open one of the cans of soda. He poured the contents into a glass and sat down, staring at her. She still hadn't woken.

Although the light was weak, he thought he saw gray roots in her black hair, something he hadn't noticed before. He sipped his soda and studied her face. There were some tiny, but clearly etched wrinkles at the base of her chin and the crow's-feet that emanated from the corners of her eyes looked deeper and longer. Perhaps he had just not noticed when he was in the dance club, he thought. He certainly wouldn't have been terribly observant afterward and he did remember that she wanted the lights out when they made love. Up until tonight, he had been too occupied to study her features.

Her lips quivered and she squinted as if in pain. He was sure she was suffering with a nightmare after the chase they had just experienced. He sipped some more soda and then unbuttoned his shirt. He took off his tie, stood up and began to take off his clothing. Naked, he went into the bathroom, took a leak and then washed his face with cold water. He stared at himself for a moment.

"What the fuck am I doing?" he asked his image. "What am I going to do tomorrow?"

"Webster?" he heard. He poked his head out of the bathroom. She was sitting up, but she had turned off the lights and she was silhouetted in the glow of light leaking from the bathroom and through the only window.

"You fell asleep."

"I know. Did you get something to drink?"

"Yep." He poured her soda over ice and brought it to her. She drank it all in one gulp.

"Any more?" she asked.

"Yes," he said, laughing. He brought her the remainder of his own and she drank that in one gulp. "I guess you were thirsty."

She handed him the glass and lay back.

"Why did you put out the lights?" he asked.

"They were hurting my eyes. Do you mind?"

"No, it's all right." He put the glass down and then came around and got into bed beside her. "I moved the car to a better spot."

"Good. Because they won't give up, you know."

"Can you tell me the rest of it now?"

"How much did I tell you?" she asked. He shook his head. She was confused, all right. How could she forget so soon?

"You were telling me about your life in Chicago. One of your husband's business friends had come to Chicago and called you."

"Right. Ben Stoddard. I was surprised he had any interest in me. My recollections of him were he was boorish, too occupied with making money. The only reason to buy art was for investment, that sort of person."

"Yeah, I know the type. So?"

"So, I was surprised but cordial, even though I really had no interest in seeing him. He caught my interest, however, when he said he had a proposal that would change my life. After I agreed to see him, I thought, he's just coming over to discuss some investment. What I didn't need and what wouldn't change my life was making more money. Not at my age, if you get my drift."

"I know. You told me. You were seventy-four?"

"I am seventy-four," she insisted.

"Right. Go ahead."

"He came. Ben Stoddard is not a good-looking man and, as I said, not very interesting to be with, but he is the sort of man who comes right to the point. We sat in what used to be my husband's den. He gazed around and laughed. 'I see you've made some changes,' he said. I thought he might ridicule what I had done, but he seemed pleased about it."

"What had you done?"

"Rid the house of every trace of Thomas. I was seeking some sort of liberation from my past, I suppose. Anyway, Stoddard liked it. He said it made me a prime candidate. I said what made me a prime candidate, and he said my desire to start over. Then he proceeded to tell me he was a trustee for a new corporation that was involved in research on the aging process. He called it the Renaissance Corporation."

"Yeah, I remember you said that name when the goons tried to get me out of the car."

"Yes. Anyway, Ben Stoddard told me they had made remarkable progress with genetics and they had come to the point where they were selecting candidates for rejuvenation. The candidates had to be very special and I fit the criteria."

"Why didn't he rejuvenate himself if it was so successful?"

"I asked him that and he said he wasn't prepared to give up his present identity just yet, but he would be following right behind me soon. Of course, I was just as skeptical as you are now and I think I even laughed. He was very indignant about that and almost walked out, but he continued to describe the project and I began to believe him. After all, Ben Stoddard was not a man to invest his time or money in anything that didn't have great potential.

"He then told me he would have the head of the research, Dr. Woodruff, come to see me personally, if I were interested in pursuing it."

"And obviously you were," Webster said.

"Yes. I really felt incarcerated in my old life, despite all the things I had done and tried to do. I was seventy-four. What was the gamble?"

"Do you have any children?" Webster asked.

"No."

"Sisters, brothers?"

"They were all older and they're dead."

Webster was quiet.

"I'm still having trouble with this story, Shelly."

"I'll get you more proof. The thing is your friend was murdered by these people and something has been done to my friend Kathleen. We've got to find her and then we'll turn it all over to the police. I'll be the chief witness. I promise," she said.

"So Kathleen is a rejuvenated person, too?"

"Yes. Her name's Kathleen Cornwall and she's from Detroit. Her husband was an executive for Chrysler. She had a far better marriage than I had and she missed him terribly after his death. Renaissance gave her a new reason to go on. She's a sweet person. I'd hate to find out anything bad had happened to her."

Webster propped himself up on his right elbow and looked down at her. He shook his head and then, with his right forefinger, he traced down her chest until he was between her breasts. He saw her smiling.

"You want me to believe I'm in love with a seventy-four-year-old woman?"

"In love?"

"Something," he said. "I couldn't get you out of my mind when I woke up in the morning and I was pretty upset that you had left without telling me enough about yourself for me to find you."

"I felt that way about you, too. Really," she said when he started to smile. "I was going to get back to you somehow, after I had returned to Renaissance and been evaluated," she said. "Really, I was," she added when he looked skeptical.

"Where is this Renaissance Corporation?"

"I don't know where the actual headquarters are, but the clinic, if you can call it that, is in a spa between Palm Springs and Rancho Mirage."

Webster shook his head.

"I think I'd rather not believe you. Do you mind if for the time being, I think you're mad as a hatter, but beautiful?" he asked.

She smiled again and then reached up to touch his face.

"No, I don't mind. But it's true, Webster, every detail; and why refuse to believe it? I've been given a new opportunity, a chance to go around again, and I can take you with me, if you want. I'm still a very wealthy woman, not that money is a problem for you. But I want to spend it and enjoy it with someone I can love and someone who can love me. Does that sound fantastic?"

"No," he said.

"Some people believe that we're all quite old, you know, that we've lived other lives. I've just been given a head start on my next life, that's all."

Webster laughed.

"This is quite a variation on the Mrs. Robinson myth, older woman, young man."

"The difference is I know I can love you and you can love me. It's not just a sexual fling, not that there's anything wrong with that part of it," she added. He smiled and kissed her on the tip of her nose. "Be gentle," she whispered. "I am a card-carrying member of the American Association of Retired Persons."

He laughed and leaned down to kiss her. Her lips were a little dry, but he pressed his firmly and then he pulled the sheet back to put his naked body against hers. Her breasts felt softer and when he ran the palm of his hand along the side of her body, he found her ribs more prominent than he recalled their being the night before, but she opened to him quickly and they began to make love with a passion that grew stronger, louder, faster until they were both crying out their pleasure.

Unlike the last time, however, she didn't turn on him when he collapsed beside her, and torment him with her desire to get right to it again. She gasped and then coughed and took deep breaths.

"You all right?"

"Yes. It's all been exhausting. I'm sorry."

"I'm not complaining about our lovemaking," he said quickly. "We both just need some rest."

"Yes, some rest," she said.

He rose to put out the bathroom lights. He would worry about the next step in the morning, he thought, when his mind was clearer and there was a calmer time to think. Probably, the best thing to do was call that detective first thing. He imagined that the police had heard about the shooting in Sherman Oaks and the chase by now anyway.

"Did you want me to get you something else to drink?"

he asked, but there was no response. "Shelly?" He walked to her side of the bed and looked at her. She was already dead asleep.

The light flowing in through the window must be playing tricks on me, he thought. She looked thinner-faced and the wrinkles he had seen at her temples before appeared deeper, longer. Not only that, but those gray roots . . . some portions of her hair now looked like gray patches, not just gray roots. He knelt down and studied her face. Her lips quivered again. They were pale in this diminished light and they parted just enough to reveal her teeth, which were more widely gapped and yellow. Her breath drove him back.

He stood up quickly. What the hell was happening here? His heart started to pound. Maybe he shouldn't wait until the morning. Was everything she told him true, as fantastic as it seemed?

He went to his pants and pulled out his wallet to find the card Chicky Siegler had given him. Then he called the number and the dispatcher answered.

"I need to speak with Detective Siegler."

"He's not on duty now."

"How about Detective . . . Torres?"

"Who is this?"

"I have to speak with one of them immediately."

"Hold on," the dispatcher said. After a moment, a different voice said, "Hello. You want to speak with Siegler or Torres?"

"Yes, please."

"I'm Chief of Detectives Kronenberg, their superior officer. Neither is available nor can be reached by telephone at the moment. Can you tell me your name and the nature of your business?"

Webster hesitated for a moment, then continued.

"I was approached by two men earlier tonight who claimed to be F.B.I. agents. They turned out to be someone different and they tried to kill me," he said. "Detective Siegler knows about it."

"Is this Webster Martin?"

A chill shot up Webster's spine.

"Yes."

"Where are you, Mr. Martin?"

"I'm . . . safe," he said. "But I want to speak with Detective Siegler or Torres."

"If you tell me where you are, I'll send a black-and-white there to get you and make sure you're protected," Kronenberg replied.

Webster looked back at the sleeping Shelly Dorset.

"I'm with someone," he said. "It's complicated. I need to speak with Detective Siegler or Detective Torres."

"They were both in a shooting a short while ago," Kronenberg said. "Detective Torres was hit. I'm actually on my way to the hospital right now."

"No."

"Yes, I'm afraid so. Mr. Webster, I must insist you come into the station right now. I believe you are in danger."

"No kidding. That's why I'd like to speak to Detective Siegler."

"I don't think you have time to wait, Mr. Webster. Your friend Phil Gold—"

"Phil? What about Phil?" Webster's heart began to thump again, cutting his breath short.

"He's dead, I'm afraid. It was at his address where the shooting occurred."

Webster squeezed his eyes shut to keep out the words, but they had already planted themselves in the garden of misery in his brain. They quickly grew in vines of panic and terror. His whole body felt on fire.

"He was shot, too?" he asked with a thin, broken voice, his eyes tearing.

"No."

"Then what happened to him?"

"Where are you, Mr. Webster? Let me send someone to get you."

His hand was trembling. The receiver felt like it had turned to lead. Carl and Phil, both dead?

"Mr. Webster!"

"I'm at a motel in Venice," he said and gave the address. "Room four."

"Don't leave, Mr. Webster. Stay right where you are."

"Right," Webster said.

He dropped the receiver into the cradle quickly and sat back, hyperventilating. Phil was dead. A wave of nausea climbed through his stomach and into his chest and throat. He gagged on the soda he had drunk. It was all acid now. Rushing to the bathroom, he nearly lost it before he reached the sink and vomited some of the drink. Then he splashed his face with cold water again and closed his eyes, willing his heart to slow down. He was so dizzy. Finally, it did slow sufficiently for him to make his way back to the chair.

He gazed at Shelly. She hadn't woken, despite the commotion. She had brought her legs up under the sheet until she was folded in a fetal position. She looked smaller.

Why would they harm Phil? He had nothing to do with either of the women.

Poor Phil, he thought, and then he thought about his own father. He had to speak with him before he found out; he had to assure him he was all right.

He sat back and closed his eyes. He was so tired. He would just rest for a while and wait for the police.

17

Tina Torres was a small, thirty-two-year-old woman, just five feet one at about ninety-eight pounds, but she was like a perfectly packed punch, tight, firm and surprisingly intimidating when she fixed those large, round dark eyes on someone, especially Charles William Siegler. He was seated in the emergency waiting room, his elbows on his knees, his hands supporting his head. He actually sensed Tina's presence before raising his eyes to see her marching toward him, her loose dark blue skirt flapping around her legs, her right hand clutching her small pocketbook as she would clutch a club.

"He was off-duty," she said before he could offer any sort of greeting. Despite her caramel-tinted complexion, her face was on fire with rage, the crests of her small, puffy cheeks crimson. "Why did you call him? Why did he have to go out?"

"I didn't call him to go out with me, Tina. He showed up on his own," Chicky protested.

"You knew he would. He idolizes you for reasons I'll never understand," she said. She twisted her head roughly to flip back the loose strands of jet black hair that had fallen over her shoulders.

"Me neither," Chicky said. "I'm sorry. Believe me, I don't do anything to encourage it."

She relaxed a bit and glared toward the doorway behind which she knew the doctors were working on her husband.

"He was afraid you would be the one who would get hurt," she said. "You're only weeks, days from your retirement and if something happened to you, he wouldn't forgive himself, he said. So who's in there being treated by the doctors? Him."

"Go figure," Chicky said. She turned sharply and looked at him. Chicky shrugged. "You married a policeman, Tina."

"I was crazy, *loco, estúpido.*"

"And in love," Chicky added. She calmed some more.

"How bad was it?"

"Shoulder wound. They didn't think the bullet had hit bone. We're waiting for X rays."

Tina took a deep breath.

"Sit down, Tina. The doctor should be out any moment now."

She looked at the chair beside him as if it were covered with grime and then sat.

"At least he won't have to work with me anymore, Tina. He'll be out of commission awhile, and by the time he returns to active duty, I'll be retired. But that won't really change things, Tina. He's a dedicated cop. A rare bird. The sort who gives a hundred and one percent and takes every crime personal."

She didn't speak for a moment. She closed her eyes and took another deep breath.

"I'm afraid," she said. "I wasn't so afraid when we were younger, even after we had children, but now . . . maybe because I'm older, I don't sleep when he's out at night."

Chicky looked at her and nodded, thinking now about Maggie. He never really considered what she was going through when he was on duty at night. She wasn't the type who would reveal her anxiety easily and somehow, she always looked fresh, busy, too wrapped up in the children to be worrying about him. But of course, she was, and keeping it internalized took its toll. He knew that now. He was wiser. Why couldn't he have had some of that wisdom when he was younger and she needed him to have more understanding, more sensitivity?

"The two of you should talk about it more," he said.

She tilted her head and looked at him.

"You telling me you did that with Maggie?"

"No, and I regret it now. It's probably why she's where she is and I'm where I am," he admitted. Tina's smirk softened into a look of sympathy.

"How is she?"

"Better, I think. There's light at the end of the tunnel."

"I should go to see her. Can she have visitors now?"

"Yeah, sure, but you have enough to do, Tina."

The door opened and the emergency room doctor appeared. They both rose to speak to with him.

"This is Mrs. Torres, Doctor."

"Hello, Mrs. Torres. The bullet passed through without touching the shoulder bone. He was lucky. He received good attention and didn't lose much blood. Give him a couple of days here."

"Can I see him?"

"Sure. I gave him something for pain so he's going to be a little groggy," the doctor warned. She started for the door. Chicky tapped her arm and she turned.

"Take it easy on him, Tina. He feels guilty as hell and it wasn't his fault."

"You would say that," she replied. "Birds of a feather."

The doctor smiled at Chicky as Tina left them.

"That's one woman you don't want to cross, Doc. So you better be right and take good care of Torres."

The doctor laughed. He saw Chicky shift weight from his bad foot to his good.

"You ought to get your foot some attention," he said. "Detective Torres told me you've been putting off seeing the podiatrist."

"Must have been babbling after you gave him the painkiller."

The doctor laughed.

"Go get some sleep, Detective."

"Thanks."

Chicky turned away and started for the emergency room entrance, but the doors slid open before he arrived and Walter Kronenberg stepped in. Chicky paused as they confronted each other. They resembled two gunfighters, each waiting for the other to start to draw.

"I thought I'd find you down here, Siegler," he said angrily.

"Torres is going to be all right. It was a clean wound. Thanks for asking," Chicky said.

"I've already received a report on his condition, Detective. Did you think I would wait for you?"

"No, I guess not. Mr. Efficiency."

Kronenberg gazed at some of the other people in the waiting room and then gestured toward the outside.

"Step out here. I want to speak to you," he said. Chicky followed him into the parking lot. They stood under the light of a pole lamp. Kronenberg had come by himself in an unmarked car, one of the rare times he didn't use a rookie as a driver.

"Care to explain what you two were doing at that address and how you managed to get into a shooting?"

"Mr. Martin called me earlier this evening to tell me he was approached by two men claiming to be F.B.I. agents."

"So?"

"From the way he spoke about them, it seemed suspicious. I spoke to a friend at the F.B.I. office in L.A. and he did some checking. There are no agents in L.A. with the names they gave Mr. Martin."

"So they came from another office. What's it your business?"

"It's easy to check the F.B.I. roster and apparently, there are no agents with those names in the Bureau at all."

"Who told you this?"

"I said a friend."

Kronenberg nodded. Chicky figured he knew he was friends with Bill Johnstone. He was the sort of administrator who made it his business to know as much as he could about his men, down to the grimiest of details.

Since he had come into the department, there was a cloud of paranoia over everyone, no one sure who wasn't being asked to spy on his fellow officers. It was part of Kronenberg's overcompensating ego to keep everyone nervous, worried and distrustful of everyone but his own partner, and even there, there was often some doubt, not that Chicky could ever have doubts about Raul.

"So how does this bring you and Raul to Mr. Gold's residence in the middle of the night?"

"When Mr. Martin phoned, he said he had been contacted by the woman he had picked up at the dance club. She was, as you know if you read our report, a friend of the woman last seen with Mr. Slotkin before he was murdered."

"Why didn't you just advise him to call the station, tell him you weren't assigned to this case any longer?"

"I did tell him the feds had the case, but you never told me which agency, so I didn't know where to send him," Chicky said. Kronenberg looked away for a second.

"Raul called me and I told him the F.B.I."

"That was afterward," Chicky said.

"Go on," Kronenberg said in a tired voice.

"I knew Mr. Martin was heading for Sherman Oaks for his rendezvous. Then I saw a television news report of a shooting there. I found out the address and took a ride to check it out. I was worried about the guy and very suspicious about the men who had gone to see him."

"But I told you that you were off the case," Kronenberg whined. "I made that point again when Torres called me tonight."

"It was on my own time. I figured the department has been so good to me, I owed the department," Chicky said dryly. Kronenberg stared at him. "Anyway, from what I learned, it was pretty clear to me Webster Martin had picked up the woman, and the men he thought were F.B.I. had shot at him and her. They pursued them, but Webster Martin and the woman apparently got away from them. I still felt he was in grave danger."

"And Raul?"

"He just showed up. I didn't tell him to, but once I told him what had occurred, we both had the idea that we should see if Webster had gone to his friend's apartment in Brentwood. That's when we came across the two men impersonating F.B.I."

"Care to tell me what's really going on, Chief?" Chicky said. Kronenberg was silent. He looked away. "You tell us the F.B.I.'s in it, the F.B.I. says no; two men impersonate F.B.I. to pursue Webster Martin—"

Kronenberg spun on him.

"There just happens to be an undercover investigation under way and you just happened to have fucked it up," he replied. "Don't worry about your retirement; you're on suspension for disobeying orders and endangering the life of your partner."

"That's bullshit. They killed Philip Gold tonight, trying, I imagine, to locate Webster Martin so they can kill him. And probably the woman he's with. There's no undercover F.B.I. investigation going on. We were pulled off because someone got to someone who got to you. It's just that simple," Chicky said.

Kronenberg shook his head.

"You're crazy as hell. I don't have to suspend you. I can have you removed for psychiatric reasons. If you so much as get within one inch of this case now, I'll have you arrested, and we won't put you in jail, we'll put you in the institution with your wife."

It was as if someone with a flashlight had come right up to Chicky, stuck the flashlight in front of his face, and turned it on. The blaze washed everything out of sight for a moment, and during that moment, he heard himself roar within, the power of that internal scream triggering his right arm to bring his clenched fist up straight and smooth into Kronenberg's left cheekbone. The collision of Chicky's knuckles with Kronenberg's face sent a shudder down Chicky's arm and into his shoulder, but Kronenberg's feet actually lifted from the walk and he flew backward to land hard on his rear.

Some people standing nearby stared in amazement, but for a moment neither man spoke. The entire event had happened so quickly it was still unreal for each. Kronenberg was actually too dazed to speak. He sat quietly, waiting for his equilibrium to return. With it came the stinging pain in his face and down the back of his neck, threading out to his shoulders. He finally gasped.

"Don't say another fucking word," Chicky said, pointing down at him, "or I'll kill you. So help me . . ."

Kronenberg had never faced such uncontrolled rage. He didn't move. Chicky turned and walked away. Once he was far enough, Kronenberg's courage returned. He struggled to his feet.

"You're finished, Siegler. I'll have your head on a pike for this."

Chicky didn't turn back. He got into his car and started the engine. He just sat there for a moment watching Kronenberg hurry into the emergency room, probably to ask for treatment so he could confirm Chicky had struck him.

It was time to retire or be thrown out, Chicky thought. He had no patience for men like Kronenberg: loyal soldiers who never questioned orders, who killed or cut or slaughtered on command and filed away their reports, and then were soon promoted, rewarded for their lack of independence and humanity.

Chicky threw his car into reverse and gunned the engine, spinning the wheels and then shooting out of the parking lot. He drove too fast for a few blocks before calming down. Fortunately, the L.A. streets were comparatively dead at this hour. He could safely go through a red light. Fifteen minutes later, he pulled into his own driveway, slammed on the brakes and cut the engine.

He got out of the car and entered his dark house, going directly to the liquor cabinet so he could pour himself a stiff bourbon. The booze burned his chest, but had a calming effect. He poured another and plopped down in his favorite overstuffed chair. For a long moment, he just stared at the shadows. He had put on only a small light by the bar.

Chicky put his head back and sighed. What a night. He came that close to being shot himself. He should have anticipated it. When that big bastard bent down to pick up the wallet . . . how could he have let that happen? It was time to retire, he thought, and took another sip of bourbon before he closed his eyes. It felt good just sink-ing into the seat, just drifting away.

He had hit Kronenberg hard. Didn't think he still had that good an uppercut. He smiled to himself, recalling his father down in the basement of their home, showing him how to throw a punch. Dad had been a Golden Gloves winner, coming out of Philadelphia. His famous story was his sparring with Kid Chocolate.

"And I held my own, too," his father had told him at least ten times. "Even the kid said so. Now look, Chicky, you got to put your shoulder into it, see. You don't just wing it out of nowhere."

"You should have seen me tonight, Dad," he muttered aloud to the darkness and laughed. He finished the bour-bon. "Maybe you did, huh? Maybe you did."

He closed his eyes again and pictured his father swim-ming with him at the lake near his uncle Charley's house in Vermont that summer when Chicky was only eight or nine. His father was a strong swimmer. He put Chicky on his back and told him to hold on. Chicky clamped his arms around his father's neck. Then his fa-ther swam halfway across the lake and back, those long, muscular arms dipping in and coming out with a smooth rhythm. That's what gave him long life and good health, the strong rhythm. He was like that in everything, old Dad, calm, collected, graceful, moving along through life with a strong, continuous stroke, no matter how thick the water, no matter how high the wave.

Chicky dreamed about swimming himself. He and

Maggie were young then, on a vacation in Mexico. For a few days, they were really lovers, cut off from the insanity with which he had surrounded himself.

"Let's not go back, Chicky," she had said. "Let's do something else. Maybe buy a place in Wyoming or Montana, live in a small town. Raise a family with a dog, eat together every night and every weekend morning, barely talk on the phone, go to dances and picnics and simple charity affairs."

"I'm a city boy, Maggie. I'd probably go blubbering down a dirt road after two weeks, and they don't need my kind of cop there. I'm no small-town sheriff, honey."

"I know. You're another Dirty Harry," she said regretfully. "It was just a thought, you know. Whenever you're on a vacation and you have time to let your mind wander, you dream things that are impossible."

She looked so sad. He had to go buy her another margarita and get the mariachis to come around again.

But that was all a thousand years ago. Now it was now. He was home alone. His partner had been shot up. His wife was being treated for acute depression, and his kids hadn't spoken to him in nearly a month.

And to top it off, he had an infected toe.

He opened his eyes when a light flashed on his window. He waited. Whoever it was had just used his driveway to turn around and was then gone.

He closed his eyes again, but instead of shutting down, his mind wandered through the events of the past few days. Who were those guys? Why would jealous husbands carry the vendetta this far? There had to be something more to this, something either Webster Martin hadn't told him and Raul or something he and his friends just didn't realize. Where was this guy now?

Chicky flipped on the lamp and dug into his pocket to pull out his note pad. He thumbed through it until he found Webster's car phone number and then he punched it out and waited. The operator reported the cellular phone client was either away from his phone or out of the calling area. He called his home and got the answering machine. He cradled the receiver and sat there, frustrated. Then he thought, if the guy was in trouble, he might just find a way to call for help. Maybe he had. It was worth a try.

He punched out the station number and got the dispatcher.

"How's Raul?" she asked.

"He's doing well. Bullet went clear through, no bone."

"Great."

"I get any calls tonight?"

"Someone called for you earlier, but Kronenberg took it," she said.

"Was his name Martin?"

"Hold on. Let me check the log." After a pause she said, "Webster Martin?"

"Yeah. How long ago?" She told him. "Did he say where he was? It's very important, Sheila."

"He didn't tell me where he was. I patched it through to Kronenberg who was on the way to the hospital and he took the call."

"He's not back there yet, is he?" Chicky asked. He couldn't imagine him returning without telling everyone what Chicky had done to him.

"No."

"Did he call anything in?"

"Hold on," she said again. Chicky sat up in anticipation.

"He sent a black-and-white to the Ocean Haven Motel in Venice. I think it's between—"

"I know it where it is. Thanks," he said.

The bastard, he thought, as he got up and hurried out. He knew all this but didn't say a word to me. Now Chicky was even happier about punching out his supervisor's lights.

18

Webster hadn't moved since he had called the police. He sat there with his heart thumping, his mind reeling, his thoughts scrambled, panic just below the surface. He had no idea how long he had been sitting there. Once in a while, Shelly would moan in her sleep and he would realize where he was and that all that had occurred was not a dream.

Suddenly, there was a knocking at the door. He nearly jumped out of his seat. He hadn't seen any car head-lights or heard any sirens.

"Who's there?"

"Mr. Martin. It's the police."

Webster hesitated, gazed back at Shelly, who incredibly remained asleep, and then opened the door. He saw the barrel of a shotgun just before it came crashing into his stomach, bending him over with pain, but he never saw the wooden stock snap up and catch him on the right side of his jaw. The blow was sharp, the pain shooting into his head and cutting off his consciousness cleanly.

He didn't open his eyes again until the cold water hit his face. For a moment he couldn't focus. Then the uniformed patrolman came into clear vision.

"Easy," he said when Webster attempted to sit up. Dizziness made him wobble. He felt nauseated and gasped for air. Then he carefully touched his jaw and felt the welt.

"Are you Webster Martin?" another patrolman to his left asked. He turned slowly.

"Yes. What happened?"

The two patrolmen laughed.

"We were hoping you could tell us, Mr. Martin. When we drove up, the door was open and you were sprawled on the floor.

"Sprawled? Shelly!"

He pushed himself to his feet and turned. The bed was empty.

"Where is she?"

"Where's who, Mr. Martin?"

"The woman who was in that bed," he said, pointing.

"There was no one in the bed when we arrived, sir."

Webster wobbled again and the officer on his right took his arm.

"Easy."

"We better take you over to the emergency room at St. John's, Mr. Martin."

"They took her back," Webster said.

"Did you see who did this to you?"

"Probably the same guys who said they were F.B.I. and chased after us. Renaissance."

"Pardon?"

"Oh God." Webster rubbed his face with his dry palms. "I need a drink of water," he said. One of the officers went to the bathroom to get him a glass.

"Just sit down for a moment, Mr. Webster. You could have a concussion," the other policeman said. "I'm just going out to the car to call in," he added after helping Webster to the chair. His partner brought Webster the water. He drank it quickly.

"You've got to look for her," he said. "Her name's Shelly Dorset."

"Uh-huh. Why don't we get you over to the emergency room first and then you can give us a full statement."

"There's no time. They're probably heading back to Palm Springs. Put out an APB. They're driving a black Lincoln. Two big men."

"Okay, Mr. Webster. Just take it easy."

"Will you do it?"

"Sure. Bob."

"Coming."

"Let's get him over to emergency. Come on, Mr. Webster. They'll look you over, take an X ray."

"I'm all right," Webster said, feeling stronger. He gazed at the bed. The blanket had been pulled back. The outline of Shelly's body still remained on the sheet. "See, she was there," he said. The two patrolmen gazed at each other.

"Right."

"No. You guys don't understand. She was afraid to go back. These guys are very dangerous."

"Okay, Mr. Martin."

"I want to speak to Detective Siegler," Webster demanded.

"Chicky Siegler?" one of the patrolmen asked.

"Yes."

"Okay, we'll try to arrange that. Come on, Mr. Martin." He took Webster's arm to help him up.

"You guys didn't see anything before you arrived? A black Lincoln pull out?"

"No, sir."

Webster gazed back at the bed as they started toward the door.

"My friend Phil was killed tonight. The same guys did it," he muttered. Just as they reached the patrol car, Chicky pulled up.

"The Lone Ranger," one of the patrolmen said. "He asked for you and here you are."

"What happened, Webster?"

"They came and took her. Shelly Dorset. I opened the door because I thought it was the police and one of them hit me with something. When I woke up, she was gone!"

"You know what he's talking about?" the patrolman holding Webster's arm asked Chicky.

"Yeah. I'll take it from here."

"He needs medical attention. We were taking him over to St. John's. I called it in."

"It's my case," Chicky said. "I'll take care of the paperwork." The two officers gazed at each other and shrugged.

"It's not that we haven't got anything else to do." He released Webster's arm. Webster took a deep breath, but held steady.

"Come on," Chicky said, guiding him to his car. He helped him into the front seat and then got behind the wheel. He backed out before the patrol car.

"I don't need to go to the hospital. I'm all right. We've got to find her."

"There's a diner here on Wilshire," Chicky said. "I'll buy you a cup of coffee and you can tell me about it."

By the time they parked and got out, Webster was feeling stronger. The clouds had thinned out in his head. There was still a sharp ache in his jawbone and a soreness in his solar plexus, but he was able to straighten up and walk steady. They took a booth quickly and Chicky ordered them coffee.

"All right, Webster. What the hell's going on?"

"Tell me what happened at Phil's," Webster demanded first.

"After you called the station and they patched you through to me to tell me about the two men who presented themselves as F.B.I. agents, I heard about the shooting up at Sherman Oaks and when I found the address corresponded with where you were going, I went to that address and spoke with the valet at the Pussycat Lounge. After I spoke to him, I knew the shooting involved you. I called a friend who works the L.A. F.B.I. office and he had no knowledge of the names you gave me," Chicky continued.

"I didn't need a friend at the F.B.I. to tell me they weren't F.B.I.," Webster said.

"Anyway, once I learned it was you in the shooting and there was a chase, Raul and I thought we should see if you had gone to your friend's apartment in Brentwood. Apparently, your so-called F.B.I. agents had the same idea and when we arrived, they were just leaving the apartment building. We stopped them and tried to I.D. them when all hell broke loose and Raul got shot. After the paramedics arrived, I entered Mr. Gold's apartment and found him on the floor. He had been struck hard on the right temple, dead at the scene. I'm sorry."

"Jesus. Poor Phil." Tears came to Webster's eyes. "Why did they have to kill him? He had nothing to do with the women."

"Probably overdid it when they tried to get him to tell them where you could be. They got away, but not before we traced the car. It belonged to some corporation that claimed it had been stolen."

"Corporation?"

"Something called . . ." Chicky took out his note pad and flipped the cover to read. "Renaissance Corporation."

Webster's face lit up.

"That's it!"

"That's what?"

"The organization, the research organization."

"Research?"

Webster told Chicky the story Shelly had told him, beginning with Ben Stoddard's visit, Dr. Woodruff, and her friend's disappearance. Chicky sat listening, shaking his head, smiling, scratching his head and finally just staring.

"And now you believe they're holding these rejuvenated women captive?"

"Shelly didn't want to go back. Not without speaking to the head honcho, Dr. Woodruff. She didn't trust these men and she was convinced they had killed Carl and done something with her girlfriend. She was terrified."

"Looks like she had reason to be. But come on, Webster, rejuvenated women?"

"I didn't believe any of it either when she first started to tell me, but now . . ."

"Now?"

"I think it might be true."

Chicky sat back and stared at him.

"Forensics found gray hairs in your friend Carl Slotkin's bed."

"See? That means something."

"Doesn't mean the woman with him was in her seventies. Lots of young people have gray hairs. I have gray hairs."

Webster glared at him.

"I believe she was telling the truth," he said.

Chicky nodded.

"Give me those names again."

Webster gave him Kathleen's and Shelly's full names and addresses, as well as the names of their husbands."

"Be right back."

Chicky went to the pay phone. Webster ordered more coffee and some cold water and waited. Nearly ten minutes later, Chicky returned. He slid into the booth and ordered himself another cup of coffee.

"Looks like this is going to be a long night."

"What did you find out?" Webster asked.

"Both women, Shelly Dorset, married to Thomas Nelson Dorset, the builder; and Kathleen Cornwall, married to Philip George Cornwall, the car executive, died this year. Recently."

"Which supports Shelly's story."

"Unless they just assumed their names."

"Why?"

"How do I know? I'm a real detective, not one of those mind readers or psychic detectives you see on television and in the movies."

Webster nodded.

"What are you going to do?"

"I don't know. I'm on suspension, maybe up on charges by now."

"What? Why?"

"For one thing, I continued to investigate the case after my superior officer took Raul and me off it, and during that investigation, Raul got shot."

"Yeah, but you had reasons and—"

"Earlier tonight I nearly stopped Chief of Detectives Kronenberg's clock for good at the hospital. Maybe I broke his cheekbone." He showed Webster his bruised knuckles."

"Why did you do that?"

"It's a bit complicated. He passed a low remark concerning my wife."

"Oh." Webster frowned. "My father's going to be very upset once he hears about Phil if I don't call him soon. And when I do, he's going to drive me crazy to leave for a while."

"Maybe you should listen to him."

"I'd like to see you nail the guys who killed my friends," Webster said.

"I've got to find out more about this Renaissance Corporation," Chicky said. "You recall anything else she told you about it?"

"Just that it was in Palm Springs and that the head of it was someone named Woodruff."

"I guess that's something to start with." He nodded and stood up.

"Where are you going?"

"I got another friend. This one's a reporter at the *L.A. Times* who usually pulls the graveyard shift. He should be there even at this hour."

"I'll go with you. I don't feel exactly safe by myself, anyway," Webster added when he saw Chicky's reluctance.

"You're sure you're all right? I was supposed to take you for medical attention. If you should collapse on me, it would be the final nail in the coffin Kronenberg has designed for me."

"I'm fine. Really."

Chicky considered.

"All right, for now. You might come up with something else you recall she said." He started to hobble toward the door.

"You're the one who needs medical attention, Detective," Webster said. Chicky smirked.

"No time for myself yet. I'm saving it all for retirement," Chicky replied. "Which looks like it will be sooner than I thought."

After they got into Chicky's car, Chicky continued to ask questions about Shelly and the story she had told Webster until that was interrupted by the dispatcher coming over his radio to issue the APB on him and his car.

"Subject is armed and dangerous," she said.

"That's you!" Webster declared.

"Kronenberg," Chicky said.

"What do we do now?"

Chicky didn't reply. He swung a sharp left, accelerated and then took another left, pulling up in front of an all-night car rental agency.

"We're going to rent a car?"

"That's what the bad guys always do. My car's hot."

"This is nuts," Webster said, getting out. "You're the police. We should be chasing them. They should be getting the rental car."

"Tell me about it," Chicky said. He hobbled forward.

Less than an hour later, they were in a conference room waiting for Gary Adler, a criminal reporter, who was a good friend of Chicky's.

Gary Adler was only in his mid-fifties, but a premature, full head of gray hair added ten years to his appearance. Chicky liked him because unlike most crime reporters, Gary had an appreciation for the nitty-gritty, day-to-day work that went into real crime solving. The reason was Gary had a brother back in Kansas City who was a policeman. Gary wrote higher quality pieces for the *L.A. Times*. He got his share of scoops, thanks to detectives like Chicky, but he didn't seek out the sensational; he sought out the facts. He and Chicky often had conversations about the role of the media in a modern technological society. The portable, inexpensive, hand-held camera had changed the face of news and information. Gary was reluctant to relinquish an iota of freedom of the press, but he was open-minded enough to accept the need for holding back information so as not to compromise an investigation or an arrest. As long as he was right up there when the time came to reveal.

"Something weird just came over my scanner," Gary said, closing the door behind him. "An APB out on you?"

"It's complicated, but yes, it's true," Chicky replied. Gary looked at Webster.

"This is going to be a big story, isn't it?"

"Potentially."

Gary hesitated, the papers in his hand.

"You'll be the first to know it all," Chicky added. Gary nodded. Then he lifted his eyebrows and handed Chicky the pages.

"Harrison Woodruff," he said. "One of those child prodigies you read about. Graduated from high school at fourteen, college with a B.S. at seventeen, doctorate by twenty-one. Molecular biologist at Johns Hopkins. Won a grant to do cancer research at Sloan-Kettering, after which he went to the National Cancer Institute in Bethesda, Maryland. From there he went to the National Institute on Aging. No forwarding address, but apparently went to work for private enterprise about a year and a half ago. Impressive. Who is he to you?"

"Not sure yet," Chicky said, perusing the papers. He held up a picture of Harrison. "Recent?"

"Relatively."

"Doesn't look more than forty."

"No. So what's with this Renaissance Corporation?"

"What do you have on it?"

"Very little. An umbrella organization for charity, debilitating diseases. Chairman is Ben Stoddard, heavy-hitter in oil, on first-name basis with dozens of senators, congressmen as well as a couple of presidents, including the incumbent. Nothing about Palm Springs in there," Gary added. "So?" He looked at Webster.

"This is Webster Martin. He lost two close friends these past couple of days, both murdered."

"One of them Carl Slotkin?"

"Yes," Webster said.

"The other was offed earlier tonight," Chicky added. Gary nodded.

"Philip Gold, Brentwood."

"The same."

"So?"

"The three apparently innocently walked into something. I'm not sure myself what it is yet, Gary."

"How'd you get an APB on you?"

"Me and my superior had a parting of the ways. I gave him a knuckle sandwich."

"What about your partner's being shot? Part of it?"

"Yes," Chicky said. Gary whistled.

"I'll be the first to know?"

"On my honor," Chicky said, raising his right hand.

"I imagine you're heading for Palm Springs," Gary said.

"I guess that's on the tour," Chicky said. He looked at Webster.

"You're not going without me," Webster said quickly.

"It'll be morning by the time we arrive."

"Who can sleep now?"

"Don't ask me. I never sleep anyway," Chicky said. "The only difference is now I have something to do during my insomnia."

Webster started to laugh, but the pain in his jaw put a hold on it. He wondered when he would feel like laughing again.

19

Shelly slept nearly the entire trip to Palm Springs. She had been almost comatose when Herbie and Mike burst into the motel room, so she never heard or realized what they had done to Webster. She vaguely realized she was being lifted from the bed and carried out to the vehicle. They put her on the rear seat and threw the blanket over her. It all happened so quickly it just seemed like part of a dream.

Twice, she awoke and called out for Webster, but someone said, "It's all right, Mrs. Dorset," and she closed her eyes again.

She fell into a deep dream. It was truly like a great descent, but she didn't plunge down; she floated and as she descended, she grew younger and younger until she was a little girl again. Her mother had woven that thick French curl. She wore a pretty pink and light blue dress with lace sleeves. They were going someplace nice for dinner. Both her parents were all dressed up, too. Her father was wearing a dark suit and her mother was wearing a long, black dress with her diamond necklace and earrings.

"I want you to meet people of substance," her mother was saying. "Right from the beginning, I want you to know what it means to have wealth and position in society. You don't want to end up like me, struggling to maintain your station in life, Shelly. You want to be secure. I know you don't understand all this yet, but you will. You will," she promised.

In this world of dreams, she really was like a balloon. She bounced from one period of her life to another. She saw herself as a teenager, saw her mother's disapproval of some of her friends because they weren't from rich and important families. Then she saw herself getting prepared for marriage. There was so much excitement around her, but she felt empty, as empty as a punctured balloon.

She started to rise through the darkness, up the tunnel of memories, and as she ascended, she grew older and older. In mirrors she saw herself as gray and wrinkled, but her eyes looked so young and so full of hope. Then she leaned back and gazed straight up to see the bright light that turned into a television screen.

Through it, she saw herself dancing with Webster at the dance club again. She was beautiful, graceful and very exciting. As they danced to the rhythm and beat of the loud music, however, she began to make longer, slower motions with her arms and her legs because her limbs felt so terribly heavy. The people around them fell out of focus. Suddenly, her face appeared to liquefy, the flesh under her skin moving like water. It shifted in one direction and then another, threatening to pour off her skull and drip to the floor. Her eyes bulged and her nostrils widened. Then, right before Webster's eyes, but apparently not noticed by anyone else on the floor, her flesh did start to drop from her bones. It fell into a puddle of blood and skin, her skeleton emerging, but her dancing continued. She tried to scream, but her tongue writhed and came tumbling forward to splash on the floor.

The effort to scream woke her and she groaned when she opened her eyes. Light flashed over her. For a long moment, she couldn't figure out where she was. She knew she was moving and finally realized she was in a car and those lights were streetlights. She tried to sit up and groaned with the effort. Mike Robbins turned around.

"She's waking up, Herbie."

"Big deal."

"Hello, Mrs. Dorset. Here we are again taking you back to Renaissance. Thirsty again?"

Herbie laughed.

"You gave us quite a time, Mrs. Dorset. I ain't used to working this hard."

Shelly rubbed her cheeks until she felt some circulation in her face. She wrapped the blanket around herself tighter and gazed out the window. She recognized the surroundings.

"We're in Palm Springs," she said.

"Very astute for a woman of your age," Herbie said. Mike laughed.

"Where's Webster? Where's Mr. Martin?"

"Webster, Webster. You know any Webster, Herbie?"

"I know a dictionary named Webster," Herbie said. They both laughed.

"What did you do to him? You didn't . . . do what you did to his friend. Did you? *Did you?*" she screamed. Her throat ached with the effort.

"Calm down, lady. We're not taking your shit now," Herbie said. "If she does that again, Mike, slap the teeth out of her mouth."

"Right."

"Please, tell me. What did you do? You didn't kill him, did you?"

"He's lucky," Herbie said. "If we did kill him."

"Oh no." She buried her face in her hands. "I want to see Dr. Woodruff," she demanded.

"You'll see him. Just shut the fuck up," Herbie replied. They turned on Ramon Road and headed toward Rancho Mirage. Shelly sat back and stared out the window, watching the scenery flow by. She took a deep breath, closed her eyes, and waited. She opened them again when they reached the main gate of Renaissance. The security guard quickly opened it and they drove right up to the main building.

Both men jumped out of the vehicle. Mike opened the rear door and reached in for her. She refused his hand and slid over the seat to step out herself. The two seized her at the elbows and practically lifted her over the walk, up the steps to the front door. Miss Kleindeist was there to open it. It was very late. No one else was there.

"Mrs. Dorset," she said. "I'm so glad you're okay."

"I'm not okay. Where's Dr. Woodruff?"

"He'll be right with us. Come, dear."

Reluctantly, Shelly permitted Miss Kleindeist to take her arm and lead her through the lobby to the infirmary and an examination room. Herbie and Mike followed up to the door. Miss Kleindeist turned to them before she opened it.

"I'll take her from here," she said. "Thank you."

"We won't be far. Mr. Steiner wants us to stay on top of the situation until he's on the scene personally."

"Wait out here," Miss Kleindeist insisted. She opened the door and led Shelly to the examination table. "Just sit up here, dear. Dr. Woodruff is on his way."

Shelly had difficulty lifting her legs and boosting herself up. Miss Kleindeist had to wrap her arms around Shelly's waist and lift her.

"I'm so weak," Shelly said. "So damn tired and weak. What's happening to me?"

Shelly looked down at her hands. The fingers looked thin, the knuckles prominent, and the skin was in folds. There were age spots over her wrists.

"I've lost so much weight so quickly," she muttered. "Haven't I?"

"You'll be all right," Miss Kleindeist said.

Shelly ran her hand through her hair. It felt like piano wire, and when she brought her hand down, there were gray strands entwined in her fingers.

"Let me look in the mirror," she cried. "Where is the mirror?"

"There's no mirror in this room, Mrs. Dorset. Please,

stay calm. Don't get yourself upset. I want to take your blood pressure," Miss Kleindeist said, and wrapped the sleeve around her arm. "Just relax," she said as she pumped it up. She put her stethoscope in her ears and listened. Shelly saw the way her eyes widened.

"It's bad, isn't it?" she asked. Miss Kleindeist did not respond. She took off the blood pressure sleeve and put it aside. "I'm thirsty, so thirsty."

"Let me get you some water," Miss Kleindeist said. As she went to the sink to turn on the faucet, the door opened and Harrison Woodruff stepped in. He took one look at Shelly and grimaced.

"Dr. Woodruff!" Shelly cried. Some tears managed to emerge and trickle down her cheeks. They felt like little beads of fire.

"There, there, Mrs. Dorset. I'm here now."

"What's happening to me? I feel terrible. My energy is gone. I'm so weak."

"You having a bad reaction to the treatments. I will take care of you," he promised. "Just lie back." He guided her shoulders. To her his fingers felt enormous. Miss Kleindeist provided a pillow.

"What's going on, Dr. Woodruff? Where's Kathleen Cornwall?"

"She's here," Dr. Woodruff said.

"Can I see her?"

"Not now. She's not feeling well either and I have her in treatment. Perhaps tomorrow," he said.

Shelly sat up again as quickly as she could.

"They killed a man. Do you know that, Doctor? They killed the man Kathleen was with and they might have killed the man I was with, Webster Martin. Can you find out what happened to him? Please."

"I will. I promise," Harrison said. "Please, try to relax, Mrs. Dorset."

"Why did they kill that man? Why did they chase after us and try to shoot us? What's going on? Who are they, really?"

"I told you before, Mrs. Dorset. They are the security people for the project. You knew from the beginning that this was a highly secretive project and that it must be protected."

"But they're killing people. I thought you were trying to help people, make life better."

"I am, but I'm not in charge of security. Remember? Now just relax," Dr. Woodruff said. He forced her to lie back.

"I don't want to lie down. I want to see Kathleen. Please."

"Be a good girl, Mrs. Dorset, and listen to Dr. Woodruff," Sandra Kleindeist said, coming behind her to place her hands on Shelly's shoulders.

Dr. Woodruff then inserted an intravenous needle and started the flow from the bag above her.

"What is that?"

"Something to help you relax and to counter the symptoms you're experiencing," he replied.

"I'm so tired and so weak. I can't stand it."

"I know. This will help." He looked at Sandra Kleindeist, who was shaking her head slowly. "I'll be right back, Miss Kleindeist. Will you be sure Mrs. Dorset is comfortable?"

"Yes, Doctor." She came around to Shelly's side and patted her right hand. Shelly gazed up at her and blinked rapidly.

"My eyesight is getting bad," she said.

"It's just the tranquillizer," Miss Kleindeist said and put her palm over Shelly's eyes and forehead. "Close your eyes. Let the medicine work."

Shelly did so. Her eyelids were feeling so heavy anyway. She heard the door open and close and then she fell into that same deep repose that had taken her wandering through her past and took her there again.

Zack Steiner was in the hallway when Harrison emerged. He was speaking with Herbie and Mike and didn't look toward Harrison even though he knew he was standing there. When he was finished listening to his men, he turned.

"What did they do to the young man who was with her?" Harrison demanded.

"Not enough," Zack replied, his eyes bright with anger. "You didn't want another young man terminated, as I recall. Now, he and the rogue detective might be heading this way."

Harrison's eyes widened.

"What does that mean?"

"It means we might be compromised out here," he said. He pivoted and marched down the corridor. Harrison looked at the two men.

"I thought I hit him pretty hard," Mike said, shrugging. "Thought it would keep him out of commission for a while and certainly discourage him. Didn't you think so, too, Herbie?"

"We should have made sure," Herbie said. "Sorry, Doc." He shrugged.

"No, you're not. None of you are really sorry about any of this," Harrison snapped back. They looked at each other and then shook their heads. Harrison hurried down the corridor toward Zack Steiner's office. Unlike him, he knocked and waited for permission to enter. It didn't come. He knocked again, harder this time.

"All right, come in," Zack called. Harrison entered.

Zack was on the phone. He held up his hand, listened and then muttered something before hanging up.

"What's happening now?" Harrison asked.

"The cop got rid of his vehicle and rented a car. They tracked his credit card. It's the electronic age," Zack added with a smile. "He ain't too smart for a detective."

"Why did he get rid of his car? I don't understand."

"There's an all-points bulletin out on him. He struck a superior officer, disobeyed orders, got his partner shot. So much for his credibility, huh?" Steiner said, sitting back. "Apparently, however, as I suspected, that man she was with is with him. I don't think there's any doubt but they're going to appear on the scene, if they avoid the highway patrol.

"Now what's with Dorset?" Zack asked, jerking his head to the right.

"She's going through the same sort of regression Kathleen Cornwall experienced, only . . . sooner," Harrison said regretfully.

"Well, what are you going to do with her?"

"Put her in the infirmary. I'm afraid in a few hours, her young man won't be able to recognize her."

"Don't be afraid. That's great."

"Not for the project," Harrison said sadly.

"All right, move her in. I'll have my men disappear. You be the only one to greet them if they get here. This is merely a spa and health club complex as far as anyone knows. They shouldn't see anything different. By then we'll have the police pick them up and it will be over."

"But what if the young man tells the police what she told him?"

"I don't know who would believe him." Zack thought for a moment. "But just in case . . ."

"Yes?"

"I suggest we move your files and equipment. I'll have a truck here by . . ." He looked at his Rolex. ". . . 0900."

"Move? But to where?"

"Storage, until Mr. Stoddard tells us what's next. Look," he added when Harrison shook his head, "I'm in charge of security and this is what has to be done to protect everyone. It's prudent, understand?"

"Maybe they'll never arrive. Maybe, as you said, the police will stop them."

"I can't take the chance. If nothing happens and Mr. Stoddard thinks we should, we'll move everything back to this site. If not, you and he will work something else out, I'm sure. I suggest you go organize your paperwork and your equipment," Zack concluded and rose.

Harrison looked at him.

"What about Mrs. Forsch in New Orleans? She's scheduled for tomorrow, isn't she?"

"I sent Satch and Tommy to New Orleans to arrange

for her delivery and death, but under the circumstances, don't you think we should put her on hold?"

"This is dreadful."

"Is it? Well, if you hadn't insisted on your stupid furloughs, you wouldn't be having this problem right now," Zack said. "Excuse me, I have lots to do."

Harrison watched him come around the desk and walk out, leaving the office door open. He sighed and then followed to have Shelly Dorset moved to a patient's room in the sick bay. She was already going in and out of consciousness when he checked on her. Miss Kleindeist looked up from gazing down at Shelly and shook her head.

"Her blood pressure's rising."

Harrison nodded.

"Her arteries are hardening again."

Sandra Kleindeist looked up at the intravenous bag.

"It's not helping."

"We've got to move her into room One B. Mr. Stone is still recuperating from indigestion in One A, right?"

"Yes. I'll have him out in the morning. Is there some other problem?" she asked softly.

"It seems a policeman and the man she was with last night might be on their way here."

"Oh, dear."

"If they come, you'll greet them first and offer to show them the complex. Give them no indication you want to hide anything."

"Fine, Doctor."

"Mr. Steiner is insisting I move my files and equipment in the morning. Maybe only for a temporary period. A little crisis, I'm afraid."

"We'll get past it," she said, smiling. "We always have."

He nodded and then moved to get the rolling gurney. They transferred Shelly to it and he opened the door so Miss Kleindeist could roll her out and to room 1B.

Harrison looked down at the pillow and saw the fallen gray hairs. It infuriated him. Sandra Kleindeist saw the frustration and anger in his face and reached out to touch his hand. He looked up at her and she offered a smile of condolence. He nodded and sighed deeply as he gazed at Shelly Dorset. Then he snapped to attention as if he felt Zack Steiner's eyes on him.

"I'll be in my office packing my paperwork into cartons for transport," he said.

"As soon as I settle her in, I'll come help you."

"No, you should try to get some sleep, Sandra."

It was the first time he had called her anything but Miss Kleindeist. She beamed.

"Nonsense. I've stayed up for days without sleeping before. It's no problem for me and you need me," she said.

"Thank you. That's very kind of you."

She flashed another smile and happily pushed Shelly Dorset to her last stop before the incinerator.

20

Why are we going back to the car rental?" Webster asked when Chicky pulled up in front of it again.

"Well, as I told you, people on the run often rent cars because their own vehicle's been identified. Only, we anticipate that and track their activities through their use of credit cards. It's how we find out they're buying plane tickets or where they've eaten last and where they are. By now I suspect they know we're in a light blue Chevy Caprice."

"So why did you rent the car?"

"It gave us a little time in the city. Now, I'm turning the car back claiming it has a mechanical problem. I'll get something comparable to replace it so they'll be no new credit card trail and we'll be in a different vehicle long enough to reach Palm Springs anyway. Hey," Chicky said, smiling. "A good cop always has to think like a good crook."

Chicky made the change of vehicles and they were on their way. Webster was afraid if he didn't stay awake, Chicky might fall asleep at the wheel. It was less than an hour to daylight, but he thought he wouldn't take any chances and practically pried his eyes open as they drove. He perused the papers Gary Adler had given Chicky and gazed at the picture of Harrison Woodruff.

"Shelly kept saying she wanted to get in touch with him," he said. "She trusted him."

Chicky shrugged.

"There's always the possibility he doesn't know the full extent of what he's into or what's happening around him. And," he added, looking at Webster, "there's always the possibility he does. At least we know what he looks like." He checked his rearview mirror. "Never thought I'd be worrying about the cops."

"Your superior officer took you guys off the case, but there wasn't any F.B.I. You think he's in on this somehow?"

"More likely he's just obeying orders from above. It's the kind of marionette he is. However, considering their influence with the police agencies, the Renaissance Corporation has some powerful supporters. I wouldn't underestimate their reach."

"How did he explain the way those so-called F.B.I. agents behaved?"

"Claims it's an undercover operation I'm fucking up."

"Could it be?"

Chicky narrowed his eyes.

"They killed your friend. That's taking undercover a bit too far in my book."

"People are sometimes expendable to covert operations."

"Tell me about it," Chicky said. "Look, I'm not any James Bond. I'm a broken down L.A. detective minutes away from retirement. My partner was shot. My career is in the toilet with my pension in jeopardy and a few people have been murdered. The trail leads to this joint in Palm Springs. So we're on our way.

"I think this Dr. Woodruff should answer some questions and if those goons are around, I'd like to have them measured for coffins. Also, I have to redeem myself." He smiled. "Justify putting my superior officer on his ass, not that I need much justification."

"Why did he make an unpleasant remark about your wife?" Webster asked.

"He hits low when he's cornered, probably always did. I think he was a rat in a previous life," Chicky added.

"Something happen to your wife?"

"She's had a mental breakdown of sorts." He turned to Webster. "She's being treated in an institution."

"I'm sorry. How is she doing?"

"Better." Chicky shook his head. "Life can wear you down," he said.

"Tell me about it. I feel like I'm in a nightmare that won't end," Webster muttered.

"Welcome to my life."

Chicky sped up. The ride from downtown L.A. on the 10 Freeway to the 111 turnoff into Palm Springs was a little over ninety miles. While they rode, Webster got Chicky to talk more about Maggie. Webster talked about his father and the way he coped with hardship.

"You're a lot alike," Webster concluded. "You both bury yourself in work to avoid thinking about your problems."

"It's called survival. Let's face it, Junior, the older generation is just tougher. You guys have problems, you turn to drugs. You party away the dark clouds. Or you go see your therapist for twenty years."

"Not me."

"You're an exception. My kids are no different. We spoiled them, made them soft, and now we wonder why they're so damn self-centered. Don't get me wrong. What's ever wrong with the young people today lies at the feet of their elders. Everyone wishes he could turn back time and do it over."

"That's what Renaissance seems to be all about," Webster said. "Shelly thought she was going to get a second chance."

"Yeah. Well, your children . . . they're your second chance, and if they screw up, it's still your fault." He looked at Webster. "Ain't you been serious about anyone? Thought about marriage, the family, mortgages, insurance . . . all that good stuff?"

"Now I know you are from my father's mold. No, not really, but not because I'm too into myself. I'm just . . ."

"What?"

"Being careful. Don't say it," he added quickly. "How did I get myself into this?"

"I won't say it. You said it."

"She was one beautiful woman, wild, fun, but yet there was that maturity."

"Boy, is that true if she's telling the truth? How old you say . . . seventy-something?"

"When you think about it, it would be quite the formula: youth with the wisdom of age. What if it worked? Would you opt for it? Would your wife?"

Chicky was quiet.

"I don't know. Maybe. Let's put it this way: I don't blame the women who volunteered; I blame the men who gave them false hope. Let's get the bad guys and then we'll talk about the perfect world." Then he looked at Webster and smiled. "I still got to see some proof of this before I'll believe any of it."

A little over an hour and a half later, they turned onto the 111 to head for Palm Springs. When they arrived, Chicky suggested they get some breakfast.

"It's too early to burst in on them, and besides, I need a surge of caffeine to keep me going," he said. They stopped at an I-Hop. While Webster waited for their breakfast, Chicky went to the phone to call a friend at the Palm Springs Police Department. He returned a few minutes later, hobbling along.

"The less sleep I get, the more this hurts and the more this hurts, the less sleep I get."

"I think your partner's right about you. You like to suffer," Webster said.

"Did Raul say that?"

"Not in so many words." Webster sipped his coffee. "Find anything out?"

"Renaissance is just another one of those health spas, according to my friend. Hot baths, mud baths, diet, exercise. One of the newer places. It doesn't sound like a clandestine laboratory creating freaks, but Brody hasn't been on the property."

"She's not a freak," Webster said firmly.

Chicky shrugged.

"A seventy-something woman who looks like that ain't exactly standard equipment. I saw the picture of her we derived from the video at Thunderbolt, remember."

Webster thought about it, but didn't say anything. He had hoped none of it was really true. It was too weird to think he had made love to and had romantic feelings for a woman that age. He really couldn't blame Chicky for his reaction.

Their breakfasts came. Chicky had a good appetite; he had ordered bacon and eggs over easy, but Webster just poked at a bowl of cold cereal and drank some grapefruit juice.

"What do we do next?" he asked.

"Well, we'll see if the good doctor will meet with us and talk to us. I don't exactly have authority to demand anything and my guess is they know it, but they might not want to attract any more attention, especially here." He checked his watch. "People at these spas are usually up early doing all sorts of healthy things. We'll go over there when we're finished here. Eat. You need your strength," Chicky said, ripping a roll in half and smearing butter over it. He dipped it into his egg yolk.

"Ever hear of something called cholesterol?"

"What's that, a breath mint?"

"If anything, it takes your breath away," Webster replied. Chicky laughed, but finished his eggs before they left.

They drove through the bright Palm Springs sunshine, past the newly constructed shopping malls and attractive condominium complexes with their gardens and pools and tennis courts, most of the complexes built near or around golf courses. There was a look of newness everywhere, a sense of rebirth.

"Logical they would choose a place like this to resurrect the aged," Chicky muttered. "I was thinking of coming down here, too, after retirement, and spending a month or so in one of the motor-home parks. Did I tell you I was getting a motor home and my wife and I were going to see America?"

"Twice."

"Maybe I am getting senile," Chicky muttered. "There it is," he said, nodding toward the gate on the right just ahead of them. The word *Renaissance* was written in black iron above the entryway. When they pulled up, they found a security guard at the main entrance. He stepped out of his booth, clipboard in hand.

"Good morning," he said. He looked like a man close to seventy.

"I guess this is the sort of work I'll be doing soon," Chicky told Webster.

"Good morning. We're here to see Dr. Woodruff." Chicky showed his badge. The security guard's eyes widened.

"Does he expect you?"

"Now, if we told people when we were coming, how would we get at the truth?" Chicky said.

"I'd better call ahead," the security guard said and returned to his booth.

"What if they just tell him not to let us in?"

Chicky looked at the ten-foot block wall surrounding the grounds.

"We'll make a reservation and check in as guests. I guess I could use it."

"Okay," the guard said, pressing the button to open the gate. "You drive straight in and park in front of the main building where it says guest parking."

"Thanks."

Chicky moved them slowly through the entrance. The grounds at Renaissance were plush, velvet lawns and beautiful gardens. Pink and bright red bougainvillaea lined the inside of the walls surrounding the property. There were stone benches in the shade of jacaranda trees and off to the left, a good-size, man-made lake with a half dozen rowboats tied to the dock. To their right as they wound their way up the circular drive toward the pink stucco structure, they saw a group of people doing calisthenics.

"Told you," Chicky said. "Looks pretty innocuous up here. I hope we have the right place."

"It's the right place," Webster assured him. They parked.

"Let me do all the talking. Just keep your eyes on everyone and everything around you."

Webster nodded. His heart began to pound as they made their way up the small stairway to the portico and then through the main entrance. It opened on a large lobby tiled with Mexican pavers and furnished with cushioned white rattan pieces, glass top tables and abstract wall art. It was bright, clean and comfortable-looking.

Sandra Kleindeist emerged from a doorway on the left to greet them. The fatigue in her face seemed well suited to her features and pale complexion. She smiled as she crossed the floor.

"I'm Miss Kleindeist, Dr. Woodruff's assistant. He'll be right with us," she said.

"Thanks," Chicky replied.

"Won't you have a seat?" She indicated the closest settee.

"Thanks," Chicky said again and sat. Webster, still gazing around, sat slowly.

"Can I get you some coffee?"

"No, we're fine. How many people stay here?"

"It varies, of course. Right now, we have about twenty-six guests. There's a brochure on the spa," she said, nodding at the stack on the table beside Chicky. He took one and gazed at it. "Are you interested in utilizing our facility?"

"Not yet," Chicky said, perusing the document. "Macrobiotic diet," he read. "Sounds small." She widened her smile.

"Small in fat and unnecessary calories."

"I see it says you give your guests a preliminary physical."

"Very important thing to do before you attempt a new exercise regimen."

"Yeah. That's what's kept me from starting. So you have medical facilities here?"

"Oh, we have a small medical complex. Nothing elaborate," she said. "But I am a nurse, an R.N."

Chicky nodded just as Harrison Woodruff came

through the doorway. His fatigue was more evident. His eyelids drooped, his face was pallid and his shoulders dipped. He looked disheveled, his hair wild, like he had just been running his fingers through it frantically. He had been working on his papers and documents, packing everything neatly in cartons for Zack Steiner's men to carry to the truck.

"Sorry to keep you waiting," he said. Chicky rose and extended his hand. "Dr. Harrison Woodruff."

"I'm Detective Charles Siegler. This is Webster Martin."

Harrison Woodruff glanced at Webster, who rose slowly, but did not extend his hand. He saw the intensity in Webster's gaze and turned his gaze back to Chicky.

"What brings a Los Angeles detective to our spa?"

"Oh, did I say I was from Los Angeles?" Chicky replied quickly. Harrison blanched and looked at Sandra Kleindeist.

"I thought someone had said that. Aren't you from Los Angeles?"

"Matter of fact, I am."

"How can I help you?"

"We're looking for a Shelly Dorset, who is supposed to be here."

"Dorset?" He looked at Sandra Kleindeist again. She shook her head. "I'm afraid that name doesn't ring a bell."

"How about Kathleen Cornwall?"

Harrison shook his head.

"Sorry, no. Someone told you they were here?"

"Shelly told me," Webster said. Chicky glared at him and then smiled at Harrison.

"There's a possibility, Doctor, that these women used false names."

"I see. What did they do?"

"Maybe nothing. But we think one of them might have witnessed a murder."

"In L.A.?"

"That's correct."

"When?"

"A few days ago."

"Well, I don't think we have any guests from L.A. who checked in during the past few days, do we, Miss Kleindeist?"

"No," she said firmly and fixed her eyes on Chicky as she folded her arms over her small bosom.

"I see. Well, I don't doubt you, but Webster here does know what they look like. Would it be all right if we just wander about? We promise not to bother any of your guests."

"No need to wander. Miss Kleindeist will give you a complete tour."

"I hate to trouble you . . ."

"No trouble," Sandra said. "We run tours daily. Maybe you'll like what you see and return as a guest," she added. Harrison smiled.

"Miss Kleindeist is one of our best spokesmen," he said. She reddened with the compliment.

"Thank you," Chicky said. "I accept your kind offer."

"Enjoy," Harrison said and started to turn away.

"Excuse me, Doctor, but aren't you the same Harrison Woodruff who did so much significant research at the Cancer Institute and the National Institute of Gerontology?"

"I have done work there, yes," Harrison replied. "I'm flattered you know about me."

"Well, I don't understand. Why would you be supervising a health spa now? Isn't that a waste of your talents?"

"No. I'm doing a different sort of research now, studying the effect of diet and exercise on health," Harrison said, smiling.

Chicky nodded.

"Let me take you through the complex," Sandra insisted. "We'll start with the exercise facilities. Right this way," she said, indicating a door on the far right.

"I'll try to see you before you leave," Harrison said.

"Right. Webster," Chicky said. He saw Webster was fuming, boiling over like a pot of milk. "Let's take it a step at a time," Chicky said under his breath. Webster turned from Harrison to him and nodded. They started after Sandra Kleindeist.

"Problem with your foot, Detective?" Harrison asked as they started away.

"Infected toe. I've just procrastinated about treating it."

"Miss Kleindeist might be able to help."

"Oh no, I—"

"I'd be glad to look at it after we tour the facilities," Sandra said, smiling.

"Thanks," Chicky said.

Sandra Kleindeist led them down a corridor and pointed out the exercise room, describing the equipment. She showed them their aerobics center, their indoor pool facility and then took them to the steam rooms and the hot baths.

"We have biking trails, walking and hiking trails," she explained. "This is our dining room. Everyone gets a personally designed diet. Our dormitories are the two buildings on the east end of the property."

"What are your medical facilities like?" Chicky asked.

"Oh, just two examination rooms, a small infirmary, nothing very elaborate."

"May we see it?"

"Of course," she replied. "And then I'll look at your foot."

Chicky looked at Webster.

"I'm getting a sick feeling," Chicky told him.

"She's here; she's got to be," he whispered.

Sandra Kleindeist led them down another corridor and around a bend to two large doors with grainy glass windows upon which was simply printed MEDICAL. She held the door open for them and they entered a smaller hallway, well-lit by neon fixtures. The hallway floor was stark white tile with the matching walls. She paused at the first doorway.

"In here we weigh the guests, take their blood pressure, do routine blood work. We do give everyone an EKG, although we don't pretend to be heart specialists. We run a fat content test. I could do that for you, if you like."

"Maybe some other time," Chicky said. "I'm limited to how much bad news I can take in a day. What's down there?" he asked, nodding toward the end of the corridor.

"Our infirmary. Just two rooms, actually. If someone has a muscle ache or any minor problem, we try to treat them here. It's not an emergency room. You can be sure of that. We never attempt to do more than we are capable of doing. Now, would you like me to look at your foot?"

"I really don't think I should trouble you."

"No trouble. We get a lot of sore feet around here," she added with a smile.

"Go ahead," Webster said. "I don't mind waiting."

"Huh?"

"Just let her look at it, you big baby."

"Detective," she said, indicating the examination table. "Just sit up there."

Chicky gazed angrily at Webster and then entered the room.

"I'll wait out here," Webster said. Miss Kleindeist started to undo Chicky's shoe.

The moment she turned her back on him, Webster started for the doorway to the infirmary. He found it was locked. Frustrated, he looked back and then took out his wallet and plucked one of his credit cards from it. He inserted it through the crack and worked it down to the door lock, pushing and twisting until he felt the doorknob give and the door open. Then he quickly entered the infirmary.

The door of the first room on his left was closed. He tried it and found it opened. He did so slowly and gazed in at an empty bed and a dark room. He found the same situation in the room on the right. Disappointed, he started to turn back when he saw another doorway toward the rear. It opened to another corridor. He followed it to a room on the left and opened the door slowly.

There was a very old woman in the bed, an intravenous plugged into her right arm. He thought she looked close to ninety, if a day. She made no movements. He listened, heard no one and entered the room. The intravenous dripped slowly. What would such an elderly woman be doing at a spa like this? he thought. Chicky's got to see her and let's see what kind of answers Miss Kleindeist has. He drew a little closer to the woman and looked at her. There was something familiar about her and yet, she was truly aged.

Her skin was pale and flaky and filled with deep wrinkles, a road map over her cheeks, across her forehead and around her dry, thin, pasty lips. Her hair was gray, with strands as thin as thread so that her dull white skull was clearly visible. Brown age spots were everywhere, on her cheeks and forehead, skull and neck.

Her hand, with its long, bony fingers and its veins raised against the wafer thin, brown-spotted skin, lay quivering over the sheet. Was this decrepit creature alive? he wondered and leaned over to see if she was still breathing. She was, but there was a hoarse sound in her throat.

He started to straighten up when her eyes opened. They were glassy. She blinked and blinked.

"Sorry," he muttered and turned away. He was nearly to the door when he heard her.

"Webster?"

21

I want you to meet someone," Webster said. He stood in the examination room doorway. Miss Kleindeist had just finished bandaging Chicky's toe and Chicky was pulling up his sock and putting on his shoe. He looked up, smiling with anticipation.

"Oh?"

"Right down the corridor here," Webster said, fixing his eyes on Sandra Kleindeist. She stood up, her hands fluttering to her throat like two small birds.

"Where did you go?" she asked, her eyes widening with a note of panic.

"Detective Siegler," Webster said, ignoring her. Chicky stood up.

"Thank you, Miss Kleindeist. It does feel better. You have the wonder touch."

She glanced at him, nodded, but then turned back to Webster quickly.

"Where did you go? Where do you think you're going?" she demanded more forcefully.

"Yes. Where did you go, Webster?" Chicky asked as he started out.

"Down this corridor," Webster instructed and walked ahead of Chicky.

"You can't go in there," Miss Kleindeist shouted. "That's not on the tour. Stop!"

They ignored her. Webster took Chicky through the first door and then through the second, turning into Shelly Dorset's room. Chicky paused in the doorway and looked at Webster.

"Who's this?" he asked.

"This is Shelly Dorset," Webster said, moving to her. He took her limp hand into his and her eyes opened with some effort. Chicky stepped closer and looked at the elderly woman.

"Huh?" He smirked at Webster. "I saw a fairly decent picture of Shelly Dorset, Webster. This can't be the woman you picked up at Thunderbolt."

"Look closely. This is Shelly Dorset," Webster said dryly.

Chicky stared, his eyes skeptical.

"But . . ."

"She says it's all gone wrong. The rejuvenation. It's having the exact opposite effect, making her older than she was, and doing it rapidly."

Chicky gazed down at the decrepit face again and shook his head.

"Good God."

Shelly's mouth writhed with the effort to speak. Her voice was barely a whisper.

"What? What's she saying?"

"Come closer. She doesn't bite," Webster said.

Chicky stepped closer and leaned over, bringing his ear close to Shelly's lips.

"I am Shelly Dorset," she said. "They did this to me."

Chicky looked up at Webster, who was nodding.

"Jesus," he said.

"I want you to see something else," Webster said, going to the window. He pulled the curtain back and pinched the venetian blinds open to peer out. Chicky gazed over his shoulder. He saw a dark brown van, the doors open. A moment later, he saw Herbie Shagan emerge from a doorway in the building, carrying a carton to the truck. Mike Robbins followed him, also carrying a carton.

"The F.B.I.," Webster said disdainfully.

"Those are our men," Chicky said nodding. He unbuttoned his jacket to get to his pistol and turned to leave Shelly Dorset's room, just as Zack Steiner appeared in the doorway, his nine-millimeter drawn. He smiled coldly, his eyes, however, hot with excitement.

"I'm afraid you're off limits here, Detective," he said.

"Who are you?" Chicky demanded.

"I'm head of security. My name's Steiner. You might as well take it with you to the next world. You," he said, waving the gun at Webster, "Webster Martin, I believe. Reach over slowly, very slowly, and take Detective Siegler's pistol from its holster. Then drop it on the bed. Go on. Mrs. Dorset won't mind," he said, widening his smile. "Slowly," he emphasized, pointing his pistol at Webster. Webster didn't move.

"Do what he says," Chicky muttered.

"Who are you people? How can you do this sort of thing to someone?" Webster asked.

"Not that it matters, but I don't have anything to do with that," he said, gesturing at Shelly Dorset with the barrel of his pistol. "Get the gun out of the holster."

Webster came over to Chicky's right side and started to reach for the pistol when Harrison Woodruff and Sandra Kleindeist appeared in the doorway, too.

"What are you doing, Mr. Steiner?"

"Just go do your work, Doctor."

"You're not going to shoot these men here, are you?"

"No. They're going to go into the truck and be shot someplace else. Does that make you happier? Get back to your office," he ordered before Harrison could speak.

Harrison hesitated.

"What happened to you, Dr. Woodruff, that you've become part of something like this?" Chicky asked. "I read your bio. You're one of our most respected and successful microbiologists, brilliant."

"I'm doing brilliant work here," Harrison said. Sandra Kleindeist appeared to be nodding behind him.

"With these kinds of people? Do you know they've killed two young men in Los Angeles these past few days and shot a policeman?"

"Killed two?"

"And shot my partner."

"Shut up!" Zack commanded. "Webster, move it. Now!"

"It's not going to end with us, Dr. Woodruff."

"Maybe we shouldn't do this," Harrison said. "Let's call Mr. Stoddard."

"You stupid . . . for such a brilliant scientist, you do the dumbest things," Zack said. "Mentioning his name, even in front of soon-to-be dead men."

He turned to Harrison.

"Now, get the hell out of here before—"

Webster lunged toward Zack and Chicky went to his left to draw his pistol. Steiner blocked Webster's assault by striking him with his left forearm, sending him to the floor. At the same time, anticipating Chicky's using his pistol, Zack pulled Dr. Woodruff in front of him as a shield. Chicky drew his gun, hesitated, but kept it pointed at Zack and Harrison. Sandra Kleindeist, seeing her beloved Dr. Woodruff in the direct line of fire, screamed and lunged at Steiner from behind, digging her fingernails into his neck, her fingers clinging like the legs of two spiders when Zack drove his right elbow back to catch her in the diaphragm. It bent her over, but she continued to cling and scream.

"Let him go!"

Chicky didn't shoot, but Harrison, anticipating that he might, turned on Steiner and pushed back. Falling against Sandra Kleindeist, Zack lost his balance for the moment. He struck Harrison on the side of the head with his pistol. Meanwhile, Webster regained his footing and tackled Steiner just under the knees. He started to point his pistol at Webster and Chicky shot, hitting him in the chest. He faltered, Chicky shot again and Steiner fell over, dead before he hit the corridor floor. Sandra Kleindeist's attention went immediately to the unconscious Dr. Woodruff.

Chicky rushed to the window, anticipating that Herbie

Shagan and Mike Robbins heard the gunfire. They had. Both men, however, instead of returning to the building, got into the van.

"What's in that van?" he asked Sandra Kleindeist. She ignored him, her attention fixed on Woodruff. "Talk!"

Sandra looked up from Dr. Woodruff, whose head she held comfortably in her lap.

"Dr. Woodruff's papers and slides," she said. "The project."

"I'm going after them," Chicky said. "That contains the proof we need."

"I'd better go with you," Webster said, prying Zack Steiner's pistol out of his hand.

"No. You stay here. Get a call out to the Palm Springs Police and have them call for an ambulance," he added, nodding toward Shelly Dorset.

"I think it's too late for her. I've come this far with you. I'd like to go all the way," Webster said.

"No time to argue," Chicky said. He paused in the doorway and looked down at Sandra. "If you have any decency left, you'll call the police and get this woman medical attention." She didn't acknowledge him. "Let's go."

They hurried down the corridor, Chicky vaguely realizing that his toe felt better.

"Got to remember to thank her for my foot," he muttered to Webster as they charged out the front entrance and to the car. They saw the van winding down the driveway toward the gate. By the time they were in their vehicle and following, the van had left the property and turned right, heading east toward the 10 Freeway. For about a minute, Shagan and Robbins didn't realize they were being pursued and kept at a reasonable speed. Chicky, on the other hand, was nearly on two wheels when he turned out of the complex and gunned the car down the highway. Herbie, who was driving, realized they were being chased and sped up, going through a red light at the next intersection.

"Shit," Chicky muttered. "I'm too old for this."

He didn't slow down, but when he passed under the red traffic light, the driver of a light blue, late-model pickup truck coming on their right had to hit his brakes and swerve to avoid crashing into the side of their car.

"Sorry," Chicky muttered to the rearview mirror and dropped the accelerator to the floor. The van picked up speed as well. Ahead of them was open road with pristine desert to the left, but they were approaching the Mission Hills Golf Club and homes, famous for the tournaments it hosted. Up ahead cars were leaving from its main gate, some of them turning west, toward the van and Chicky and Webster. As the van barreled down the highway, Mike Robbins leaned out of the window and opened fire with his nine-millimeter semiautomatic. One of the bullets hit the hood of Chicky's car. He swerved to the left to get out of the line of fire and almost went head-on into an oncoming vehicle. The driver leaned on his horn angrily.

Webster screamed as they careened back into their lane. He leaned out of his window and pulled the trigger of Zack Steiner's pistol.

"Easy," Chicky said. "You don't know how to use that. You might hit an innocent bystander."

Nevertheless, Webster held his finger on the trigger
and one of his bullets hit the rear of the van and continued through to catch Herbie Shagan in the back, tearing
cleanly through his lung. He collapsed over the steering
wheel and the van spun to the left, to the right and then
to the left, going over the highway and catching its
wheels on the shoulder of the road. The van turned over
and bounced hard to turn over again. On its second rev-
olution, its gas tank exploded and the walls of the van
came apart as the vehicle shattered under the pressure.
It stopped against what seemed to be a wall of flame, emanating thick black smoke into the desert breeze. The
flames roared.

"Jesus, talk about your lucky shots," Chicky shouted
as he slowed down.

"That was for Carl and Phil," Webster said.

Chicky brought their car to a stop and they got out,
but they couldn't get very close to the burning vehicle.

"Sweet revenge, but so much for our evidence," he
muttered. In the distance they could see a California
highway patrolman rushing toward them on the 10
Freeway.

There were a half dozen police cars at the Renaissance Spa when Chicky and Webster returned. Some
were from the sheriff's department. Chicky had had the
highway patrolman call in the scene at the spa. Brody
Ralston, Chicky Siegler's friend in the Palm Springs Police Department, stepped toward them when they
emerged from their vehicle. He was a man in his early
fifties, tall, with a stomach that looked like it contained a

regulation NBA basketball. His hair was thin, a mixture of gray and light brown, and he had a face that looked carved from seasoned leather.

"What the hell's going on here, Siegler?" he demanded.

"Here?" Chicky looked around. "Mud baths, low fat diets, exercise. People are getting younger, healthier, aren't they? I'm seriously thinking about checking in."

"Huh?"

Two Palm Springs detectives joined them and Brody made the introductions.

"I'm going in to see about Shelly Dorset," Webster said. He left the explanations to Chicky.

Inside, there were patrolmen everywhere. Two of them were standing beside Dr. Woodruff, who sat on a settee holding an ice pack against his left temple. He looked up sadly as Webster approached.

"What happened to the van?" he asked.

"It turned over during the chase and caught fire."

"What?"

"Dr. Woodruff's things?" Sandra said, grimacing in anticipation of bad news.

"Up in smoke," Webster replied. "Maybe where they belong."

Harrison Woodruff turned a shade of white, his lips becoming so pale they were indistinguishable from the rest of his complexion. He moaned and permitted himself to collapse into Sandra Kleindeist's eagerly hospitable arms. She held him to her, letting his head fall to her bony shoulder and pressing her lips against his hair. He closed his eyes.

"You don't know what you've done," she said hatefully, "what a horrible thing you've done."

"You took the words right out of my mouth," Webster said dryly.

He continued through the spa's main building, down the corridor toward the room in which he had left Shelly. Two patrolmen and a forensics detective were standing over Zack Steiner's body. The door to Shelly's room was closed. Webster started toward it.

"Who are you?" the patrolman on the left asked. He was the taller of the two. His name plate read CARSON.

"I'm Webster Martin. I know the woman in here," he said.

"You know something about this?" the other patrolman asked, nodding down at Zack Steiner.

"Detective Siegler of the LAPD is right behind me. He's giving the details to the Palm Springs detectives. Excuse me, I have to see Mrs. Dorset," Webster continued. He reached for the doorknob.

The forensics man stood up. He was tall, at least six feet four, with intense dark eyes and dark brown hair cut in a military style.

"You say you knew the woman in there?" he asked.

"Knew?"

"She's been dead some time," he said. "Do you know why they kept a corpse in this room this long? Are you related?"

"She's died?"

"Some time ago, yes." Webster looked down and then up as the forensics man's words registered.

"She can't be dead that long. I was just speaking to

her, less than an hour ago," Webster explained. The forensics man looked at the patrolmen, who stared at Webster.

"The woman in that room has been dead days, maybe a week," the forensics man said firmly.

"That can't be," Webster insisted and opened the door. The stench hit him first. He saw that Shelly's body had the sheet drawn over it. He held his breath and approached. He hesitated, looked back at the policemen in the doorway, and then reached out slowly and inched the sheet back. The sight churned his stomach. He dropped the sheet as if it were on fire and turned away from the decaying corpse.

"You see," the forensics man said with a certain degree of arrogance, "she's been dead longer than an hour."

"I know," Webster said, gazing back at her. "She died months ago . . . in Chicago."

"Huh?"

"I thought you said you had spoken to her less than an hour ago," Carson said.

"I did. But she was on dead time," Webster replied.

"What? What the hell does that mean?" He looked at the forensics man, who shrugged.

Webster didn't reply. He took a deep breath and started away, leaving the three of them looking after him.

Ben Stoddard heard the phone ringing on his private line. He didn't want to pick it up, but it was relentless, the ringing piercing through his very soul.

Bad news never procrastinates, he thought. It has a life of its own, working its way into your heart like determined termites hollowing out the structure of a building.

"Hello," he said softly. He wanted to rage, to scream, but the strength seemed to have been sapped out of him. He was sinking in his office chair, beginning his descent into hell. Maybe that was what really had driven him to invest in and believe in this project: his fear that if he died, he would go straight to the eternal fires.

"Is it true?" he heard.

Funny, he didn't even recognize the voice, although he knew it had to be one of his board of directors.

"Yes," he said.

"What's going to happen?"

"You're going to die on time," he replied, and slammed the phone down.

Not that it mattered, but every trace of anything that linked the project to him went up in that van. In a way that was good, of course, but in a sense, it was bad. If they only knew how close we had come. Maybe . . .

He shook his head. Whatever happens now, it won't happen in his lifetime, he thought. He felt like an astronaut who had just seen his tether rip. He was going back, falling into space. The gauge told him just how much oxygen he had left and after that, he was going to die. It isn't that often that we look right into the face of our own death. We spend our lives ignoring its existence, distracting ourselves any way we can and living with the hope that somehow, some way, science will keep us alive.

He rose from his chair slowly. Now, more than ever, he felt like an old man.

He was unable to avoid being his age.

He paused and looked out his window at the setting sun, feeling like he was looking at his life's gauge and watching it tick down.

Then he would float off and be forgotten.

Epilogue

Raul, Tina and the children were there to help Chicky and Maggie load the motor home with their things. The house had been sold.

"Our children presented us with a check this morning intended to cover our expenses for a year. Think that's a hint?" Chicky joked.

"Hint?" Tina smiled.

"To stay away," Chicky replied.

"Oh." Tina looked at Maggie first before she permitted herself to laugh. Maggie was shaking her head. She looked more vibrant than she had looked for months.

"Dirty Harry can never accept a gift without making a comment," she said. It was Raul's turn to laugh.

"Go on. Enjoy yourself at my expense, Torres. Your day will come."

"Hey, I've got a lot to thank you for, Chicky. You got rid of Kronenberg."

"What did happen to him?" Tina wondered.

"Transferred. I don't care what happens after that. He's out of my casa," Raul said.

"It's enough to make me reconsider my retirement," Chicky quipped. Maggie gave him the eye. "Just kidding." He sighed and looked at the house. "It's like taking off your most comfortable shoes even though they're worn out, but . . . time to move on."

"You'll send us beautiful postcards from everywhere," Tina told Maggie. They hugged.

Chicky and Raul stared at each other for a moment. Then Chicky extended his hand.

"How's the new guy?"

"Wet behind the ears."

"Mexican?"

"Very funny. Get the hell out of here," Raul said. They embraced and Chicky opened the motor-home door. He helped Maggie in and got behind the steering wheel.

"How's it feel up there?"

"Like I'm finally someplace," Chicky said.

"Don't stop along the way and start solving crimes."

"Hey, that's not a bad idea. The Motor Home Detective. Could be bigger than Dick Tracy." He started the engine.

"Bye," Tina called. Maggie gazed out at her and smiled tentatively. The mixture of fear and hope created a soft look in her eyes. She mouthed a good-bye and turned to look toward the future as Chicky pulled away from the house, honking his funny-sounding horn.

Raul stood there, his arm around Tina, the twins at their side.

"I wish we were going with them," she said. Her words

drifted away like leaves in an autumn breeze as the motor home went around the corner and disappeared.

Up at the Martins' Sherman Oaks building site, Webster completed the checklist with the building inspector and headed for the office trailer. Just two days prior, his father had hired a new secretary. His father's attempts at subtle matchmaking had always failed, but Webster had to admit the old man finally had found an interesting prospect.

Diana Wilson was a lithe brunette, two inches shorter than Webster, with the brightest blue eyes he had ever seen. She was efficient, intelligent and very professional. Finding quality secretarial help was always a problem. He hated to do anything to threaten the business relationship, and he knew that's just what a romantic relationship would do. But to be honest with himself, he would have to admit he was simply afraid.

He hadn't seen or pursued anyone since Renaissance and Shelly. He was still recuperating from the deaths of his friends and the horror of what had been conducted on the Palm Springs site.

He entered the trailer and Diana looked up from her computer keyboard. She was wearing an eggshell-white dress, the hem of which reached just a few inches from her ankles. Her rich, soft hair lay gently over her shoulders. She wasn't tan, but she had a dark complexion, which only emphasized her bright blue eyes more.

"I put your phone messages on the desk," she said.

"Oh. Thanks." He sat down and glanced at them. Then he looked at her. She smiled. It was the sort of smile that could warm a cold, cold heart and initiate his own, private renaissance.

He sighed and pulled out the side drawer to flip through the files until he found her résumé. He pulled it out and perused it, centering his attention on date of birth.

She claimed to be twenty-four.

"Let me ask you something, Diana," he said. She paused and turned to him.

"Yes?"

"When you moved here from Topeka, did you happen to bring along your birth certificate?"

"Birth certificate? Yes, I did. Why?"

"Nothing. I'd like to see it."

"Why?" she asked, laughing.

"Just curious. Maybe you could bring it along tonight if you're free."

"Tonight?"

"Uh-huh. Are you free?"

"Yes. But where am I going?"

"I know this terrific small Italian restaurant in Venice using treasured family recipes, spectacular food, cozy place. How's it sound?"

She laughed.

"Fine. What time?"

"I'll pick you up at seven."

"Okay," she said.

"Only be sure you bring your birth certificate along," he added. She stared at him. "You have it, right?"

"I have it," she said.

"Good." He leaned back and closed his eyes for a moment. "Good," he said.

Pocket Books proudly presents
a preview of the next thrilling
novel by

ANDREW NEIDERMAN

UNDER
ABDUCTION

Coming in December 2002

Anna Gold stared at the telephone on her light maple wood secretary in the den as she slipped her left arm into her navy blue wool coat. She thought she could will the phone to ring, will her lover to follow through, and as he had promised, make her the most important person in his life. He should have called this morning to confirm their plans, all that they would do to make a future together now that he knew she was pregnant with his child.

She had waited until after lunch to go for groceries because she didn't want to miss him, but here it was nearly one and he still hadn't called. In fact, no one had called this morning and the silence of her solitude hung in the air of her apartment with a heaviness that resembled the aftermath of a funeral.

The lines were dead now between her and the people she loved and the people who should love her. She had acquaintances, superficial friendships with girlfriends who were citizens of the same country of loneliness, young women about her age who were searching for some meaningful relationship, too. Her work as a paralegal at the public defender's office had brought her into contact with many different kinds of people, but she had yet to find the close friend with whom she was comfortable enough to share intimacies, intimacies that up until now she had shared only with her sister. She had told no one except her lover and her sister that she was nearly two months pregnant. She had confirmed it herself with one of those home-test kits.

Almost immediately in a panic, she had made inquiries about having an abortion and had even gone so far as to have an appointment with Doctor Carla Williams at the Mountain Clinic. But then she had calmed down and thought, if he loves me as much as he says he does and is ready to make this change in his life, why have an abortion? She never even told him she had gone to find out about it. As far as he knew, that wasn't a choice, not with her religious background. And she was encouraged by the fact that he had never even suggested it.

Instead, he had sat there with that same sweet smile on his face, his hazel eyes brightening when she had told him, and he had nodded and said, "Well, I guess this means we'll just have to move things along a little faster than I had anticipated. Nothing to worry about. I'll be here for you; I'll always be here for you."

He brought her to tears when he added, "You've given me a new lease on life just when I thought I had made tragic mistakes and buried myself in misery.

Thank you, Anna. Thank you for being here." And they kissed.

But that had been days ago, and he hadn't called her this morning as he had promised.

She began to button her coat, her fingers trembling with the disappointment that filled her with an emptiness, a hollowness in her chest. The third button from the top on her coat dangled ominously on loose threads. Anna was not the homemaker her mother had been and her sister was; she couldn't mend clothing and she was, at best, a mediocre cook. Her mind had always been on what she considered more lofty endeavors. She wasn't going to be frustrated in her pursuit of a career and a more cosmopolitan life, no matter what her family's traditions were.

She would have been a full attorney by now if her father hadn't discouraged her and pulled back on the little support he had given her soon after her mother's death. The estrangement that followed was destined. She believed it was built into her genes: she had inherited her father's strong determination, and that, perhaps, was why they had been combatants for so long—they were too alike. Of course, her father would never admit to such a thing. She was merely rebellious, foolish, ungrateful. She couldn't have a sensible discussion with such a man.

Yet his face haunted her at times like these. The vision of him furiously standing before her remained vivid. There were those big dark eyes of his, tragic eyes that saw the world through shattered glasses. His shoulders, powerful though they were because of the work he did with stone, still always seemed sloped with the burden that followed two thousand years of persecution.

"You are like their Christ," she once accused, which brightened his face with the blood beneath his skin like she had never seen it brighten before. "You take all the misery onto yourself. You crucify yourself. Instead of nails in your hands, you pierce your soul with the pictures of the Holocaust or daily examples of anti-Semitism. You want me to march through endless cemeteries with you."

After the initial shock of her words, her father's shoulders swelled, moving up and back as if they were being pumped full of air, and he glared at her with that face of the prophets he often assumed and said, "You can run; you can hide. You can put a cross around your neck, if you like, but you can never deny who you are and what you are."

Was he right? One of the things she had done when she first moved in here was put a mezuzah on the door jamb. She couldn't help it. It just seemed natural and she wasn't ready to spit in the face of her faith. She simply wanted breathing room to become her own person. Was that such a terrible thing?

At the door of her apartment, she paused and glanced at the phone on the side table in the living room. That one didn't ring either. Of course, there was the answering machine, but her lover rarely left a message on it, and she knew that even if he did, she wouldn't be able to get back to him.

She hated herself for being so dependent on someone else's schedule, responsibilities, and whims. How had she grown after escaping the confinement in her father's house? Where was this precious freedom she had dreamed she would have?

"I'm still no better than a puppet, and this time I have no one to blame but myself," she muttered and opened the door.

Her apartment was in one of the new complexes built outside of Monticello, New York, the biggest village in Sullivan county and the center of county government. These were advertised and sold as garden apartments, each with its own small balcony overlooking the pool and landscaped commons. But being in upstate New York, the pool was utilized for only eight to ten weeks, if they were lucky; and during the long winter months, the flower beds were dead or brown, the bushes were thin, and the walkways were usually streaked with mud, ice, or snow. Now the pool was an empty shell gathering debris.

Except for attending Yeshiva University in New York and spending a year at the Benjamin N. Cardoza School of Law, she had spent all of her twenty-six years in this area, the Catskill Mountains, known as the borscht belt. But she was comfortable here and she could be on her own here; she still felt protected by familiarity. Setting out to start a new life in a completely new vicinity after cutting herself off from her father was too terrifying. Despite her need to be cosmopolitan, she was handicapped by her need for stability. It was part of the contradiction, the confusion of identity that kept her searching for answers.

Did she, as she naggingly feared, grab on too quickly to someone else's affection?

She had fallen in love, depended on someone's promises, surrendered to passion, and now she was in trouble because the clock was ticking. The magic of life, the making of a baby had started. It wasn't something planned, but the impulsiveness with which she and her lover had begun their relationship permeated everything they did. Everything they did was on the spur of the moment, which made it even more exciting. She was tired of being the well-organized, sensible young woman. One minute she was planning to make a cup of tea, read a book, and go to sleep; and the next moment, she was rushing off to meet him at a motel or out-of-the-way bar and then a motel. It was wonderful to be taken by surprise, to defy what was sensible, to be carefree and throw caution overboard with the frenzy of one desperately trying to stay afloat.

Sometimes, they would be riding along talking and, suddenly, he would stop, pull onto a side road, and they would be at each other. She had never known such passion. She had had crushes on boys, but never developed a real relationship with anyone, even at the university. Maybe she was inexperienced and naive, more like an adolescent when it came to matters of the heart, but she truly believed her lover was just as taken with her as she was with him. In fact, he appeared to love her more for her simplicity and innocence. How many times had he told her she made him feel like a young man again, falling in love for the first time himself?

If all that is so true, Anna, why the delay? Let's get this life started, she thought. But now, with his hesitation, his long list of excuses, she had grave doubts gnawing at her insides.

And so, to abort or not to abort, that was the question, the question of the age, it seemed; only now, it was, dreadfully, a personal question.

She had been impressed with Doctor Carla Williams. The head of the clinic had taken great pains not to influence her one way or the other. "This has to be your sole decision, Anna," she told her. "I just give you the facts. I'm not anyone's priest, minister, or rabbi. I have enough trouble looking after my own soul," she said. Anna liked her. If she was going to have it done, Carla Williams was the sort of doctor she'd want doing it, she thought.

Anna knew what her sister Miriam had thought about it, but this wasn't happening to Miriam; it was happening to her. Miriam couldn't begin to understand, even though she was older. Miriam was even more cloistered and inexperienced at matters of the heart than she was. Miriam could only gasp or exclaim or cry.

Well, she wasn't Miriam. She was her own person and she would make up her own mind. She vowed she would do whatever she had to do and be persuaded by nothing except her own feelings.

"Don't quote scripture at me, Miriam," she told her. "This is the real world I'm in."

But her bravado weakened when she gazed at the

mezuzah in the doorway. Despite her protest, moral law weighed heavily on her conscience. Independence and finding her identity was one thing; defiance was another. She closed her eyes, kissed the tips of her fingers, and then opened her eyes and touched the mezuzah before walking out and closing the door behind her.

Anna moved quickly down the walkway toward the covered parking spaces. Each tenant had two spaces, but she needed only one for her late model Honda, which she had leased. Everything in her life was leased right now, including the furniture and the kitchenware in the apartment. She had even rented her television set on an option to buy deal. At least she owned her clothes, some not very valuable jewelry, and the towels and linens.

When she had left home, she had little more than a thousand dollars, but she had the job and the promise of some sort of future doing work she felt gave her life more meaning. It was enough to give her the courage to be on her own, and she had been for nearly a year; but now she was also in trouble.

Or was she? Perhaps he would fulfill his promises. Perhaps he was as deeply in love with her as she thought, hoped. If only he had called this morning, if only she had some concrete reason to be optimistic, if only . . .

She started the engine and drove the mile and a half to the supermarket. Saturday was supermarket day for her now, but it wasn't always. In fact, she never rode in a car on Saturdays, much less go shopping. As she drove through the quiet streets, she envisioned her father's face again, his grimace, the dark way his eyes turned down because of the shameful burden she had become.

Even now, after all this time and all she had done and said, she couldn't keep out the tiny pinpricks of guilt that stabbed her heart. It was as if God were looking down on this stupid supermarket parking lot and making notes in his Divine notebook.

Anna Gold shopped and rode in her car on the Sabbath, and after I had strictly told them all . . . remember the Sabbath day, keep it holy. This is keeping it holy? Comparing prices, clipping coupons, squeezing fruit?

Anna laughed at her own imaginative dialogue. She didn't intend to be irreverent or blasphemous, but as she had told Miriam, she simply wasn't going to live in the Middle Ages, or even before the Middle Ages, which was how she characterized her father's faith. Her sister stood in the hallway of their house with her mouth agape as Anna vehemently espoused her beliefs the day she left.

"Religion has nothing in common with reality. One church still prohibits the use of condoms even though a storm of dire disease, AIDS, rains down on humanity; while another prohibits sick children from getting the medicine they need or the blood transfusion they need. And we're no better with our archaic kosher laws and our fanatical adherence to the Sabbath. The world still turns on Saturday, Miriam!"

"Anna," she gasped, "God is listening."

"If He's listening," she said, "he must be hysterical with laughter watching these holy men twist and turn what He created into their own creations."

Her sister's face whitened. She looked to the living room where their father sat fuming.

Poor Miriam, Anna thought, she hated leaving her behind, but maybe that was where her sister would rather be, maybe that was where she belonged. They were sisters, but they really were two different people. Miriam wouldn't be caught dead pushing a cart down a supermarket aisle on Saturday. She would be afraid her hands would burn.

Anna smiled and shook her head at the thought as she moved along, pulling boxes rapidly from the shelves, pushing the cart down the aisle, nearly knocking over an elderly lady who was comparing prices. It wasn't that crowded, however, so she was able to get to a check-out counter sooner than she thought. She wanted to get home just in case he called. This was the weekend he was supposedly telling his wife. This was the weekend it would really begin for them. Monday she would be able to walk with her head high and stop feeling like a sneak.

As she pushed her cart through the entrance of the supermarket and toward her car, she caught sight of a late model Ford sedan parked to her left in a No Parking zone. The two people who sat up front, a young man and a young woman, were staring at her. The woman was driving. Anna thought nothing of it until she paused at her car, opened her trunk, and turned to see the sedan come up the lot toward her. She put her pocketbook in the trunk and loaded in the first bag. But then she paused again when the Ford came to a stop right behind her.

The man stepped out quickly, a Smith & Wesson .38 caliber pistol clutched in his right hand. To Anna, it looked like a cannon. She gasped at the sight of the gun. Her experience with weapons was practically nonexistent. In fact, she could count on her one hand how many times she had actually seen a gun in real life. She even hated seeing violence on television or in the movies and usually had her head down during those scenes. Some soldier in Israel she would make.

Anna held her breath, her right palm over her heart. A holdup in broad daylight? These things happened only to other people and rarely in this semirural, laid-back world miles and miles from urban centers. At least that was what she had believed up to this moment.

Without saying anything, the man with the gun opened the side door of the car.

"Get in," he ordered. "Quickly."

Anna didn't move. It was enough of a shock to think she was being robbed, but what he demanded now turned her heart to stone and made her tremble so, she thought her teeth would soon begin to chatter. She shook her head. It was all she was capable of doing. If she tried to run, she was sure to stumble.

"Get in or I'll kill you right here," he said firmly. He had blue eyes that turned into glass. He looked younger than he apparently was; he had a baby face, soft cheeks, and thick red lips, but he looked hypnotized, crazed, far from an innocent, harmless child.

"Who are you? What is this?" she asked and at the same time gazed around for someone to help her.

There was no one nearby. It was fall in the Catskills. Whatever tourists and summer visitors there had been were long gone, and the area had been returned to its small population of year-round residents. In some nearby hamlets, a good twenty minutes could pass before a car would roll down Main Street.

There was a woman two rows down in the parking lot just getting out of a car with her little girl, hardly anyone to come to the rescue, Anna thought, and the people in front of the supermarket were too far away and too distracted to be of any assistance either.

"Last chance," the baby-faced man said and pushed the barrel of the pistol into her stomach. His lips writhed and his eyes were full of purpose. There was no bluff to call here. "Get in," he ordered and pulled the front of her coat. The loose button popped off.

Terrified, Anna obeyed and got into the car. He slammed the door closed and got into the front. The female driver accelerated and they pulled out of the parking lot quickly, speeding up the street toward the main highway, New York Route 17.

"Who are you? What do you want?"

"Put your hands up here," he ordered in response. He indicated the back of the seat. "Do it!" he shouted.

She did so and he quickly wrapped fish line around her wrists to bind her. It was so tight that if she moved one hand an eighth of an inch, the fish line cut into her skin. She grimaced and complained.

"It hurts!"

"Just for a little while," he said, smiling.

Who were these people? What did they want with her?

She gazed back at the fast-fading sight of the parking lot. The trunk of her leased automobile was still open, and most of her groceries were still in the cart.

A chill of terror tightened around her waist. It resembled the labor pains she anticipated would come. Her throat tightened; tears came to her eyes.

The man turned around.

"Thank you for being cooperative, Anna," he said.

"Yes, thank you," the female driver parroted.

As they drove on, Anna was unable to see that they were looking forward with the same ecstatic smile on their faces, each reflecting the other's overwhelming sense of happiness.

MORE CHILLS AND THRILLS
FROM
ANDREW NEIDERMAN

AMNESIA
THE DEVIL'S ADVOCATE
IN DOUBLE JEOPARDY
NEIGHBORHOOD WATCH
SURROGATE CHILD
THE DARK

Visit
❖ **Pocket Books** ❖
online at

....

www.SimonSays.com

....

Keep up on the latest new
releases from your favorite
authors, as well as author
appearances, news, chats,
special offers and more.

SIMON & SCHUSTER
A VIACOM COMPANY
www.SimonSays.com

Pocket
Books

2381-01